Who has seen the wind?
  Neither you nor I:
But when the trees bow down their heads,
  The wind is passing by.

WHO HAS SEEN THE WIND

W.O. MITCHELL
WHO HAS SEEN THE WIND

ILLUSTRATED BY WILLIAM KURELEK

Macmillan of Canada   Toronto

Canadian Cataloguing in Publication Data

Mitchell, William O., 1914-
  Who has seen the wind

ISBN 0-7705-1324-7

I. Kurelek, William, 1927- II. Title.

PS8525.I88W62 1976 C813'.5'4 C76-017145-9
PR9199.3.M59W66 1976

First published by Macmillan of Canada 1947
This edition first published 1976

Printed in Canada
for The Macmillan Company of Canada Limited
70 Bond Street, Toronto M5B 1X3

To
O. S. MITCHELL
my father and my son

As for man, his days are as grass: as a flower of the field, so he flourisheth.

For the wind passeth over it, and it is gone; and the place thereof shall know it no more.

Psalms CIII: 15-16

Many interpreters of the Bible believe the wind to be symbolic of Godhood. In this story I have tried to present sympathetically the struggle of a boy to understand what still defeats mature and learned men—the ultimate meaning of the cycle of life. To him are revealed in moments of fleeting vision the realities of birth, hunger, satiety, eternity, death. They are moments when an inquiring heart seeks finality, and the chain of darkness is broken.

This is the story of a boy and the wind.

WHO HAS SEEN THE WIND

PART ONE

ONE

Here was the least common denominator of nature, the skeleton requirements simply, of land and sky — Saskatchewan prairie. It lay wide around the town, stretching tan to the far line of the sky, shimmering under the June sun and waiting for the unfailing visitation of wind, gentle at first, barely stroking the long grasses and giving them life; later, a long hot gusting that would lift the black topsoil and pile it in barrow pits along the roads, or in deep banks against the fences.

Over the prairie, cattle stood listless beside the dried-up slough beds which held no water for them. Where the snow-white of alkali edged the course of the river, a thin trickle of water made its way toward the town low upon the horizon. Silver willow, heavy with dust, grew along the riverbanks, perfuming the air with its honey smell.

Just before the town the river took a wide loop and entered at the eastern edge. Inhabited now by some eighteen hundred souls, it had grown up on either side of the river from the seed of one homesteader's sod hut built in the spring of eighteen seventy-five. It was made up largely of frame buildings with high, peaked roofs, each with an expanse of lawn in front and a garden in the back; they lined avenues with prairie names: Bison, Riel, Qu'Appelle, Blackfoot, Fort. Cement sidewalks extended from First Street to Sixth Street at MacTaggart's Corner; from that point to the prairie a boardwalk ran.

Lawn sprinklers sparkled in the sun; Russian poplars stood along either side of Sixth Street. Five houses up from MacTaggart's Corner stood the O'Connal home, a three-storied house lifting high above the white cottage to the left of it. Virginia creepers had almost smothered the veranda; honeysuckle and spirea grew on either side of the steps. A tricycle with its front wheel sharply turned stood in the middle of the walk.

The tricycle belonged to Brian Sean MacMurray O'Connal, the four-year-old son of Gerald O'Connal, druggist, and Maggie O'Connal, formerly Maggie MacMurray of Trossachs, Ontario. Brian at the moment was in the breakfast room. He sat under the table at the window, imagining himself an ant deep in a dark cave. Ants, he had decided, saw things tiny and grass-colored, and his father and mother would never know about it. He hated his mother and his father and his grandmother for spending so much time with the baby, for making it a blanket tent and none for him. Not that he cared; he needed no one to play with him now that he was an ant. He was a smart ant.

He hadn't asked Dr. Svarich, with his bitter smell, to play with him. He would never again ask anyone to play with him. He would make them wish they had never been mean to him.

4

"Brian!"

His grandmother stood high above him. Looking up to her he could see her face turned down, could see the dark velvet band circling high around her throat, hooping in the twin folds of skin that hung from under her chin. Light stabbed out from her silver-rimmed glasses.

"I told ye to go outside!"

He crawled from under the table and stood by her hand with large liver spots spattering its back, and blue veins writhing under the thin skin. Her hand had great knotted knuckles. When her stomach sang after dinner, Brian promised himself, he would not listen.

"I will not speak to ye again!" The loose folds of her cheeks shook slightly as she spoke. The winy bouquet of tonic was about her, reminding him of apples. Behind the spectacles her eyes looked forbidding to him. "If ye stay inside ye'll disturb the baby. Ye must go out!"

"Can I have a tent like the baby has?"

"Ye cannot. 'Tis bad enough having the baby ill without—"

"Is he ill bad?"

"Aye," said his grandmother. "Now, be a good boy and do as ye're told."

He would get Jake Harris, the town policeman, after her. He hoped Jake would bring his policeman's knife and chop her into little pieces and cut her head off, for making him go outside to play.

He stood on the step of the back porch a moment, feeling the warmth of the sun against his cheek, the wind, which was beginning to rise now that it was late afternoon, delicately active about his ears and at his nostrils.

Slowly he walked to the sand pile by the high Caragana hedge that separated the O'Connal back yard from that of Sherry next door. He hated his grandmother. She made him go out to a sand pile where there was nobody but an old shovel to play with. Reflectively he stared down at the sand hump in one corner of the box. It was like an ant pile, he thought; perhaps if he waited an ant might come out. He watched impatiently, and then as no ant emerged, he took up the shovel that lay at his feet. He hit the bump, and wished that it were his grandmother. He hit the bump again, being careful that it was with the sharp edge and not the flat bottom of the shovel. He was hitting his grandmother so awful she was bawling her head off.

He stopped.

Directly opposite him, and low in the hedge, was a round and freckled face—a new face to Brian. He began again to punish the sand pile.

The boy came to the edge of the sand pile. Hedge leaves hung to his sweater and to his hat, a blue sailor hat bearing the legend H.M.S. THUNDERBOLT. It had got twisted so that the ribbon hung down his snub nose.

"I'm coming into the sand pile." As he stepped over, Brian saw that his knees were scratched, that his hands were fat with deep crease-lines at the wrists, like the baby's. "Let me hit some," the boy said.

"No," Brian said.

"I'm Benny Banana."

"Benny Banana—Benny Banana," chanted Brian; "Banana-Benny-Banana."

The boy sat down; he picked up a thin pebble from the sand. "What's your name?"

Brian plumped himself down by the boy. "Brian Sean Mac-Murray O'Connal," he said.

"I'm Forbsie Hoffman." The boy touched the tip of his tongue with the pebble he had picked up. The pebble hung. To Brian it was magic.

"I'm going to do that. I'm going to hang to my tongue." He tried it. "Mine won't hang at all."

"Naw 'hinny enouch," said Forbsie, with the pebble still clinging to the tip of his protruding tongue.

Brian found that a skinnier pebble hung.

Forbsie said, *"Thpt."*

Brian said, *"Thpt."*

"Do you know anything more?" asked Brian.

"I'm hungry. Maybe if you was to ask, your maw'd give us a piece."

6

"The baby's going to heaven," explained Brian.

"My Dad's a conductor," Forbsie said, "on the C.P.R. He has got silver buttons."

"It's where God stays," said Brian, "heaven."

"No it ain't," said Forbsie. He lifted his arm and pointed. "God lives right in town. Over there. I seen Him lots of times."

"Where?"

"At His house."

"You have not!"

"Oh, yes! He's all grapes and bloody. He carries around a lamb."

Brian got up. "Let's us go over to His place."

Forbsie got up. "I guess I'll go home. I don't feel so much like going."

"I've got something to say to Him. I'm going to get Him after my gramma. You show me where He lives."

"All right," said Forbsie.

The wind had strengthened; it had begun to snap the clothes on Sherry's line, where Mrs. Sherry, a tall, spare woman, was in the act of hanging up her washing. She took a clothespin from her mouth. "How is the baby today, Brian?"

"He's very sick," Brian told her. "This is Forbsie. We're going to see Someone."

Mrs. Sherry, with limp underwear in her hands, stared after the boys as they walked toward the front of the house.

At MacTaggart's Corner a tall man in shirt sleeves greeted them: Mr. Digby, Principal of the school. He walked a block west with them from the corner. Digby could not be called a handsome man, largely because of the angularity of his face. His skin had the weathered look of split rock that has lain long under sun and wind. His sandy eyebrows were unruly over eyes of startling blueness; his hair lay in one fair shock over his forehead.

"We're going to see Somebody," Brian told him.

"Are you," said Digby.

"Yes," said Brian: "God."

The schoolmaster showed no surprise. "I'd like to come with you, but I have a previous engagement."

"What's that?" asked Brian.

"It means that I can't go," said Digby.

When the boys had turned off Bison Avenue and left the Principal, they walked in silence over the cement sidewalk. Once they bent down to watch a bee crawl over a Canadian thistle, his licorice-all-sorts stripes showing through the cellophane of folded wings. Down the road, from time to time, a dust-devil spun — snatching up papers, dust, and debris, lifting them up, carrying them high into the air, and leaving them finally to sink slowly down again.

"Step on a crack," Forbsie sang, "break your mother's back!"

Brian sang, "Step on a crack, break my gramma's back!" He did not miss stepping upon a single crack in the three blocks that took them to the great, gray, sandstone church: KNOX PRESBYTERIAN — 1902.

"Is this it?" asked Brian.

Forbsie said that it was.

"Let's go see Him, then."

"I'm going home, I think. It's suppertime, and I better get home."

"Not yet." Brian started up the stone steps; when he turned at the top, he saw that Forbsie was halfway down the block, his head turned back over his shoulder. Brian knocked on the church door. As he did, he felt the wind ruffling his hair. Forbsie was down by the corner now.

A woman came out of the little brown house next to the church. She shook a mop, then turned to re-enter the house. She stopped as she saw Brian; stood watching him. A fervent whirlwind passed the brown house with the woman standing on the porch; at the trees before the church, it rose suddenly, setting every leaf in violent motion, as though an invisible hand had gripped the trunks and shaken them.

Brian wondered why Forbsie had not wanted to come. He knocked again. It was simply that God was in the bathroom and couldn't come right away.

As he turned away from the door, he saw the woman staring at

8

him. She ought to know if God was in. He went down the steps and to the opening in the hedge.

"I guess God isn't anywhere around."

"Why — what do you mean?"

"That's His house, isn't it?"

"Yes."

"I'm going to see Him."

The woman stared at him silently a moment; under the slightly gray hair pulled severely back, her face wore an intense look. "God isn't — He isn't the same as other people, you know. He's a spirit."

"What's that?"

"It's someone—something you can't hear—or see, or touch." Her gray eyes were steady upon his face; he noted that her teeth had pushed back her upper lip slightly, giving her a permanent smile.

"Does He smell?"

"No, he doesn't. I think you better talk with my husband. He's the minister and he could tell you much more about this than I could," she said, with relief loosening the words.

"Does he know God pretty well?"

"Pretty well. He — he tells people about Him."

"Better than you do? Does he know better than you do?"

"It's — it's his job to know God."

"My dad is a druggist. He works for God, I guess."

"He works for God," the woman agreed.

"My Uncle Sean isn't a sheepherder—neither is Ab. Ab's got a thing on his foot, and one foot is shorter, so he goes up and down when he walks."

"And who is Ab?" the woman asked him.

"Uncle Sean's hired man that feeds the pigs and helps grow the wheat whenever there isn't any goddam-drought."

The woman looked startled.

"Has your husband got calfs?" Brian asked her.

"No—he hasn't any calfs—calves." She looked quickly back over her shoulder.

"He looks after the sheep and the sheep pups."

"Looks after the . . . !"

"I'm going to get God after my gramma," Brian confided. "She has a thing on her leg too. It is not the same as Ab's. You only see it on the heel. She's got room-a-ticks in a leg."

The woman cast another anxious look over her shoulder.

"She belshes," said Brian, "a lot."

"Perhaps your grandmother has stomach trouble."

"If your husband works for God, then he could take me in His house for a while, couldn't he?"

"Perhaps he could. Tomorrow."

"Not now?"

"Tomorrow — in the morning — after breakfast." She turned to the doorway.

"Does God like to be all grapes and bloody?"

"All what?"

"That's what I want to see."

"But what do you mean . . . ?"

"Something's burning," said Brian. "I'll come back."

She hurried in to her burning dinner.

Brian walked back towards his home. He did not turn down Bison Avenue where it crossed the street upon which the church was, but continued on, a dark wishbone of a child wrapped in reflection.

The wind was persistent now, a steady urgency upon his straight back, smoking up the dust from the road along the walk, lifting it and carrying it out to the prairie beyond. Several times Brian stopped: once to look up into the sun's unbearable radiance and then away with the lingering glow stubborn in his eyes; another time when he came upon a fox-red caterpillar making a procession of itself over a crack that snaked along the walk. He squashed it with his foot. Further on he paused at a spider that carried its bead of a body between hurrying thread-legs. Death came for the spider too.

He looked up to find that the street had stopped. Ahead lay the sudden emptiness of the prairie. For the first time in his four years of life he was alone on the prairie.

He had seen it often, from the veranda of his uncle's farm-house, or at the end of a long street, but till now he had never heard it. The hum of telephone wires along the road, the ring of hidden crickets, the stitching sound of grasshoppers, the sudden relief of a meadow lark's song, were deliciously strange to him. Without hesitation he crossed the road and walked out through the hip-deep grass stirring in the steady wind; the grass clung at his legs; haloed fox-tails bowed before him; grasshoppers sprang from hidden places in the grass, clicketing ahead of him to disappear, then lift again.

A gopher squeaked questioningly as Brian sat down upon a rock warm to the backs of his thighs. He picked a pale blue flax-flower at his feet, stared long at the stripings in its shallow throat, then looked up to see a dragonfly hanging on shimmering wings directly in front of him. The gopher squeaked again, and he saw it a few yards away, sitting up, watching him from its pulpit hole. A suave-winged hawk chose that moment to slip its shadow over the face of the prairie.

And all about him was the wind now, a pervasive sighing through great emptiness, unhampered by the buildings of the town, warm and living against his face and in his hair.

Then for the second time that day he saw a strange boy — one who came from behind him soundlessly, who stood and stared at him with steady gray eyes in a face of remarkable broadness, with cheekbones circling high under a dark and freckled skin. He saw that the boy's hair, bleached as the dead prairie grass itself, lay across his forehead in an all-round cowlick curling under at the edge. His faded blue pants hung open in two tears just below the knees. He was barefooted.

Brian was not startled; he simply accepted the boy's presence out here as he had accepted that of the gopher and the hawk and the dragonfly.

"This is your prairie," Brian said.

The boy did not answer him. He turned and walked as silently as he had come, out over the prairie. His walk was smooth.

After the boy's figure had become just a speck in the distance, Brian looked up into the sky, now filled with a soft expanse of cloud, the higher edges luminous and startling against the blue. It stretched to the prairie's rim. As he stared, the gray underside carded out, and through the cloud's softness was revealed a blue well shot with sunlight. Almost as soon as it had cleared, a whisking of cloud stole over it.

For one moment no wind stirred. A butterfly went pelting past. God, Brian decided, must like the boy's prairie.

TWO

The clock in the O'Connal living room ticked on in the silence as Sean O'Connal sat uncomfortably in the presence of Brian's grandmother. Against the dark brown drapes behind the chair, his hair and mustaches showed a carrot-red. He was a large man in blue overalls and work smock with flat, brass buttons, his solid hands resting upon great knees.

"When do you figger he'll be back?" he asked.

The grandmother looked up from her sewing. "He should be home any minute now. Ye could phone the store if ye like."

"I'll wait," said Sean. From a pants pocket he pulled out his pipe. He sucked on the amber stem to find it plugged. His face reddened slightly. He took out a jackknife and opened it. The grandmother worked on, with her head bent.

"Got no goddam ash trays around here?"

"Your elbow."

"Huh?"

"Right behind your elbow," said the grandmother.

Sean turned his head to the small octagonal table at his chair-arm and deposited a tarry mess of dottle on the tray there. He drew a length of haywire from his coat pocket and rammed it through the pipe several times.

Relaxing with the first puff, he said, "And what would you be makin'?"

Mrs. MacMurray bent her head to her work and bit off a thread. "A middy." She held it up.

Sean eyed the square, broad collar. "Who's to wear that?"

"Brian."

"I like to see a kid in overalls."

The grandmother wound thread deftly around her finger tip and into a knot. She began to sew again. Sean cleared his throat loudly. "Where's Maggie?"

"Upstairs. She's steaming Bobbie."

"How is he?"

"He's a sick baby." She looked up at Sean. "Dr. Svarich was here to see him yesterday and he thinks there's the possibility of pneumonia."

"The hell there is!" ejaculated Sean. "How — what are they doin' for him?"

"There isn't so much can be done," said the grandmother. "Steaming him." She looked to the hallway door. "There's someone now."

Brian entered the room with his pants and jacket bristling spear grass. "Hello, Uncle Sean."

Sean greeted the boy and turned back to the grandmother.

"Anything I can do to help at all?"

"I don't think so," she said; then, "thanks."

"Got any wheat, Uncle Sean?"

"Why, sure." Sean put his hand into his pocket and brought out a few grains. "Chew it up good, and it'll make wheat gum for you."

Brian began dutifully to chew. His grandmother called him to her chair to try on the middy. She looked it over, took several tucks in with pins. Sean watched, then suggested, "Little full under the armpits, ain't it?"

The grandmother ignored the remark.

"Ain't them cuffs tight fer the widtha the sleeves?"

"I think I have an idea what the pattern calls for," she said. "Don't wriggle."

"I'm not," said Brian.

"All right," said Sean. "I just thought it looked kinda funny the way she hung down like a puhtatuh sack from under his—"

"I don't want to wear any potato sack, Gramma!"

"'Tisn't!" said Mrs. MacMurray, twitching him around. "Pay no attention to what he says."

"Now that's not the sort of thing to be tellin' me own nephew. Goddamdest—"

"And that's not the sort of language to be using before your own nephew!"

"What's wrong with my language?"

"It belongs to the barroom," said the grandmother, stung by Sean's criticism of her handiwork.

"It does not!"

"But it does, Mr. O'Connal."

"Oh." Sean's voice dropped to crooning level. With a magnificent effort at restraint he relaxed into his chair. "I will not argue it with you. I'm not like some that have to always be havin' the last word."

"I do not!"

"Oh, yes, you do."

"You have just said it yourself," accused the grandmother.

"The hell I did!"

"There — you've done it again."

Sean fixed his eye upon the grandmother with a significant nod of his head, leaving her thus with the guilt of having said the last word. His face reddened in the punishing silence as she worked over the middy upon the patient Brian. He threw restraint to the winds.

"Last goddam word or no last goddam word, I wouldn't put that — that — thing upon a dead goddam gopher!"

Without a word the grandmother reached behind her for the cane by her chair. She left the room. Brian looked up to his uncle's face with plain worship in his eyes.

"I was out on the prairie today," he said.

"Were you now," said Sean.

"Yes, and I saw a woman."

"On the prairie?" Sean took him upon his broad knee.

"No. She was at the house. I'm going tomorrow. It didn't make any gum, Uncle Sean. It swallowed." He opened his mouth to show Sean. His uncle gave him more wheat.

"Sort of make more spit as you chew it," advised Sean.

He looked down at the boy upon his knee. "Did you see the little man while you were on the prairie?"

"No," said Brian. "I saw a boy but he wasn't little. Tell about the little man, Uncle Sean."

"Saw him just the day before yesterday," said the uncle, laying his pipe upon the table. "Monday it was. He popped out of a gopher hole in my south forty. I'd just climbed down from the rod weeder to untangle her, and there he was, standing in front of a Roosian thistle—wearin' two-inch overhawls and with a rabbit's-foot fob to his watch. 'God bless this fine summer fallow and us two that's on it,' he sez, 'an' good mornin'.'

"Well, I don't make a hobby out of talkin' to little men standin' about as high as a sprig of pigweed and picking their teeth with the fine hair off a crocus near by. I stood there without sayin' a word for a minute, then I sez, 'Good mornin'. You're a stranger around here, are you?'

" 'Oh, no,' he sez. 'I come to the districk in 'eighty-five—after they hung Looie Riel for startin' that rebellion.'

16

" 'Not much here then,' I sez.

" 'No town at all,' he sez. 'Just the river an' little green frogs hoppin' up an' down on the banks. The town came later.'

" 'By the way it jumps on its *r*'s, yer voice sounds familiar,' I sez.

" 'Does it?' he sez.

" 'Yes,' I sez. 'You wouldn't be a County Down little man, would you?'

" 'I am,' he sez.

"Well, we talked an' it turned out he come over third-class — spent some time in Ontario, then come West to the end of the steel — the C.P.R. wasn't finished in them days. From there he come on a three-gaited sorrel grasshopper that went lame in the Moose Mountain country. He turned him loose an' come the rest of the way on foot.

" 'What the hell made you pick this country?' I asked him.

" 'I liked the look of her in them days,' he sez.

" 'Look at her now,' I sez.

" 'You look,' sez he, 'she gives me the heartburn!' An' with that he — "

Sean looked up as the hallway door opened and Gerald O'Connal entered. Like Sean, Gerald was one of the red O'Connals, and like Sean too he was well over six feet, but there the similarity ended. Gerald's hair was a dark auburn; his face was clean-shaven, his skin showing a faint underblush of red, his blue eyes having the lashless look about them that often goes with red hair. Whereas Sean was the possessor of a volatile temper, which had never truly subsided during the dry years of the late twenties and this heartbreaking one of the thirties, Gerald was a quiet, slow-smiling, and almost shy individual. There was fifteen years' difference in their ages, a difference which gave to the rough Sean a feeling of protectiveness for his younger brother; at the same time he stood in awe of Gerald with his university education, his fine business, and his fine home.

"And how's the baby?" said Sean, letting Brian off his knee.

"Not so good," said Brian's father. "Svarich was around to see him yesterday. God — I — hope he pulls through it all right!"

"He will," boomed Sean. He stood up. One broad, freckled hand, with gold-red hairs on its back, gripped his brother's shoulder. "I — if there's anything I can do — Gerald."

"Thanks, Sean."

"One hell of a good toot? I've got a crock out in the car."

"What's a toot, Uncle Sean?"

"No thanks, Sean."

"He'll be all right. Isn't going to do any good to get yer britchin' all tangled up. He'll be all right."

"I hope so. Will you stay for supper?"

"No," said Sean. "And there's reasons fer that. The old — Mrs. MacMurray ain't — I'll be gettin' out to the farm."

"How's it going?" asked Gerald, taking a cigar from his vest pocket.

The concern that had been in Sean's eyes was replaced by a sudden intense light. In the course of the drought years Sean had changed from a bewildered man, watching dry winds lick up the topsoil from his land, to a man with a message. He was the keeper of the Lord's Vineyard, literally.

And now, as he often did, he launched into one of his evangelistic denunciations.

"Awful! She's plum awful, Gerald! Stupid!" he cried. "They never hearda strip farmin' an' they don't wanta hear! 'Plant yer crops,' I tell 'em, 'in strips acrosst the prevailin' winds — fight the wind an' fight the driftin' — stop clawin' her plumb back fer wheat or oats or barley or flax! Farm her with her hearts an' brains, you stubble-jumpin' sonsa hunyacks! Git off yer black prats an' raise some pigs an' cattle too! Fergit yer goddam little red tractors an' yer goddam yella-wheeled cars an' yer trips to Washington an' Oregon an' California!

" 'Jist look at her—creased an' pocked an' cracked—no grass to hold the topsoil down! That's what happens when you crop her out an' away fer the winter—then back agin in the spring to scratch at her agin—on agin off agin an' away agin! You wanta travel an' so does she! I seen her travelin' on a first-class ticket by air—she's bin to the Coast with you—a thousand million sections of her—

18

black cloudsa dust blacker than all yer greedy souls—lifted up an' travelin' — travelin' clear to Jesus!' "

Brian watched his uncle, open-mouthed. Then he turned to see his grandmother in the kitchen doorway, her mouth down-curving in bitter disapproval.

"Come into the kitchen! Yer bread an' milk's ready!"

Brian moved slowly towards her, still half-dazed and hypnotized by the spell of his uncle's words.

THREE

The day after his visit to the prairie,
Brian stood upon a chair in the kitchen. His grandmother was
going to be bossy again, he supposed. He looked down at the
porridge cooking on the stove. When porridge cooked, it went *bup
bup*, very slowly at first, then faster; there were old men's mouths
opening and closing as it boiled.

Brian heard the door open; he looked up to see his father
enter.

20

"See the little old men, Dad," said Brian.

His father looked over at him, and upon his face was a strained and worried look. "Not this morning, Spalpeen." He hurried out the back door with his hat in his hand.

The baby was no better, decided Brian. It had been very sick when he went to bed last night. No one had come to tuck him in.

For a long time he had lain listening to the night noises that stole out of the dark to him. He heard the sound of grown-up voices casual in the silence, welling up almost to spilling over, then subsiding. The cuckoo clock poked the stillness nine times; the house cracked its knuckles; and the night wind, stirring through the leaves of the poplar just outside this room on the third floor, strengthened until it was wild at his screen. He thought again of the strange boy on the prairie and felt, as he did, a stirring of excitement within himself, a feeling of intimacy. The wind cried long at the eave troughing outside, then was suddenly sibilant again at the screen. It was a frightening and lonely sound, fading into nothingness. Brian threw back the covers. He got out of bed. When it came again, he wouldn't be there.

He crossed the hall in front of his grandmother's room, then descended the stairs to the second floor. *Their* light was on. The brightness had leaked out under their door. He pushed it slightly open to peek in. He could see his father's broad back with suspenders running over the shoulders. His mother, dark and small, stood by the crib with the blanket tent over it, and on the hot plate beside it was a steaming kettle. His mother was holding the baby with one small arm outflung and hanging limp.

"I'd better get Svarich," his father was saying.

His mother continued to look into the baby's face.

"If we could only do something — " Brian's father said.

Then, although he could not see his father after he had moved out of line with the crack of the door, he heard him say jerkily, "I'll cut out through the back — no — better phone — get him to drink something!"

"He can't keep it down."

Brian had gone back through the darkness to his bed, where the wind waited for him. He fell asleep thinking of the boy on the prairie.

21

"Get down from that chair!"

She *was* going to be bossy again today. Several times — as she put wood in the stove, as she poured the cream off the milk and dished out his porridge — she told him to be still.

The first mouthful of oatmeal was hot; he reached for the cooling milk. He made a gutter with his spoon, deep to the bottom of the plate. When God ate His porridge He had a dish as big as the prairie. He had to squirt milk onto it from a long hose; if it was hot He turned a cooling wind on it. They would all be sorry when he got back from God's house. He began to eat his porridge.

"Are ye not through yet?" She was back again.

"I'm nearly." She would squeal out loud when God got ahold of her.

"Outside with ye, boy."

"The baby's still sick, I suppose."

The lines on his grandmother's face softened. "Poor wee thing," she said. "It look as though his time has come."

"He's going to heaven?"

"Aye. Away with ye now. Ye must not come to the house till noon. Yer squealin' — "

"I don't *squeal!*"

His grandmother picked up the empty dish before him.

Brian had to knock twice at the brown house by the church before anyone came to the door. A man opened it, and Brian's eyes went immediately to the pince-nez glasses with their black cord looping down his vest.

"Yes?"

"I'm visiting God today."

"Oh," the man said, and smiled a slow smile that made round muscle-curves of his cheeks. "I'm at breakfast right now, but I think we could make it after another piece of toast. Whose boy are you?"

"My Dad's. I'm Brian."

"Brian who?"

"Brian Sean MacMurray O'Connal. What's your name?"

22

"John Hewlett Hislop," said the minister, "B.A., B.D. Come inside."

Mrs. Hislop was sitting at the kitchen table. Brian waited impatiently while the minister ate another piece of toast and then got up. "Where are the keys, dear?"

"Hanging behind the front door — or on the hall table," she said. "Look in the top drawer of the sewing machine — I can't — they might be on the mantel. I don't remember exactly where I put them after Mrs. Abercrombie borrowed them for Auxiliary."

By the time the keys were found, Brian could hardly contain himself. He ran down the house steps and up those of the church.

Mr. Hislop looked through the keys on the ring. They crossed a short hallway and entered the church.

Through the stained-glass window the morning sunshine streamed, a fluted bar of light shearing the church dusk. Drifting motes traveled from outer darkness, across the light, and into nothingness again. Flies flew into the light, had bright life, and lost it.

Their footsteps stopped echoing through the empty church. Brian looked up to the window's blue-and-ruby glow.

"How do you like it?" Mr. Hislop's voice seemed to bounce off the quiet.

"I don't see any sheep — or sheep pups."

"They only come here once a week," said the minister.

"Is God busy right now?"

"Yes. He's busy. Just what did you have in mind?"

"Where — where is He? That's just His picture — all grapes and bloody."

"Lemon-colored, too," pointed out Mr. Hislop. "Why do you want to see — "

"What are those — with things to their backs — wings?"

"Angels," said Mr. Hislop.

"And wherever they go they fly there — all the time up in the sky, and there's sunshine, and it's blue, and heaven's where God is. He's in heaven — that's just like a picture of Him — isn't it?"

The minister nodded.

"He has lots of fun." Brian turned. "He has lots of fun up there."

"He looks after things."

"Does He? What things?"

"Flowers — birds — people — things. He makes meadow larks sing. If an ant climbs a grass-blade — a — a grasshopper spits tobacco juice — that's God."

"Spiders and buffalo beans?"

"When a butterfly winks his wings — that's God too," said Hislop. "Ladybugs, kittens, pups, gophers: they're all — "

"Trees — trees — does He do trees?"

"He makes leaves from buds — men from boys. He hands out the colors and the sounds and tastes and feels. He makes hungry — loving — sleeping — waking — "

"Everything?"

Mr. Hislop nodded.

"The boy on the prairie?"

The minister looked puzzled. "The boy on the prairie?"

"He's on the prairie — that's where he is — he's bare feet."

"Yes — I — God made him."

"He doesn't live in a house — I'm not going to live in any house any more — I don't have to if I don't want to. The boy has — I wish I had prairie hair. He has wind on him all the time — it gets in his hair."

Brian was silent a moment while he stared up at the window. "What are their wings made out of?"

"Feathers," said the minister. "I think."

"Their nests are white too. They lay very white eggs. Are there any little boy angels like I am?"

"There are some. When a little boy dies, he becomes a boy angel."

"Oh," said Brian.

Outside, the sunlight was bright in Brian's eyes; he stood on the church steps a moment, thanked Mr. Hislop. Then he started home.

Mr. Hislop, herder of God's Presbyterian sheep, watched Brian as far as the corner; he turned to the house, then through to

24

the back where the lawn mower waited. As he pushed it ahead of him over the back lawn, he thought of the boy. Something had been proved, he supposed. He bent down to extricate a piece of twine that had wound itself up in one of the mower wheels. He straightened up. Digby wouldn't agree. He stared down at the lawn mower. Too bad Digby wasn't here; be rather nice to squat down in the shade of the poplar and talk. Digby might even push the lawn mower a couple of rounds.

He sat down in the grass and stared out over the untidy yard. No two ways about it: it was messy, with its litter of papers, its grass growing rank along the edges, its old bones that dogs had left. It had offended Mrs. Abercrombie to the point of her mentioning it to his wife as she left church last Sunday. That old girl had her knife into him all right.

It all went back to that business the Christmas before, the difference of opinion over Romona. A slightly fey derelict, Romona had resided in a gray shack at the end of the First Street, next to the *Times* building and near the railroad tracks and the river. She spent most of her time wandering down back alleys in search of whatever town shopkeepers might have left out for her. At Wong's Bluebird Café she often found vegetables and sliced bread, left over by café diners; at Funder's Meat Market, slightly tainted meat. Her shack was the mecca for the lean and hungry alley-cat men who swung down from the long grain freights. Romona fed them; she did their washing for them, so that her line was continuously masculine. At Christmas-time Romona, in a burst of festive spirit, covered her window with red tissue paper picked up at the back of O'Connal's drugstore. The light of her shack showed through for all to see, a rich and glowing red. An immoral red, Mrs. Abercrombie decided. Straightway she went to Romona's shack, knocked on the door, and told her to take the paper down. "You," Romona told her, "kin go plump to hell."

That Christmas, as every Christmas, Mrs. Abercrombie was head of the church hamper committee. She told the other members that unless Romona took down the offending paper, her name must be struck from the list. Mr. Hislop had suggested that he might call on Romona.

The scarlet woman, her hennaed hair glinting mahogany in its tight coils, told Mr. Hislop that she was not taking down the paper, hamper or no hamper. Mr. Hislop asked her if she wouldn't consider green tissue paper.

"Green," said Romona, "jist ain't Crissmuss to me. I'm fussy about red, so green don't mean a good goddam, Rev-rund."

The next night at the hamper meeting, the minister insisted that Romona's name stay on the list. For one of the very few times in her life, Mrs. Abercrombie had to admit herself beaten. The red glow stayed on in the window long after New Year's; the fact that Romona left town in the spring was not enough to remove the sting of defeat from Mrs. Abercrombie's soul.

Hislop stared now at the yard. The place was untidy and must be unpleasant in the sight of the Lord. It made him feel uncomfortable, made him conscious of what it was and what he would like it to be.

Self and not-self; what was the relationship? He had separated himself from the phenomena of his experience. He could say to himself, "I see the yard — John Hislop sees the yard and the lawn mower." But — who was John Hislop? What was "seeing"? Was the chipped greenness of the mower a quality inherent in the mower, or was it only . . .

The screen door slapped the stillness. He saw his wife standing on the back porch. He got up and began to push.

At MacTaggart's Corner, several blocks away from the Presbyterian manse, Brian and Forbsie Hoffman sat on the top rail of the fence upon which Arthur Sherry had left part of his tongue the winter before.

"I wish I knew where we could get some feathers from," Brian was saying.

"I busted a pillow once."

"We could start from the garage and get there quick."

"Get there — get there," said Forbsie, "quick there — quick there — quick."

"We could bounce on the clouds."

"Pillows' stummicks is full of feathers," said Forbsie. "Little curly ones."

Brian got down from the fence. "With string we could make them."

Forbsie jumped down, his fat cheeks jouncing as he landed. "They snowed all over my room."

"We'll tie them together," explained Brian with excitement, "and that'll be wings for us. You can have wings too — string and feather wings. I'll get some string. You get the pillow — "

"You better get the pillow too," said Forbsie as they turned into the O'Connal yard. "I'd get licked."

"How do you get their feathers out?"

"Paring knife. They don't bust so easy. I'm not getting any pillow!"

"Wait here," Brian told him. "I'm going into the house. You wait here."

His grandmother was ironing in the breakfast room; he saw only her erect back as he went silently through the smell of newly-ironed clothes and into the living room. He did not stop to see her spit a live bubble on the iron's smooth bottom, to watch it jump lively there as it always did when she tested it. From the living room couch he took a pillow with raised orange flowers, then went out the front door and around to the back where Forbsie waited.

He made two more trips into the house without his grandmother's knowing it, once for the paring knife, again for string.

The feathers, as Forbsie had told him, were very tiny, hundreds of them spreading themselves over the sand, stirring to the slightest breeze, lifting and drifting over the yard. Several clung to Brian's dark hair; one, sucked in by Forbsie's breath, went up his nose, and made him sneeze three times.

"What yuh doin'?"

Arthur Sherry, a six-year-old cynic in overall pants and sleeveless, faded blue shirt, looked down at them. As though in irritation at the thick-lensed glasses which blew up his eyes remarkably, his face convulsed from time to time in sudden, twitching grimaces.

"Making wings," Brian told him. "We're going to fly."

A sound of disgust issued from Arthur's lips at the same moment that his face decided to twitch. "Anybody knows you can't make wings to fly."

"Yes, we can," said Brian. "We can if we want to."

"Nah, you can't." The glasses jumped slightly on the bridge of his nose. "It's dumb to think that."

"It is not," Brian insisted. "Go on and tie," he advised Forbsie. "Don't listen to Artie — to what he says. He doesn't know!"

"Maybe they won't work," said Forbsie.

"Yes, they will," Brian said with fervor. "They will so work." Even as he said it he was aware of a sinking feeling in his stomach, a sudden and very physical loss.

Arthur made a snorting noise; he kicked lazily at the spread feathers, and the air current stirred thereby lifted them and let them sink slowly back to the ground. "Just with airplanes — that's all."

"And wings! Angels got wings! They fly too!"

"Not made outa string — with pillow feathers," Artie added as he saw the deflated pillow on the sand. "They grow 'em."

Brian was silent. He had not thought of that.

Arthur went on: "Outa their shoulders. They always had 'em —like a sparrow — not outa chicken feathers tied with string. Store string," he added disgustedly.

Brian faced Arthur. "Well, I'm going to heaven!"

"Artie — dinner!" called Mrs. Sherry across the hedge.

Arthur looked back over his shoulder and saw that his mother had gone back into the house. He pushed Brian in the chest with both hands so that he sat down. "No, you ain't. Not with string an' feathers."

And Brian, staring down at the pitifully few feathers they had tied, knew that Arthur was perfectly right.

28

FOUR

Under the manse poplars it was moderately cool for the first day of July. With his friend Hislop, Digby sprawled on the grass near the lawn mower, its handle waiting at an expectant angle. Digby was a contented man; his end-of-the-term forms had been completed and found correct by the school board; he could look forward now to a summer holiday two months long. It was true that he drew no salary for that time, that he had made no provision for living expenses, and that it would take him till next Christmas to get out of debt to Mrs. Geddes, with whom he boarded; but as long as he was regularly supplied with the plug tobacco he smoked in his curve-stemmed pipe, and had the leisure to talk with men like Hislop and Milt Palmer, the town shoe and harness maker, he was contented.

A gentle wind stirred the leaves on the poplars, setting disks of shadow dancing over Hislop's earnest face. "They were no different from men today," he was saying. "Just as imaginative—as sensitive. There hasn't been any advance in the things that count—not in generalizations—it was all there with Plato—with Christ."

"*Mmh*," said Digby.

"Men look a little closer — that's all. They've narrowed it down—and—and the cause-and-effect relationship isn't quite so shaky. But in the field of moral values — "

"Blocks." Digby sat up with the quickness so characteristic of him. "Just blocks."

"Blocks!"

"According to my friend Milt Palmer. He says it's just playing with blocks — moral law — convention."

"But — it isn't!" said Hislop. "Righteousness, goodness, beauty, and — and truth — they all have their prototypes in God! God is — the world is of God — they've got to have some foundation — "

"You hope," said Digby. He pulled a blade of grass, chewed on the tender end of it a moment. "Funny fellows—shoemakers—lots of salt. Not like the Bens. No volunteer values in the Bens."

"I know," said Hislop.

"Looks as though that seed fell on stony ground." Digby knew what he was talking about: for the past year he'd had the Young Ben in his school. The boy was the son of a spare, gray bird of a man, surrounded always by the sour-sweet aroma of brew tanged with a gallop of manure and spiced with natural leaf tobacco. The Ben had about as much moral conscience as the prairie wind that lifted over the edge of the prairie world to sing mortality to every living thing. "In the Young Ben too," Digby pointed out.

30

The Young Ben's pre-school environment had not been fertile for the social graces; until he had come to school—a year late, and then forced to do so by the school board's insistence—he had never entered the town, though he had often accompanied his father from Haggerty's Coulee, where they lived, to the town's eastern edge, where the prairie swelled gently. There he would sit watching, his chin in his hands, his elbows on his knees. At other times, before he had come in to school, he had been observed, as Joe Pivott, drayman for Sherry's mill, had put it, "a-runnin' acrosst the bald-headed prairie with no more clo'es than tuh wad a four-ten shotgun."

"I think," said Hislop, "we'd better get to this lawn. I started it last Monday—it's got to be done before I meet Mrs. Abercrombie at the door on Sunday."

As he walked to the lawn mower he was not thinking of the Bens; he was remembering the visit from the O'Connal boy with the dark and serious eyes. He found that memory comforting.

Brian was wishing too that Forbsie didn't have the mumps. Without Forbsie he was alone; he couldn't play with Arthur Sherry, since Arthur was at that moment waiting in the next yard to wrestle him down. He wished that he could get on their vacuum cleaner— ride it out the front door, down the steps, and along the street. Artie would run after him, but he wouldn't let him on. He'd lie back and ride all the way past the poplars to the clouds — God's clouds where it was blue and sunshiny. It would be fun.

He looked down at the white paper on the rug before him. He didn't want to draw men; he wanted to ride a vacuum cleaner up into the sky where it was blue—blue like . . . On the paper he made blue with his crayon. And God was there. He made a yellow God, yellow for the round part, and green legs, and purple eyes, and red arms, and that was God. He made another God and another and another till there were Gods all over the paper. He added arms and more arms, legs and more legs; those were spider Gods, of course.

As he drew, the curtains on the open window bellied gently out; from the high den window dropped staining light, the beveled glass breaking it up into violet, blue, and red. Brian laid down his crayons and stared at the colored patch on the rug.

The man standing in the center of the light colors, decided Brian, was about as high as a person's knee, his own knee. He wore a hat like Uncle Sean's, uncreased just as it had come from the store shelf—a blue gumdrop hat. He wore white rubber boots, and He held a very small, very white lamb in His arms. Brian said:

"I am pleased to meet you."

The man wiggled the black string that hung down from his glasses. "You are welcome," He said. "I am God. I am Mr. R. W. God, B.V.D. You call me R. W."

"I knew you were. What did you leave heaven for?"

"I am going to get after Artie Sherry for you," God said. "And I will get after your grandmother too."

"No," Brian said. "You can let her alone now. She isn't so bossy now the baby is better."

"Has the baby been sick?"

"Oh, yes, but he has had his Crissmuss, so he is almost all right again. What will you do to him?"

"It will be awful," said God. "I will get Artie to look through a hole in a fence, and then I will kick him real hard."

"Thank you very much for what you will do to Artie. When?"

"Soon. I am busy now. I will fix up Artie later on."

"You won't kick him a little?" said Brian anxiously.

"I will give him thousands of kicks. I will give him hundreds."

Brian heard the sound of footsteps behind him.

"Good-bye, God," he said.

"I thought you'd gone out to play, Son." With a towel around her head, her face no longer looking as strained as it had when the baby was sick, Maggie O'Connal stared down at her son. The shadows of fatigue had not quite disappeared from under her eyes in the week since the sleepless nights with the baby.

Maggie O'Connal had been one of the prettiest things to come to the town after she married Gerald O'Connal in the early twenties. She met him in the Ontario town where he came for his apprenticeship after a pharmacy course at the University and three years overseas in the war. Maggie had been born on a homestead in

32

Saskatchewan, and had been homesick for the West during a two-year stay in Ontario with her mother. One year after Gerald and Maggie came to the district in which Sean was farming, Mrs. MacMurray had come to stay with them.

Maggie O'Connal was still pretty: dark of hair and of eyes, slight and small-boned, she had the same dignity of posture that was both Brian's and her mother's. Her speech was quick, but definite and sure too, with now and again a hint of Scottish accent showing itself, sometimes in a slight lift at the ends of sentences, often in a deepening of the flatter vowel sounds and a lingering over the "l"'s. From her Brian had inherited his dark eyes and hair, and learned his careful enunciation.

"I feel more like playing inside," Brian was saying to his mother, "so I'm playing inside." He did not bother to tell her that Artie was waiting for him.

"Better try the back veranda then. Den's next for cleaning. Take your crayons with you."

"Can I help?"

"Just stay out of Mother's way." She gave him an affectionate pat on the rump as he passed her on his way to the living room he must cross to reach the back veranda. In the breakfast room he passed his grandmother at the sewing machine, bent over and threading the needle.

At the dinner table that evening, Brian bowed his head, his hands held palms together against his breastbone, as his father said Grace.

"For what we are about to receive at this time, O Lord, make us truly thankful."

"R. W.," said Brian upon the heels of his father's deep "Amen."

"Just wait until your father's said Grace," his mother admonished him gently. "Your plate, Mother."

Tonight was the baby's first meal with them, and he sat in his high chair between his grandmother and his father. His illness had given his usually pale face a waxen quality; it was white with the stark whiteness of egg white. He looked far from fragile, however, for he was a chunk of a child with fat legs like hams, his face not so plump as it had been, but still round and full. Orange-red hair was like froth on the top of his head, and his blue eyes were almost wild with devilishness.

"Ye need not give me any of the carrots, thank ye, Maggie," said Brian's grandmother. "We're a wee bit short on material—ye should have read what the pattern called for." She had been working on another suit for Brian.

"You'll need all the cloth before you're through," said Brian's mother. "Put your plate down, Brian."

"You needn't give me any of the carrots, Mother."

"Carrots are good for you, Son," she said as she heaped his plate.

"They make ye grow," his grandmother said. "I'm fond of them myself — "

"You can have mine."

"But they disagree with me."

"Carrots are bloody."

"Where did you pick that up?" That was his father, large at the end of the table, his coat off, his white shirt with its turned-back sleeves setting off the rich mahogany of his hair.

"Nowhere," said Brian. "Beets bleed. Carrots got blood — they're colored too."

"Does Artie use words like that?" his mother asked him.

"Don't say it any more, Spalpeen," his father told him. "It isn't nice."

"Why?"

"It just isn't."

"Then, I don't have to eat my carrots?"

Gerald O'Connal looked down the table to his wife. He saw what might have been amusement in her dark eyes, and with a slight shrug of his shoulders and a nod of his head in Brian's direction he indicated that it was time for her to take over. He was fond of his sons, with a consistently deep emotion that he knew made him helplessly indulgent; he had often blessed the vein of iron that enabled his wife to deal with them more firmly than he.

"Eat your carrots," said Brian's mother. Brian picked up his fork.

34

"Isn't he the comical one, though!" exclaimed the grandmother. Butter and jam were smeared around the baby's mouth and on the tip of his nose. He wore an oilcloth bib decorated with kittens and a great deal of the egg he'd had for his dinner. He was holding out what had once been bread and butter to his grandmother.

"Dere — brea'."

"He's an O'Connal, though," she said.

" 'Connal dough," echoed the baby, and held out his mug. The grandmother took it.

"The other's MacMurray to the gizzard."

The baby threw his spoon. He had very bad manners, decided Brian.

The sun poured brightly through his window; sparrows were shrill and pigeons hiccoughed on the small projection of roof that separated the second and third floors. For a moment Brian lay watching the small boys on his wallpaper. They were all fishing with bent rods.

At breakfast his grandmother told him twice not to bolt his food. He set his empty glass on the table, and wiped off the milk mustache.

By the hedge that ran along the side of the house away from Sherry's, he took God from his pocket and placed Him on a clean poplar leaf that had dropped on the grass. There was R. W. God on a green poplar leaf, and the leaf was on the lawn, and God was nice to play with, and he was going to make what he called a "song-one" about God.

"Now God is on a leaf—and the leaf is on a lawn—on a lawn —on a lawn—and He's got cuff links—He's got them on—on the lawn—and they are gold—they are gold cuff links—and they're yellow—so are the dandelions—and that's how God is—with gas on His stomach—with gas on His stomach—so He can belch if He wants to."

He played all morning with God, and at lunch when his father said, "Amen," Brian said "R. W." again.

"What is it, Spalpeen?" asked his father.

"A little man," said Brian. "Forbsie has the mumps."

"Has he?" said Mr. O'Connal. They ate their lunch.

It was unfortunate that Mrs. O'Connal chose that afternoon to hang out a washing. She picked the time when R. W. had a gas attack necessitating a particularly large belch.

"Don't you ever let me hear you doing that again!" Her eyes were startled as she stood by the line with one of the baby's small sweaters in her hand.

Brian looked up to her. "I didn't do anything."

"But — I just heard you! Don't tell stories, Son."

"It wasn't me," insisted Brian. "R. W. — "

"Brian! Get into the house!"

She made him stay in his room until his father came home. He was allowed down to dinner; his father walked back up the stairs with him. As he pulled up the covers, his father sat on the edge of the bed.

"What's this about fibs, Spalpeen?"

"But, I didn't."

"Your mother says — "

"God did it."

"Just a minute — "

"Mr. R. W. God. I call Him R. W. like you do with Judge Mortimer 'E. L.', and Mr. Hoffman 'S. F.', and like that."

"All right. Just — could you tell me about R. W.?"

"He rides a vacuum cleaner."

"Does He!"

"Yes — with rubber boots on."

"Go on."

"A pipe ... gold cuff links ... He recites."

His father fumbled a moment with the cuff of his shirt.

"He's up to my knee."

"What does He recite?"

" 'Casey at the Bat', and 'When Father Rode the Goat'."

"As well as I do?"

"He can't remember sometimes — all the things."

"I see." For several long moments, Brian's father was silent,

36

his eyes on the bed quilt. He cleared his throat. "Spalpeen, God is —He isn't . . . It's not the thing for little boys to think that God's a — a gentleman who rides vacuum cleaners. It's not right."

"Why?"

"It's sort of silly, isn't it?" Brian still said nothing. "You don't really talk to Him, do you?"

Brian's dark eyes, steady on his father's face now, were disconcerting. They said that it was not silly, that he did see Him, that he did talk to Him.

"We'll just forget about Him. Say your prayers and go to sleep."

As his father listened, Brian said, "Now I lay me down to sleep.

" . . . Bless Mother and Daddy and Gramma and the baby and Uncle Sean and Ab and Forbsie; not Artie — the — the —"

He cast about for someone to fill the gap that Artie Sherry had left—"the boy on the prairie." He looked up at his father. "Is that all?"

"Better stick Artie back in. Who's the boy on the prairie?"

"I saw him once—he's always on the prairie—he likes it."

Mr. O'Connal got up. "Good night, Spalpeen."

"I didn't say, 'Amen.' "

"Didn't you? Well — go ahead."

"Amen," said Brian fervently, "R. W."

FIVE

The puppy's feet were spraddled out, the grass brushing his fat stomach. He was red and white. He was Brian's.

"He's the jeezliest thing."

"What's that?" Brian asked quickly.

"I dunno," said Forbsie, his fat face bent over the pup. "I just made it up."

"His ears flop," pointed out Artie Sherry.

"But they will stick up," Brian assured him. "He'll get older. He's a fox terrier. He's a fox terrier pup."

"I like his belly," said Forbsie.

"He has a very pretty inside to his mouth," Brian said. "Freckles — black ones. Look." The puppy tried to get away from him, but he managed to hold its jaws apart for the other boys to see. "There's tiny, tiny waves," he explained to them. "They're hard ones. You stick your finger in and you'll feel them. I'll let you feel."

Forbsie and Artie felt.

"He's got a candy tongue," said Forbsie as he wiped his fingers on the grass. "How do you get them?"

"I got him a funny way. My dad didn't want me to play with a Friend. I don't play with R. W. any more."

"Who's R. W.?" asked Artie.

"Somebody my dad didn't like."

"Where did your dad get him?" said Forbsie.

"He just brought him home for dinner."

"Where do they get pups?" Forbsie wondered.

"I dunno," said Artie.

"Sash and Door Factory — they might," suggested Brian.

"That ain't right," said Artie.

The puppy's attention was taken by a white butterfly that went scattering past him; he galloped awkwardly after it. An empty matchbox caught his eye; halfway to it he was attracted by a dandelion. He snarled at it.

"He don't seem so bright to me," Artie said. "Is he house-broke?"

"He doesn't do it on rugs. Just on bare floors."

"Do you rub his nose into it?" asked Artie.

"Uh-uh!"

"You're s'posed to."

"I don't care! Nobody's rubbing my dog's nose into anything! I'll fix her!"

"Your maw?" asked Forbsie.

"Gramma. He gets under her feet all the time. He chewed up a lot of squares she was saving for a log-cabin quilt. He coughed them all up in her room. She says he's yappy."

The puppy was yapping shrilly now — at Artie's boot. He stopped to look under his stub tail. He sat up. He yawned. He turned his head over his shoulder, saw Brian, ran to him with his stern wiggling, and climbed up into his lap. Brian tried to hold his head out of reach, but the puppy licked at his nose and tried to get his ear to chew.

It was a shame that he liked to chew things. It was a shame that the grandmother's dresses were so close to the floor and that they rustled. Several times the puppy had got his teeth into the hem and had leaned back tugging. When she had scolded him, he had simply growled puppy growls at her. It was bad enough, she said, having one leg in a brace without having a pup try to upend her every time she turned around.

Three weeks after Brian got his dog, the grandmother's patience almost reached the breaking point. She was crotchety one day at lunchtime when she was unable to find the pillow she usually sat on.

"I've not used it all morning," she said. "I left it on my chair right here in the breakfast room. It is not here now."

"Well," said Brian, "the pup didn't get it."

"I did not say that he did. But if he did not, has it grown legs and walked away?"

"Perhaps it's on your rocker, Mother, in your room."

"It is not there, I tell you."

"I'll just take a look," said Mr. O'Connal.

When Brian's father had brought the pillow downstairs from her room, she did not tell Brian she was sorry. Throughout the meal she complained of the dog. She had never known a smellier dog; as she said this, she lifted her head and sniffed loudly. Brian's mother asked him to leave the table and wash his hands.

Just as dessert was brought to the table, the grandmother's stomach rumbled distantly, ending on a high, singing note much like the ricochet sound of a bullet. It left Brian open-mouthed.

" 'Tis my nervous indigestion," she excused herself. "The dog has done it."

40

"Has the pup been chewing that too?" asked Brian's father jokingly.

The grandmother chose to be hurt. "Go ahead. Poke fun at an old woman while ye still have time for it. Do it now, for I will not be with ye long."

Mr. O'Connal apologized immediately, but the harm had been done. To mollify her mother's feelings, Mrs. O'Connal announced that from now on the dog was not to enter the house; he was to sleep outside — in the garage.

That night, with Brian's help, Mr. O'Connal tied the puppy with a length of binder twine in one corner of the garage. The puppy twisted and turned in frenzy, tugging at the twine around his neck. He bit vainly at it, jumped from it again and again. Then he sat and cried pitiful, squeaking cries.

Brian could hear the puppy long after he had gone to bed, its cries borne to him on the rising wind. Then, after his father and mother had left to visit the Abercrombies, and the wind keening along the eave troughing outside his window had drowned out the dog's howls, Brian was filled with loneliness.

When he was sure that he could stand it no longer, the memory of the boy on the prairie came to him suddenly. He thought of him with his pale hair and his torn, bleached pants, curled up on the prairie, sleeping alone while the wind rushed over the dark face of the prairie to him. He took two blankets from his bed, sneaked down the two flights of stairs and out of the house. He had difficulty in getting the wide garage doors open, and as he struggled he could hear the dog scratching frantically on the other side. One of the doors came open suddenly, and the puppy was jumping up on him. It had chewed through the twine.

It took the dog some time to quiet down; for a while it wriggled ecstatically on Brian's stomach, then curled up in the curve of his elbow. Finally it laid its chin over his shoulder, took one deep breath, nudged Brian's neck with its cold nose, and went to sleep.

It was nice, thought Brian, that his parents had gone to the Abercrombies' for bridge. The dog's stomach rumbled twice. Brian put his arms around its neck. He went to sleep too.

Mr. Abercrombie dealt the cards with deft little flicks that sent them round the table to drop in piles as accurate as the man himself. His hands, thought Mrs. O'Connal, were bank-manager hands, square in their palms and finger tips, the knuckles sharply angled. Their backs were covered with hair like wire, jet against the pale skin; it curled crisply over the edge of his white shirt cuffs. Mrs. O'Connal stirred uncomfortably, small and dark, almost lost in her throne chair with its plum-colored upholstery of Venetian cut-velvet. She hoped that her sons were all right, that if the baby cried her mother would not be sleeping too soundly to hear him.

To Mrs. O'Connal's right, Mrs. Abercrombie was having some difficulty in concealing the irritation she felt at seeing Mr. O'Connal absent-mindedly picking up one by one the cards her husband dealt. . . . Gerald O'Connal's mind was not on bridge. It was in the office of Dr. Svarich, where he had spent part of that afternoon.

As he had linked up his sleeves, Peter Svarich, a thin-faced man with an air of discontent, had watched him, one leg over the corner of the table. "Bit of gastritis, I'd say."

"Serious?" Mr. O'Connal had asked him.

"No — not yet. Might bloom into an ulcer. You could try relaxing a bit," he had gone on in his dry and slightly nasal voice. "Stay away from liquor—pastries—fried stuff; take a quart or two of warm cocoa to the store with you—drink it in the middle of the morning and the afternoon. That'll put out the fire." He got up.

"How old are you?"

"Forty."

"Might be change of life," Svarich had said.

"Had it twice," Mr. O'Connal had told him. . . .

The sound of Abercrombie's flat voice brought him back to the room. "The trouble with the West," Abercrombie was saying, "has been threefold." He paused in dealing the cards. "A — too much credit in the beginning—an unhealthy amount of it through the twenties. B—farmers are not a thrifty lot. C—the wealth of the country doesn't come from sufficiently diversified sources." The cards took up their snickering again.

"We need an up-and-coming man in the church," said Mrs.

Abercrombie. "Just look at the condition of that yard. There's no rhyme or reason to his calls."

She's on poor Hislop again, thought Mrs. O'Connal wearily.

"And then there was that C.G.I.T. thing last Sunday," said Mrs. Abercrombie.

"Why — I thought it a lovely service," said Mrs. O'Connal.

"Did you?" said Mrs. Abercrombie.

Mrs. Abercrombie was as shapeless as her husband was angular; there was a blown softness about her, in her large arms with their dimpled elbows, in the rounding bosom that gave no hint of plurality, in the plump hands that stabbed out blue-white fire whenever she moved them.

Mentally Mrs. O'Connal tried to sort out the rings: one had belonged to Mrs. Abercrombie's mother, and had replaced the cheap one that Mr. Abercrombie had given her when he had been simply a bank clerk in a town without running water or electricity; the large solitaire commemorated his getting a bank of his own; he had given his wife the last one when she had presented him with their daughter, Mariel.

The dealing over, they began to play. Again Mr. O'Connal's mind was not on the cards.

"You might try golf," Svarich had said. "Take a couple of nights off from the drugstore — won't hurt you." He had straightened up and gone to the cupboard in the corner. He took out a jug with brown neck and shoulders. "Drink?"

"No thanks," Brian's father had said, then watched Dr. Svarich fill a glass for himself. The small consultation room had been suddenly filled with wild and alcoholic pungency. "What is it?"

"The Ben's own tonic. Compounded, I believe, of gopher sweat, skunk civet, the plasma of a pregnant weasel — seasoned in prairie sod, guaranteed to make a Tory scream for low tariff — given in payment of an account."

Brian's father had said, "How do you play golf?"

Dr. Svarich had stopped pouring another glass of the Ben's brew. "I don't know. I play chess." He had downed the drink. "Golf is Scotch. I'm Ukrainian."

"Your play, Gerald." His wife's face bore a gently chiding

look; Mrs. Abercrombie's, open impatience.

It was a large face, its largeness made more noticeable by the smallness of each feature in it. Or *on* it, thought Maggie O'Connal; it gave one the feeling that it was embossed. Strange that so large a woman was so energetic; she was active in church work, the Red Cross, the Daughters of the Empire, the Eastern Star, the library board, the local relief committee for the unfortunates of the dried-out area. Through these committees she picked her way with a deliberateness that brooked no contradiction. By virtue of her rings, the dignity of her husband's work, a trip they had taken to Europe six years before, and a certain insensitivity to what others thought, her social position in the town was unassailable.

"What we need is an up-and-coming man in the church," said Mrs. Abercrombie, "a man who will take time by the fetlock."

"I hope the children are covered," thought Mrs. O'Connal, and she forgot to return her husband's lead.

Jake Harris, the town garbage collector, fireman, and policeman, was the possessor of a remarkably ugly face, a series of bumps from forehead to Adam's apple; even Jake's eyes bulged.

He stood in the O'Connal garage with a flashlight turned on Brian and the dog asleep on the floor. He had been summoned from his room on the second floor of the town hall, above the two roan fire- and garbage-wagon horses stabled below. Mrs. O'Connal's usually contained voice had been frantic.

"So this is where you got to."

Brian concerned himself with getting sleep from his eyes.

"You've give yer maw an' paw quite a start."

"I just thought I'd sleep with my pup," Brian said. "He's a fox terrier."

The puppy was awake; he stood for a moment with his feet apart, then went to smell the bottoms of Jake's pants. He wagged his tail. He liked the bottoms of Jake Harris's pants.

"Nice-lookin' pup." Jake leaned down. "I fancy the red an' white myself." He straightened up. "Better git in the house an' let your maw know you're all right."

From the darkness of the front veranda, Brian's mother came

out to meet him; her arms around him were convulsively tight.

Within the house, his grandmother embraced him; but his father, when he had returned from downtown where he had been looking for Brian, was not quite so effusive.

"Why did you ever do a thing like that? Why did you go out to the garage to sleep? Why did you scare the life out of us?"

"I wanted to sleep with my pup," said Brian. "I went out and slept with him."

"I don't suppose it occurred to you that we might worry about you?"

"I just wanted to be with my pup, that's all."

His father looked at him seriously. "Look, Spalpeen, I got that puppy against your mother's wishes. Now—there's been nothing but trouble ever since that dog came to the house—if I hear of any more, there isn't going to be any puppy around the house. Understand?"

Brian nodded.

"I'd hate to do it, Brian."

Over near the eastern edge of the town, darkness was thinning to the pale violet of dawn as Brian got into bed. From behind the O'Connal house came the self-assured crow of one of Gaffer Thomas's roosters. The leaves on the tall poplar that rose outside Brian's window were perfectly still.

SIX

Mr. Hislop laid the letter down on the desk in his study; he stared for a moment at the worn back of the *Harmony of the Gospels*, took the pince-nez glasses from their place on his nose, let them drop to hang down his vest front. He looked at the letter half-folded on the desk.

It was a protesting letter. It had been written by the Ladies' Auxiliary and was signed by Mrs. Abercrombie. The candlelight service of the Canadian Girls in Training had not found favor with the Ladies' Auxiliary. The letter had come as a shock to Hislop, who had assumed that everyone in the congregation had been as pleased as he with the service, with the white middies, blue skirts, and blue ties of the C.G.I.T. girls. They had filed down both aisles of the church, each carrying a candle, their young voices lifted in "Follow the Gleam". To Hislop it had been a moving ceremony; he felt that his sermon had carried a little added fire that day.

Now, he felt rather sick. He had not thought that any members of his congregation would consider the candle ceremony an indication that Knox Presbyterian Church was turning Roman Catholic.

But he might have known, he thought bitterly. Mrs. Abercrombie's intolerance was an evil force in the town; he had known it very soon after taking over the church, when he had been indiscreet enough to play tennis with Father Cochran, and later when she had bucked combining services in the summer with the Baptist church. He got up and went to the study window; there he stood looking out to the hedge and the street beyond.

How could a person be content with the husk, the dry appearances, that gave shape to a religion? What was the sense in his standing up there week after week talking to people who followed such a woman, who looked up to her, envied and admired her? He looked back to the letter on the desk. He wondered if he should show it to his wife, then decided immediately not to. It wasn't just Mrs. Abercrombie; it was the Auxiliary.

Perhaps he should call a meeting of the elders tonight. He could use the assurance of their confidence in him. There had been none of this in the Peace River country, he thought; and his mind went back to his mission field there, the log cabin with its clearing in the bush, the long rides on horseback to reach four churches on a Sunday. Communities had personalities too, and that one had a naïve and simple friendliness that seemed to go with the newness of the country.

He'd better phone Judge Mortimer and ask him to have a few of the elders come over to the house tonight, then drop over to Digby's; that would help. He walked over to the wall by the desk and turned the crank on the telephone before he lifted the receiver.

As he put the receiver back on the hook, he felt a wave of futility pass over him, a despondency deeper than any he had known in his life; he knew that his faith had been badly shaken, faith in the people he preached to, faith in his work, and faith even in — No, that was still solid; they couldn't shake that.

He'd go over and see Digby.

Brian O'Connal, his puppy in his arms, walked down Sixth Street in the direction of MacTaggart's Corner. It had not been the dog's fault: the chain his father had got for it should not have been long enough to reach the washing; the clothesline should have been stronger too. He was remembering the conversation he had overheard between his father and his grandmother after she had found the washing in the dust. "Ye said ye'd send the dog away. If that animal does not go, I will!"

"All right," he had heard his father say. "All right."

Then that night, last night, his father had said to him, "Remember what I told you, Spalpeen?"

"Yes," Brian had said, "I remember."

"There was some trouble this morning."

"He just pulled the clothesline down."

"I have to do something about it."

"Send him away?"

"Well — I've thought of a pretty good idea."

"What?"

"I've had a talk with Forbsie's father. Hoffmans haven't a grandmother staying with them, you know."

"I know."

"A puppy wouldn't cause such a rumpus in a house where there wasn't a grandmother, would he?"

"He wouldn't stop chewing things just because there wasn't any grandmother around."

"I thought that if we were to send the puppy away until it wasn't so much of a pup, it would be a good idea."

"For all the time?"

"No."

48

"Just for a long time," Brian had said, aware that his eyes were stinging.

"Not for a long time," his father assured him — "until he has grown up. Mr. Hoffman says that they'd be glad to look after him for us. I think that's pretty fine of the Hoffmans, don't you?"

"No," Brian got out with difficulty, "I don't."

"Well, Spalpeen, there's nothing else we can do. I can't think of anything else."

"We — couldn't — send Gramma away till — till — he — "

His father had reached into his hip pocket and handed him a handkerchief. He had said, "Damn!"

And after his father had left, Brian had heard him in their bedroom below; he had sounded a lot like Uncle Sean.

Forbsie was standing at MacTaggart's Corner; he had evidently been told of the arrangement made for the dog.

"I'm taking my pup over to stay with you," Brian told him. "Not very long. It's not for good."

"That's dandy," said Forbsie, his fat face shining. "Our pigeon's got some eggs now."

"He's only staying till he gets bigger."

"The eggs are in a nest, and I'm going to have your pup to play with, and — "

"You got to feed him at morning and noon and afternoon and at night too. Give him milk."

"All right," said Forbsie. "Can I carry him a ways?"

"No."

Forbsie was silent a moment. "The eggs are sort of warm if you touch them. The mother pigeon sits on them."

"Don't feed him more than what I say. He'll get fat. His legs will go funny."

"All right. There's going to be baby pigeons come out of those eggs. Could I carry him for a ways now?"

"He's kind of heavy."

"He doesn't look heavy. I could carry him all right."

"No."

"They're in the loft. They — "

"Don't give him a big bone. He's just a pup. Don't give him a big bone. He'll choke."

Mrs. Hoffman, when Brian had taken the puppy into the house, promised him that it would be allowed to sleep by the stove in the kitchen. It would not have to sleep alone out in the barn.

All morning Brian played with the puppy.

All afternoon he played with the puppy.

After dinner he missed the dog badly. He went down to the coal room in the cellar and sat on a chunk of wood there. When he was through, he went up to bed.

About an hour after Brian O'Connal had gone to bed, Mr. Hislop received Judge Mortimer and five elders into his study. Judge Mortimer, agent for the MacDougall Implement Company and police magistrate for the district; Mr. Funder, father of eight children, and owner of the butcher shop; Mr. Nightingale, retired farmer; Mr. Thorborn, owner of the livery stable behind the church and also chairman of the school board; Mr. Jaques, the undertaker for the town; Mr. Jenkins, who owned the dairy: these were the men who listened gravely as Mr. Hislop read them Mrs. Abercrombie's letter.

A stiff and uncomfortable silence had descended on the room as Hislop put down the letter. He looked to his elders questioningly. Judge Mortimer stepped forward slightly from the rest, a broad, gray-mustached man with the impressive dignity that came of presiding in court, and of being sublimely ignorant. He felt the same as Mrs. Abercrombie about the candlelight service. In turn, the other elders expressed their agreement with the sentiment of the letter; only Mr. Nightingale, who was slightly deaf and had not heard enough of the letter to trust himself in a statement, failed to support Mrs. Abercrombie and the Ladies' Auxiliary.

Rather dazedly Mr. Hislop bade his elders goodnight.

In the days that followed, Brian O'Connal came to accept his dog's exile, after he found that he could see him daily. He spent his entire mornings and afternoons over at the Hoffmans'. It was a week later that he and Forbsie first saw the baby pigeons.

The hay in the Hoffmans' loft was piled up at one end; the sunlight, slanting down from a window high in the peak, was almost solid with dust. Upon their stomachs, their chins in their hands, Forbsie and Brian gazed from the top of the hay hill and into the nest on one of the two-by-fours between the barn wall studding.

In the nest were open mouths, eager and unsteady upon wormlike necks.

"They came out of the eggs," Forbsie said with a proprietary ring in his voice.

"Will their mother sit on them like she did on the eggs?"

"I wonder how they got in there in the first place?" said Forbsie. "There weren't any holes for them to crawl into that I could see. How did they do it?"

"I'll ask my dad."

Brian did not climb through the hole in the loft floor when Forbsie left. He watched the baby pigeons for a long time. He was still there when Forbsie returned. Throughout the morning, while he played with the dog and paid numerous visits to the pigeons, he pondered over the question of their origin.

He was still considering it as he walked home to lunch. The morning, which had been a bright one, had now turned dull with the sky dark to the southwest, the sun overhead almost completely obscured. The wind had risen earlier than usual and had an unusual coolness about it. Brian met his father returning from work, just as he came to MacTaggart's Corner.

"Dad," he said as he walked by his side, "I want to ask you about some pigeons. How did they get in there?"

"Where, Spalpeen?"

"Those eggs. How did they get in there in the first place?"

"The father pigeon put them there."

"How?"

"Well, at first there wasn't any egg. Then the mother pigeon put the egg around it."

"She built it?"

"Yes, she built it."

"I guess that's right," said Brian. "I'm going to tell Forbsie."

But Brian was not able to get over to Forbsie's after lunch; it began to rain. It began furiously, a breath-taking downpour at first that settled down to the monotonous, businesslike rain that farmers had looked for ever since spring seeding. At no time during the rest of the day did it look as though it intended clearing up.

When Brian awoke the next morning, it was still raining. His mother insisted that he stay in the house for the rest of the day. And the rain was still falling the next afternoon as he sat disconsolately at the living room window. It was a long, bay window with a built-in seat, facing Artie Sherry's house to the south.

Brian watched the drops gather and slide, slowly at first, then faster, down the pane. The sky over Sherry's low house was the color of lead; the sodden leaves of the hedge were dripping. He felt inexplicably sad. The pictures in the family Bible and in the *Book of Knowledge* no longer held any interest for him. He had not seen his dog for three days.

He had asked his mother time and again if he could go over to Forbsie's to see the puppy and the baby pigeons; he had been told just as often that he could not go out until the rain had stopped. He hated the rain.

His eyes rested on the leaves of the shamrock plant in its red clay pot on the window sill. Perhaps if he had a baby pigeon at home, he wouldn't miss his pup so much; baby pigeons didn't chew things. His grandmother couldn't kick up a fuss about a little baby pigeon. He wished that his mother would let him go over to Forbsie's so he could bring back a baby pigeon until it had stopped raining.

He got up and went through the archway and into the living room, where the baby stood in his play pen.

"B'ian," his brother said and held out his arms to be picked up.

Brian turned away from him. The baby began to cry. His mother came out of the breakfast room. "Leave the baby alone, Son."

"I didn't do anything to him."

"Well, stay in the den, or the dining room, so that he won't cry. You can come into the breakfast room with me if you want to."

He shook his head. He felt as though he were going to burst into tears at any minute. He went back to the dining room window and looked out at the rain again.

In the Presbyterian manse study, Mr. Hislop turned away from the window. "There's nothing else I can do," he said to Digby.

"It's a damn shame!" said the schoolteacher. "You don't make it any better — you should have ignored the letter."

"You can't," said Hislop. "You can't ignore a thing like that. It's not just the letter—it's what's behind it. I couldn't get up each Sunday and preach to them, knowing they—that they all felt as she did —"

"The trouble with you," said Digby, "is that you're too thin-skinned. You're tender. That's no good if you're a minister—or a schoolteacher. You've got to be tough — good and tough. I'm tough. You're not."

"And my elders—I never thought for a minute they'd take the stand they did. I'll have to resign."

"Fight 'em," said Digby. "Get up there and give it to them. You're lucky; you've got them where you want them. How I'd like to have my school board in front of me once a week — unable to talk back!"

"If it only hadn't happened," said Hislop. "It makes me feel like a fool — stupid — blind — gullible fool! I knew they thought I was impractical—you can always expect a certain amused patronizing from your congregation—but—"

Digby got up from his chair; he went over to Hislop and put his arm over the minister's shoulder. The two stood silently side by side looking out at the rain.

On Hoffman's barn roof, the rain was loud; the hayloft was dim. Brian had not called in at Forbsie's house. No one knew that he was up here. In the dusk of the loft he could just see the heads of the baby pigeons. They were partly feathered, their eyes opened. The mother pigeon had left the nest, slapping her wings frantically at

Brian's approach. She walked back and forth now, cooing anxiously on a rafter at the other end of the loft.

Brian reached out and touched the head of one of the baby pigeons; it was blood-warm. He stroked the weaving head with his finger. He slid his hand under the pigeon and took it from the nest, cheeping loudly.

He held it to his chest, his head bent over it. He put it inside his shirt, then buttoned up his coat.

A baby pigeon was almost as good as a pup.

SEVEN

The rain had stopped, and the air had
the clear coolness that belongs to it after rain. Over the prairie,
shallow sloughs were filled to their edges; the thirsty earth had
drunk up the water and left much of it to lie in clear puddles
between the hummocks; summer fallow fields were welters of
gumbo mud; clear drops beaded the foxtail, wild oats, and
buckbrush; they sparkled diamondlike from the lupine that spread

a purple shadow over the prairie; they gleamed from Sean O'Connal's wheat, brown and wilted, five miles south of the town. Sean, with his weathered hat sodden and his fierce red mustaches dripping, stared down at the crop soaked with moisture that had come too late to do it any good.

"Goddam them!" he cried. "Goddam their souls as green and hard as God's little green apples! Goddam their goddam souls!"

In town the air had a fresh and sparkling quality; eaves dripped steadily into rain barrels overflowing. In the running gutters could be seen the reflection of the sun, now a clean, whole disk, now a broken, quicksilver thing that joined, then broke again into rippling bars. Water lay in a wide sheet on the road before the Presbyterian manse.

Within the study, Mr. Hislop looked over the letter of resignation he had written to his elders.

Rain still streaked the windows of the O'Connal back porch where Brian O'Connal sat on the floor, staring down at the baby pigeon in his hand. His father stood tall above him. The bird's skin lids were closed over its eyes; the bald head, with its tiny plowshare beak edged with yellow, hung down.

The little sack of a body was not warm.

"It's dead, Spalpeen," Brian's father said gently.

"Why?"

"It happens to things," his father said.

"Why does it happen to things?" He turned up his face to his father, cheeks stained with drying tears.

"That's the way they end up."

Brian looked down again at the baby pigeon in his hand. "It was in an egg. Now it's stopped."

"Yes, Spalpeen, it's stopped."

"I want my pup."

"All right. We'll bring him back."

"Why did it — "

"Let me have it, Spalpeen."

"What are you going to do?"

58

"I'll bury it for you."

"What's that?"

"Dig a hole for it. Cover it with earth."

"Why?"

"That's what you do when things die. They call it 'burying'."

"Where will you do it?"

"Where do you want me to?"

"I don't know."

"The back garden?"

"I guess so." He looked down at the baby pigeon's limp body again; it was just like dirt, he thought, like prairie dirt that wasn't alive at all. He looked up to his father again. "I know where. The prairie — dig a hole for it in the prairie."

"All right," his father said.

"Where the boy is," said Brian. "There is where — not with houses." He was aware of a sudden relief; the sadness over the death of the baby pigeon lifted from him.

"After dinner, then, Spalpeen," his father promised.

The late evening sun lay dilute on the flat fronts of the houses along Sixth Street as Brian and his father walked out to the prairie. They felt the washed coolness of the air against their skin; they saw summer lightning far off on the horizon, bright against the dark purple of clouds banked there.

By a pile of field stone just outside the town's edge, the father turned to the boy. The son lifted his arm with the bird's neck lank from his small fist. The father knelt, placed the dead pigeon on the sod beside him, and began to dig with the small, green garden trowel he had brought out.

He stood up, brushed the dirt from his hands, looked into his son's face. As he did, he caught a flicker of movement in a clump of buckbrush to the left. He walked toward it, his son behind him. He bent down and carefully parted the bushes.

Crouched there, looking up, was the boy that Brian had met out on the prairie earlier in the summer. His eyes were wild.

The father let the branches go back together.

"He was watching," said the son as they walked back to the town. "He does that all the time."

"Do you know him?"

"I knew him a long time ago."

"But when have you ever known—you've never seen him in town, have you?"

"He's a lot different. He said we could bring the pigeon out here."

"Did he?"

"Yes. He told me to. It's his."

"What is, Spalpeen?"

"The prairie is."

"How is it his?"

"He lies down on top of it."

"But—how is it *his* prairie?"

"I don't know. It just is. What's his name?"

The father looked down at his son, a puzzled look upon his face. "That's the Young Ben."

At the edge of the town, they turned and stood, looking out over the prairie, to its far line where sheet lightning winked up the world's dark rim. Here and there, low along the horizon, pygmy farm buildings stood out momentarily—were quickly blotted. The soft and distant explosions of light were accompanied by a sound as of lumber being carelessly dropped.

Father and son began to walk home.

Two days later, Brian lay under the hedge on the Sherry side of the house, his puppy in his arms. Sun streamed through the chinks in the Caragana leaves; a light breeze stirred them; Brian could see part of the road in front of the house; he could see two butterflies in lifting falling flight over the lawn patched with shade, briefly together, briefly apart. He lost sight of them by the spirea at the veranda.

The puppy whimpered slightly in its sleep; it nudged its head further into Brian's neck. The boy was aware that the yard was not still. Every grass-blade and leaf and flower seemed to be breathing, or perhaps, whispering—something to him—something for him. The puppy's ear was inside out. Within himself, Brian felt a soft explosion of feeling. It was one of completion and of culmination.

The poplars along the road shook light from their leaves. A tin can rolled in the street; a newspaper plastered itself against the base of a telephone pole; loose dust lifted. Dancing down the road appeared a dust-devil. It stopped, took up again, and went whirling out to the prairie.

In the summer sky there, stark blue, a lonely goshawk hung. It drifted low in lazing circles. A pause—one swoop—galvanic death to a tan burgher no more to sit amid his city's grained heaps and squeak a question to the wind.

Shadows lengthen; the sunlight fades from cloud to cloud, kindling their torn edges as it dies from softness to softness down the prairie sky. A lone farmhouse window briefly blazes; the prairie bathes in mellower, yellower light, and the sinking sun becomes a low and golden glowing on the prairie's edge.

Leaning slightly backward against the reins looped round his waist, a man walks homeward from the fields. The horses' heads move gently up and down; their hoofs drop tired sound; the jingle of the traces swinging at their sides is clear against the evening hush. The stubble crackles; a killdeer calls. Stooks, fences, horses, man, have clarity that was not theirs throughout the day.

PART TWO

EIGHT

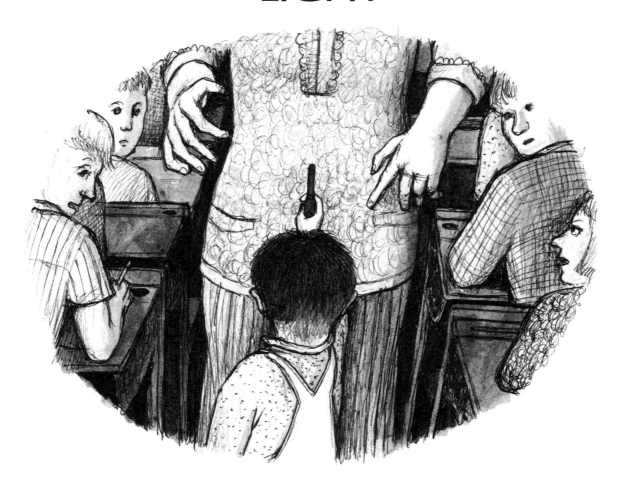

Although two years of wind had piled the black dust even higher against the fences and farm buildings, and the yellow-stubbled fields were thinly stooked with the meager stooks of lean times, the fall of 1931 still brought the excitement of harvest with it. The baize-green of young wheat no longer spread over the flat expanse of prairie; the incessant winds rolled waves no longer through the darker green of June growth. For several weeks men had been busy in the fields, following the binders, stooping to pick up the sheaves and pile them into the stooks that thimbled the land.

It was an urgent time of the year for the town, whose livelihood depended upon the prairie. Down the streets on both sides of the river, tractors hauled threshing machines with feeders turned back upon themselves, linked to cook-cars and followed in turn by the wheeled half-cylinders of water wagons. High, spreading grain wagons passed through on grinding wheels; long caterpillars of grain freights often blocked First Street with their slow passage for minutes at a time.

Strange men swung down from the trains, their blanket rolls slung over one shoulder, bright flannel shirts open at the neck, their lean faces dark with coal dust. They stood before the beer parlor of the Royal Hotel, in front of Drew's Pool and Snooker Hall, or on the bank corner, waiting for the farmers who came into town, looking for bundle pitchers, spikers, and team skinners. There was harvest work for perhaps half the men who came to the town, at a dollar and a half a day, the day lasting from five in the morning to seven at night.

The crop was poor and the wheat would bring only twenty-five cents a bushel. It cost thirty cents to grow, but it must be harvested.

On the morning of the first day of September, the bright noise of sparrows woke Brian. The curtains in his room breathed in and out with the fall breeze as he lay still beside his brother; he could see his clothes folded over the foot of the white-enameled iron bed. His mother had put them there the night before. Today was to be his first day in school.

From under the bed came a frantic scrabbling of sound; the red and white fox terrier jumped up. His one red ear gave to his head an archly tilted look; a saddle-shaped patch of red spread over his back. "Down, Jappy." Brian pushed him from the bed; he flung back the covers. Bobbie slept on, his plump fist against his fat face, his tightly curled red hair bright against the rumpled pillow.

The dog jumped against Brian's leg as the boy stood a moment

66

by the side of the bed. Brian O'Connal was short for his six years and slight with the leanness and darkness of an Indian boy; as his grandmother had often said, it was the black Scotch MacMurray in him. He held his head back and upright with a sureness that was also his grandmother's.

With the dog trotting after him, he went to the open window. He would not have to say that next year he was going to school, thought Brian—or next fall, or next week: he was going today. He was going to school just as Artie Sherry did. He was old enough now. He would find out all about things. He would learn. He wouldn't get the strap.

"You up?" Bobbie was sitting, his red hair tousled, the sleep in his blue eyes not quite able to dim their wild twinkle. He was a chunky boy, four now, and solid, in his Uncle Sean's words, as a brick outhouse. "I wish I was going to school."

"You will when you get old enough." Brian turned from the window. He began to dress while Bobbie watched him from the bed.

Downstairs Maggie O'Connal stood at the stove in the kitchen; she prepared the family breakfast with quick, bird-like movements. Brian said good morning to her as though it were any morning, trying his best to hide the excitement that was in him, to act as though he were used to going to school every morning. He was not very successful. There was a strange tightness in his mother's face; a look of concern in her brown eyes with their fine crow's-feet at the corners.

"Off to school, Spalpeen?" Brian felt a rush of emotion, as he always did when his father spoke to him. Gerald O'Connal ruffled his son's hair as he passed Brian; he sat down at the opposite end of the table. His dark red hair with gray beginning to grizzle it had a roan look along the sides of his head. In the last year his complexion had lost the blood-flush that had warmed it. He cleared his throat. "You—uh—do as they tell you, Brian."

"He will," Brian's mother said quickly. "I'm sure he will."

"I'm six now," said Brian as he picked up his spoon.

"I'm four," Bobbie said. "I'm going to school next year. I don't want any porridge."

"Porridge makes ye grow," said the grandmother, who had come in with him. Her hair was thinner now; her skin had taken on a transparency new to it. Lace hung from the velvet band around her throat; it failed to hide completely the gentle swell of a goiter there.

"I still think I should go with him — "

"No, Maggie," Brian's father interrupted her.

"You don't have to go," said Brian. "Forbsie's starting too, and his mother isn't going with him."

The look upon Maggie O'Connal's small face deepened; it was not a happy one.

"I'm not very fussy about porridge," Bobbie announced.

"Well, ye must eat it," said the grandmother; "it makes ye grow."

"I'm not fussy about growing."

"Eat it up, Son," his mother said with the tone in her voice that Bobbie knew meant no further argument. He began to eat his oatmeal, stuffing it in with great, heaping spoonfuls. Actually he was very fond of it.

As he broke up stale bread and poured milk over it for his dog, Brian wished that parents wouldn't act as they were doing. They seemed to think it was awful to go to school. He'd heard Artie talk of getting the strap, and of Mr. Digby's getting after a person for shouting in the halls; still, that was no reason for his mother and father's acting as they were. He straightened up from the dog's dish by the sink.

"It's not time yet," said his mother.

"I know. I'm going upstairs a minute."

In his room he picked up the pistol that lay on the table by the bed; it was a water pistol with a rubber bulb for a handle, cross-hatched with creases, the rest of it cast-lead. He carried it with him always and was not truly dressed without it, or without the gloves that had red stars sewn on the fringed, funnel-shaped parts that covered his sleeves. He went downstairs again.

" . . . He's so young," he heard his mother saying.

"She says you're awful young to go alone," said Bobbie.

"No, I'm not. What time is it?"

70

His father looked at his watch. "Half-past eight."

"I better be going."

His mother went over to him quickly and bent down. He kissed her and felt her arm tighten on his shoulder. When he straightened up and felt that his cheek was damp, he was impatient with her.

He left the kitchen after instructing Bobbie to hold the dog until he'd got away from the house. Dogs did not go to school.

"I thought," Gerald O'Connal said when Brian had gone, "that it was only the Irish who were sentimental."

Maggie O'Connal, with her back to him as she faced the stove, did not answer him.

"There's only one kind of Irishman," said the grandmother, "shanty Irish. They're not sentimental. They're dirty."

"And the Scots are tight," said O'Connal.

"Not tight," returned the grandmother, "canny."

"Another name for it," said Brian's father.

"He's so—so—*damned* independent," said Maggie O'Connal. She turned to Bobbie and spoke with unusual sharpness. "Don't you go any farther than MacTaggart's Corner — understand?"

Bobbie, who frequently strayed far from home, was intent on his porridge.

Forbsie's fat face shone. "Do we have to line up?" he said to Artie.

"Everybody does," Artie answered, his face contorting at the offending glasses. "The girls go in the girls' door an' the boys go in the boys' door. You better not let 'em catch you going in the girls' door."

"Why not?" asked Brian.

"You're not s'posed to. There's two toilets. There's the girls' toilet on the girls' side — an' the boys' on the boys' side — in the basement."

"Is there!" said Forbsie.

"That's where old Tinhead is." Artie referred to Mr. Briggs, the school janitor, said to have a silver plate in his head ever since he had served with the Princess Pats in the war.

Ahead of them and behind them small groups of children made their way to the school on the eastern edge of the town. "There's the China Kids," said Artie.

Brian saw them, the Wongs, Tang and Vooie. It was Vooie's first day at school, and his sister, Tang, with the protectiveness of an older sister, had the collar of his coat clenched tight in her hand. Brian had seen the Wong children often, for they had grown up on that section of gray cement that ran before their father's Bluebird Café. Now that the mother, a small amber woman brought from China by Wong to bear him Tang and Vooie, had died, the father had left Vooie to his sister's care. He cooked meals for the children, and that was all. Brian knew Wong too, a small, stooped Chinese with a white mustache, who wore summer and winter a rooster-comb-red toque. Brian had seen him often behind the café counter with its welter of cigarette and tobacco packets, its jaw breakers, licorice plugs, whips, pipes, and staring fried-egg candies.

Brian's confidence ebbed as they neared the schoolyard on the prairie edge and as Artie regaled the other boys with stories of the terrible Miss MacDonald. She was cranky; she hated kids; it was she, he told Forbsie and Brian, who would be their teacher.

Until the bell rang, Forbsie and Brian stood with their backs to the orange brick of Lord Roberts School, watching other boys play catch, or wrestle in the bare dirt. The swings on the town side were occupied; girls swinging idly with one foot trailing, the boys pumping high and mightily. When the bell rang somewhere in the depths of the school, the children formed reluctantly into two lines at the doors; those left outside the lines were the beginners, forlorn little souls whom Miss MacDonald came out to shepherd in to the school. She assigned them their seats in the lower grades room, at the head of the stairs, told them to sit quietly and play with the colored plasticine Mariel Abercrombie had passed out. Then she turned to hand out the readers to the Grade Threes, of which Artie Sherry was a member.

The first excitement over, Brian began to find school a rather disappointing affair. Forbsie sat across from him, Artie two rows over. He would go over and see Artie for a while, Brian decided; he got up and started down the aisle. Miss MacDonald, at the board, turned and saw him. "Sit down, Brian."

"I'm just going over to see Artie."

"You'll have to sit down." She turned back to the board.

Brian continued on his journey to Artie. She wasn't his mother; he wasn't hurting anything; he wasn't doing anything wrong.

"I said to sit down!"

He stopped at the end of the aisle. "I just want to see Artie for a minute."

"You must put up your hand if you want something. Then I'll give you permission to see Artie."

He stood watching her.

"Sit down in your seat!"

He continued to stand. Miss MacDonald's thin face reddened slightly. She bit her lip. *Sit down!*"

Brian stood. Utter classroom quiet had descended. Outside the window a meadow lark went up his bright scale with a *one-two-three-and-here-I-go*. Miss MacDonald began to walk down the aisle in which Brian was standing. He reached into his hip pocket and felt the comfort of the water pistol there. Miss Mac-Donald stopped three seats ahead of him. "Will you sit down!"

Wordlessly he drew the pistol out, being careful not to squeeze the butt. He held it behind his back. Miss MacDonald reached out her hand to guide him back to his seat. It paused in midair as Brian brought the water pistol to view. One clear drop of water hung from the end pointing at Miss MacDonald's midriff. Her mouth flew open. She stared at the pistol and at the slight drip of water from the small hand holding it.

"I filled it," Brian assured her, "out of the fountain."

Her face flamed. "Give me that pistol!"

He made no move to hand it to her.

Her hand darted out to the water pistol. Startled, Brian squeezed. The pistol squirted. Miss MacDonald, with her dripping hand, jerked the pistol from his grasp. She propelled him from the room.

As he walked ahead of her to the end of the hall where the Principal's office was, Brian's heart pounded; he was in for it. The front of her dress dripping, Miss MacDonald knocked on the Principal's door. It opened, and Mr. Digby, tall and sandy-haired, a questioning look upon his rough face, stood there.

With emotion poorly concealed, Miss MacDonald told him what had happened, the indignant spray of saliva from her thin lips unheeded, the corners of her mouth quivering. When she had finished, Digby said:

"You'd better let your classes go. Miss Spencer has, hers. I'll attend to Brian."

The door closed on Miss MacDonald's outraged back.

Mr. Digby walked to the desk, sat down; he leaned forward with his elbows on the top. "Well, Brian?"

The boy stared at him.

"Little trouble?"

With his dark gaze deliberately unflinching, Brian continued to stare.

Mr. Digby's long fingers began to drum the desk top. He leaned back in the chair; the fingers drummed on. He cleared his throat. "Don't — Won't you talk to me?"

Unchanged, Brian's face looked up to the Principal; no expression was there, certainly no inclination to talk was indicated. Mr. Digby rose from his chair, Brian's eyes lifting with him.

"You — Don't you like school, Brian?"

No sign betrayed Brian's response one way or the other to the institution of education.

"We're only trying to — to — " What were they trying to do? He'd talked it over enough with Hislop when he'd been here. Each year a new crop. Teach them to line up six times a day, regulate their lives with bells, trim off the uncomfortable habits, the unsocial ones — or was it simply the ones that interfered with . . . ? "We . . . want to help you. You want people to like you, don't you?"

He could see the gentle swell and ebb of the boy's chest under his sweater, that and nothing more.

"You want to get along with people. You want to grow up to be . . . " An individual whose every emotion, wish, action, was the resultant of two forces: what he felt and truly wanted, what he

74

thought he should feel and ought to want. Give him the faiths that belonged to all other men.

His mind shied from his thinking like a horse from too high a jump. The thing was to get the child to talk—without frightening it out of him. "Miss MacDonald is your teacher now. You must do as she says. It's—it's like . . . " He cast about for something to say, any wedge to slip under the barrier between them. "You do what your mother tells you," he pried. "You don't disobey her."

Still no interest or understanding showed in the boy's dark eyes.

What would the boy understand?

"Have you a dog, Brian?"

There was a flicker of the boy's eyes. That was it.

"He does what you tell him. You expect him to do what you want him to. A dog isn't much good if he won't do what he's told." He looked for a moment at the boy with his erect back, his legs slightly apart. "Does he do any tricks?"

"He can jump over—" The words spilled out, then stopped.

"Over your arms if you hold them out?"

"Over a stick," Brian corrected him.

"Oh." The teacher was silent because he knew it was the right moment to say nothing.

"Tricks aren't any good. He's going to catch gophers. That isn't a trick."

The Principal nodded.

"They're *for* catching gophers."

"That's right."

"Fox terriers. He's a fox terrier. I don't like her."

"Don't you?"

"She tried to make me sit down. I didn't feel like sitting down. I wasn't hurting anything."

"What if everyone in the room wanted to stand up? She couldn't teach very well then, could she?"

Brian considered a moment. "She stands up."

"That's because she's the teacher."

"Does she have to stand up to teach people things?"

Digby nodded.

"Maybe I have to stand up to learn things," suggested Brian.

"Do you *have* to?"

"Maybe I do," said Brian. "Does she?"

"Maybe she does," said Digby.

"Well, I don't."

"You could learn anyway," suggested Digby, "couldn't you?"

"Yes, I could. But I don't think I'll learn from her. I better have another teacher."

"I don't think that could be arranged," Digby explained to him. "You see, she's the only one we have for Grade One. You want to go to school, don't you?"

"Oh, yes, I'm going to find out about things."

"Then you'd better try to get along with Miss MacDonald." There was a note of firmness in Digby's voice.

Brian was silent. Digby reached into his desk drawer; he drew out the water pistol and handed it to Brian. "She'd like you to have this back," he said, knowing that it was the farthest thing from Miss MacDonald's desires.

"Thank you. It doesn't work very good anyway."

"All right. No more school today — this afternoon. Think about what I said."

For some time after Brian had left, Digby sat at his desk. On the half-opened window behind him a fly, lulled to languor by the morning sun, bunted crazily up the pane, fell protestingly, and lay half-paralyzed on the sill, the numbness of his sound lost in the emptiness of the office.

With a feeling of helplessness that couldn't come quite into focus, Digby thought of his perennial problem — the Young Ben. In looking down on that broad-boned face with its gray eyes and the cheeks nutmegged with freckles, he had wondered often if the Young Ben were a child. Digby reached out and straightened *The Highroad to Learning* on his desk. As at the beginning of every term the Young Ben had attended school, he had not showed up for registration. The Principal would have to go out to the Bens.

76

The feeling of helplessness flooded over him as he thought of the Ben, the boy's father; the drunken, irresponsible and utterly mindless Ben, always at odds with some rule, law, or convention; shooting prairie chicken out of season or without a licence, running his still, completely unaware of the demands of family or community. The Ben was seldom sober; he knew only two stages of drunkenness, the dramatic and the unconscious. The first was loud with an obscenity expressed best in song; the second, final — leaving him sprawled in a snowdrift in the deep of winter, or draped over a downtown curb at the mercy of botflies in summer. From either of these positions he was usually rescued by the town constable, Jake Harris, or by the Young Ben.

With a feeling of relief Digby turned his thoughts to the boy who had just left the office; and then, with irritation, to Miss MacDonald. The damn woman needed a refresher course — Child Mediumship — something.

He got up. He'd have to call on the Bens after lunch.

NINE

Without seeing either Forbsie or Artie, Brian walked to MacTaggart's Corner, then turned south on the cement walk. He turned again at the corner, and continued on to First Street with its false-fronted stores.

O'Connal's Drugstore stood next to Harris's Hardware; across the alleyway on the other side was Drew's Pool and Snooker Hall. Along the base of the plate-glass windows, on either side of the door, ran the legend, G. L. O'CONNAL—DRUGS. A jar ornate with gilt, and with ruby twilight glowing in its heart, hung over the doorway. Brian opened the screen.

Leon, his father's clerk, stood by the magazine rack, waiting on Mrs. Abercrombie. At the counter along the back, upon which the cash register stood, Brian paused. He looked up to the black-framed diploma on the wall. At the bottom was a shining red cogwheel seal. Brian went round the end of the counter and into the dispensary. He never did this without experiencing a slight proprietary thrill; as he looked along the rows of labeled bottles, at the white pestle and mortar, the pan scales, and the ranks of drawers also labeled, it was with the knowledge that these were his father's.

His white jacket gleaming under the light bulb hung from the ceiling, Brian's father glanced up from Svarich's chicken-track writing on a prescription. "School out, Spalpeen?"

Brian's eyes were on one of the drawers; an old friend was there—"lick-rish" root. He looked up to his father. He'd have to tell of what had happened this morning, sooner or later. With a rush of words he described for his father the morning's events. When he had finished, his father said:

"You'll just have to make sure it doesn't happen again."

"I'll try," Brian promised him. "May I have a chocolate bar?"

"Spoil your dinner. I'll bring one home for you. Told your mother?"

"Not yet. I thought I'd tell you. You tell her for me."

"All right. Better head for home now. Oh—see if you can find Bobbie. Mother phoned."

Slightly lighter of heart, Brian left the store. It was always easier to explain to his father. With the discernment that children have, Brian and Bobbie had both measured the indulgence of their father. They felt in their mother an immutability that made the consequences of wrongdoing inevitable.

In Maggie O'Connal there was a vein of Gaelic "gumption". Unstained by the sin of oversimplifying, she had at an early age arrived at an appreciation of life's complexity and the contrariness of the world's contents, animal, vegetable, mineral, spiritual, and economic. Because there was not in her the slightest trace of conceit, she could not count her chickens before they were hatched; she could not take the easy way with her children. She expected much of them; her punishment seldom went beyond the coolness of disapproval. She had plans for her sons; she wanted them to be as neat as a stooked field, as sweet as a loft of hay, but above all — mature.

At the moment that Brian stood outside the drugstore, looking up and down the street for his brother's wagon, Bobbie was three blocks over on the high station platform, sitting in his red wagon under the broad eave of the station building. The eleven-fifteen train had just come in, and the express agent, Mr. MacKellar, with two helpers, was in the act of unloading the town's express into a high-wheeled cart. Bobbie watched the unloading; he watched the cart being wheeled to the express shed. He watched Mr. Stapells shoulder the mailbags and carry them to the light delivery truck that bore the royal coat of arms on its door, signifying that it carried His Majesty's mail. As the truck drove away he turned the tongue of his wagon and went down from the platform.

During the summer, the business district had become the scene of Bobbie's daily Odyssey; a small, red-haired Ulysses, he traveled by red wagon, one knee up, one leg propelling him along as he steered with the tongue in his fat fist. On his way to the post office from the station, he left his wagon in front of Drew's Pool Hall. Inside, he watched billiards, snooker, pea-pool, skittles, played under the green-shaded lights where men made and missed shots, cursed and spit into gleaming brass spittoons. After leaving the pool hall he traveled on to the post office, and there watched people take mail from the glassed doors that lined one wall, then down the post office steps and past the bank corner to the town hall. He ran his wagon through the open double doors next to the town secretary's office just as the noon whistle sounded.

As he entered, a bell in the back broke into the hard and sustained clangor of daily fire drill. Two doors opened out; two great-rumped, roan horses emerged and stood patiently under the harness that hung from the ceiling, before red fire-wagons gleaming with polished brass. The fire hall was a place that Bobbie left out of his travels on Thursdays and Saturdays; Thursday was garbage day; Saturday was sprinkle day, when Jake Harris hitched up the roan horses to the town water wagon and went up and down the streets, combing them with two curved sprays. On Thursdays Bobbie visited the low brick building at the end of First Street, with its larger-than-life-size picture of the Prince of Wales over the door; for a moment he would watch it shake visibly, then he would go inside to see the presses run off the four-page *Times*, which Mr. Stickle edited.

For now, he watched the standing fire- and garbage-wagon horses, his mouth slightly parted in his round and freckled face, savoring the smell of horse, hay, and manure. This was the climax of his travels. That morning he had visited and watched Allie Gatenby working on a kitchen cabinet for Mrs. Baine, the workshop littered with plane shavings, a redolent pot of glue thickly bubbling on the small stove in the middle of the floor. He had watched Milt Palmer cover a rawhide saddle-tree, had heard a horseshoe hiss when plunged into the round tub outside the blacksmith shop, had seen the shaving of a man, the greasing of a car, the assembling of a threshing machine, and the pasting-up of an Old Stag Chewing Tobacco poster. Not one of these had approached the delight of watching the fire horses at noon drill.

He heard a shout, and looked up to see his brother, Brian.

"C'mon home — you're going to get it."

As they came to the bank corner, Bobbie stopped his wagon to stare at the bathtub body of an old Ford, naked of any top. "That's Uncle Sean's car," he said.

Brian looked at the car a moment, then remembered he had been charged with getting his brother home. "I know it — c'mon home." With his hand on Bobbie's shoulder, he began to walk up the street in the direction of the house.

Just as his wife was the most imposing woman in the town, Mr. Abercrombie's bank was its most pretentious building. It was not false-fronted, it was not of wood, but of a pure and shining terra cotta, hinting at the classical in its architecture.

In his office next to the grilled PAYING AND RECEIVING cages,

Mr. Abercrombie sat in a square, leather chair behind a broad desk upon which his angular hands toyed with the pen from the desk set there. Sean O'Connal, his pale red mustaches tinted slightly darker where tobacco juice had been, sat on an inadequate wooden chair before the desk.

"I'm sorry," Abercrombie was saying flatly. "My reason is threefold. A — you can offer no security. B — you owe the bank more than you can hope to repay. C — it is not practical."

"But — it is," said Sean, with difficulty keeping his temper under control. "If it hadn't bin fer the goddam drought this year, I'd bin able to swing it myself. It's jist — all I need is three hunderd — with that I kin git the lumber fer the snow fences, dig the dugout fer to catch the run-off in spring —"

"I'm not saying it wouldn't work," said the manager, "but I fail to see just how it would increase your income, so that you'd be able to — "

"I don't give a good goddam if it increases any income! It's jist to show them what a fella kin do if he wants: irrigation — garden irrigation — enough to have a garden green! Why — if every farmer in this district was to — "

"I say again — my reason is threefold. A — "

"An' what you say is stupid!" roared Sean. "Threefold stupid fer threefold stupid reasons! A — hen manure! B — heifer dust! C — buffalo chips!"

Brian's mother met her sons at the door of the house. Her husband had told her of Brian's morning at school; she made no mention of it as she led the boys in to the breakfast room, or throughout the lunch. The meal over, she took a length of clothesline rope, tied one end of it to the fence at the back of the house, the other around Bobbie's middle; she placed a little wicker chair by the garage wall for him to sit on.

When she returned to the house she took Brian with her into his father's den.

"Now, Son," she said to him, "Daddy's told me. I just wanted to tell you one thing. School's important. I want you to learn whatever there is to learn."

82

"I don't like her."

"That makes no difference. You've always done what I've told you—you know that Mother loves you—that . . . Oh, Son, I don't want you to be a *gowk*!"

Brian received her outburst with a sudden thrill of feeling at the unusualness of it.

"I won't," he said fervently. "I won't, Mother!"

The swarming hum of telephone wires was vibrant in the afternoon silence; the stooked fields on either side of him shifted and changed as Digby walked out to Haggerty's Coulee, where the Bens lived. As he walked, the schoolmaster thought of the Young Ben's school record, of the interminable whippings he had given the boy. He had known it was useless as he sweated over the ritual, the Young Ben lifting one hand after the other, high to the sting of the regulation length of breeching harness given the Principal by Mr. Thorborn, chairman of the school board and owner of the draying business and livery barn behind the Presbyterian church. The whippings were only in deference to the public opinion of the town, which felt that the Young Ben was a bad actor like his father and that he should be sent to "an institution".

Mr. Digby stepped off the road to let a car pass, and as he did he saw that he had reached the turn in the road and the river that marked Haggerty's Coulee. In a moment he was looking down on the Ben establishment with its weather-grayed sheds, its shack walls piled with dirt for warmth's sake, its yard given to unbelievable piles of manure steaming in the fall sun. Several of the ten cows in the herd that the Mrs. Ben had managed to build up from one Holstein — legacy of an older Ben, who had been hit on the head with a bucket while cleaning out a well — could be seen below. There was no sign of the Ben himself, but as Digby stood at the top of the trail he heard the slapping sound of a screen door, and then saw the figure of Mrs. Ben in a shapeless black gown, picking her barefooted way across the yard. He hailed her. She looked up, shading her eyes against the sun with her hand.

In the yard a-tremble with midges dancing, humming with the lazy monotone of flies on the manure heaps, Digby told Mrs. Ben why he had come. When he had finished, she shrugged her shoulders.

"Ain't seen the Young Ben tuhday. Ain't seen him all day. Did school start up tuhday?"

"Do you think—will you see that he gets there tomorrow?"

"I kin start him out," she said. "No tellin' whether er not he'll end up there."

"The Ben — is he — "

"He ain't bin home neither—bin tuh the cemetery, I guess." She looked up at Digby. "Somebuddy died."

The woman talked as though her voice were wading against a current. She pushed back a hank of limp hair with her wrist. "Not much good talkin' tuh thuh Ben tuhday. Not ona grave day. Can't git nowheres with him ona grave day." Her eyes were steady on his face, lifeless eyes as gray as the Young Ben's. "Might fin' him down tuh thuh Royal."

Then it wasn't any use, thought Digby, not today. In the course of trying to understand the Young Ben, he had come to know much about the boy's father. A great deal of his information had come from Mr. Briggs, the school janitor, in bits picked from that man's magpie mind, gleaned during recesses when he had smoked in the janitor's retreat off the boys' lavatory. In the twilight of the furnace room, with its hung gray dust and its spun gray intricacies of spider webbing, he had found out that the Ben did little work, condescending only occasionally to dig a grave. If he had dug one today, he would be in the beer parlor, drinking up the remuneration.

"Mrs. Ben," Digby said, "will you please try to get the—your son to school tomorrow? I—there are penalties for parents whose children do not come to school — you know."

"I'll start him out."

"Thank you," he said. He admired the woman for her honesty that would not let her promise more.

As he walked back to the town, he thought of his friend Hislop, the minister who had left town two years before. He had never been able to get Hislop to commit himself on the Bens. What moral yardstick could one use with such people? They understood

84

no rules; nothing they did considered other people; they were as naked of right and wrong as a coyote howling on a still fall night, a plague of grasshoppers attacking every green thing, the sun cracking the face of the prairie.

It was a losing battle, he decided, as he turned into Mrs. Geddes's, where he boarded.

At his table in the Royal Hotel beer parlor, the Ben was accompanied by Mr. Cobb, the town plumber and a mild man, Allie Gatenby, Joe Pivott, and seven of Joe's Llewellyn setters. A week-old gray stubble meticulously followed the creases in the Ben's much-creased face. His eyes stared from rims as red as fanned coals. They made Mr. Cobb wince as he drank his beer; even when he looked away from the Ben and down at the table top, he was uncomfortable with the mental image of the Ben's eyes burning deep in their raw rims.

Upon the Ben's head rested a fifty-pound sack of chicken feed.

"Kids," he was saying, "I got 'em—a hunderd an' thirty-three a the barstards — spread clear from Haluhfax tuh Vancouver."

"None on the Island?" said Joe. Joe Pivott drove the dray for Sherry's mill. He was a bachelor and the owner of twenty-one setters.

"I meant in Canada," said the Ben. He tipped up his glass of beer without moving his head, then in order to drain it completely, placed his hand behind the sack, and tilted his head back. He set the glass down empty; the sack remained on top of his head. "That don't count the Ben," he said. "The Ben was borned growed-up." This was a favorite theory of the Ben, one that he had expounded many times over beer, brew, or, on one occasion, a bottle of Cobb's Blistering Remedy for Horses, which he had mistaken for Lister's Household Lemon Essence.

"Thuh Ol' Lady she come tuh me," he went on, "an' she sez, 'Ben,' she sez, 'yuh better go git Doc. I ain't feelin' none too good. The pains is comin' on real frequent now.' So I go out to ketch Dolly, an' her not havin' thuh harness ontuh her sence thuh fall buhfore, I chase her clear down thuh other enda thuh goddam pasture witha panna goddam oats behin' my goddam back. After 'bout a hour I come back tuh thuh house fer tuh git my goddam hat. There is thuh Ol' Lady a-settin' ona goddam apple-box a-peelin' some goddam puhtatuhs intuh thuh goddam slop-pail. 'Where's my goddam hat?' I sez. 'Yuh don't need her,' she sez. 'The kid's already bin borned.' 'What is it?' I sez, an' she sez, 'A boy — han' me that there pot offa thuh table.' I asked where was he at. 'After he finished separatin' thuh cream,' she sez, 'he went out fer tuh chop me some kendlin' fer thuh stove.' Thuh goddam kid was borned growed-up."

"He's queer anyways," said Joe. "About them hunderd an' thirty other kids you was talkin' about. Missis Ben — she know about them?" As a result of the faint dusting of flour that paled his boots, his overalls, his whole being, Joe achieved an other-worldly appearance. His cap, pulled over one ear, gave to his narrow face a slightly tilted look. He was the town's practical joker.

"Goddam rights, she don't know," said the Ben. "Two things I'm a-scairt of — the Ol' Lady an' ghosts."

"Hell," said Allie Gatenby, "I thought you wasn't scareda nothin'."

"I'm a-scairt of a goddam ghost," said the Ben seriously. "So scairt I git thuh shiverin' diaree by thuh time I git tuh thuh hardpan." He belched and said reflectively as he stared at his empty glass, "I don't know jist which one I'm a-scairt of thuh most — thuh goddam Ol' Lady er a goddam ghost." He stood up, knocking the table as he did, slopping Mr. Cobb's beer over. "I'm hungry — anybuddy comin' tuh thuh Bloobird?"

"Later," said Joe Pivott. "We'll see yuh there later."

The sack of chicken feed still on his head, the Ben staggered out the open door. Joe leaned over to Allie Gatenby. "Ben's got him quite a load on an' I got a idee. Figger you could git a-holt of some sheets?"

"Might," said Allie, who lived in the Royal Hotel.

"Dandy," said Joe. "That's jist dandy."

Hours later, the feed sack still on his head, the Ben staggered down the moonlit road that led to the crease of Haggerty's Coulee, his voice raised in song.

86

"Thuh puh-ride of thuh puh-raireeees — thuh cowpuncher's hoo-er!"

He stopped, was sick in a congregation of goldenrod tall in the moonlight, straightened up refreshed, and continued down the pale and dusty road.

"High-ho, Kaaaaaathoooozalum — thuh dotter of Jaaaah-roooozalum —"

Two white figures rose eerily from the buckbrush on either side of the road ahead. Arms lifted up and out menacingly, they advanced upon the Ben.

He stopped; his stubbled chin shot out.

What followed took Joe Pivott and Allie Gatenby by surprise. They knew that the Ben was superstitious, but they were not prepared for his response.

He raised his nail-kegs of fists and shouted hoarsely and alarmingly, "C'mon yuh buggers — botha yuh! I berried yuh this mornin' — I'm a-gonna berry yuh agin tuhnight!"

TEN

Brian no longer sat across the aisle from Forbsie; on the second day of school, the Young Ben showed up and was given Forbsie's seat. Ten years old, a child all elbows, shoulder blades, and knees, he lifted his blond head high above the children in seats around him.

He could not read; he did not write, either in a scribbler at his desk, or with chalk at the board. He sat always with his narrow, gray eyes distant, one arm over the back of his seat as he stared out the school window to the prairie stretching from the schoolyard edge. He was barefooted. In the rope that served him as a belt, he carried a leather-handled hunting knife. Sometimes, always with his strange eyes on the window, he would whittle—a piece of wolf willow, a length of saskatoon, the lid of his desk. This was the Young Ben's third year in Grade One.

And Brian O'Connal across the aisle was aware of a strange attraction to the Young Ben. At no time had he played with him in the town; he had seen him seldom, having caught a glimpse of him only now and again, hauling bundles of washing to and from town families; yet it seemed to him that at some time he had known him intimately. Fascinated and confused, he would stare often and long across the aisle at the Young Ben; and on one occasion the Young Ben had turned his head from the window to gaze at Brian, without curiosity, in his eyes simply the wild and natural candor of one prairie creature looking at another.

Brian never talked or whispered to the Young Ben, as he did to Charles Funder ahead of him or Vooie Wong behind him; he never smiled to him, nor the Young Ben to *him*; yet as the term wore on, there grew a strengthening bond between them, an extrasensory brothership whose first empirical evidence came one morning early in January.

In his first few months of school, things had gone well enough for Brian; actually, like all children after the first blush of individuality at three, he was malleable and would remain so until perhaps the age of eight, when he would again try to impress his personality upon the world he had come to dissociate from himself. So it was that he learned easily to put up his hand when he wanted to leave the room; one finger for renal reasons, two for the other. He learned to stand up when he answered Miss MacDonald, to line up with the boys at noon, at recesses, and after four. In spite of all this, however, a slight tension existed between him and Miss Mac-Donald; it was seldom evident, perhaps only in a special little note of her voice, saved for when she spoke to him.

Brian was a Gopher; Forbsie and Artie were Ants; Mariel Abercrombie was a Grasshopper — Miss MacDonald had the children divided into three groups. Brian took great pride in the fact that the Gophers were ahead of the rest of the room in Health. The Gophers chewed their food more and harder than the Ants or the Grasshoppers; they neglected fewer times to sleep with their windows open; they brushed their teeth more religiously. In the matter of vitamins they were slightly behind the Grasshoppers, but they were still ahead on the over-all count.

Each morning after the Lord's Prayer, Miss MacDonald would ask for the hands of those who had brushed their teeth twenty strokes the previous day, those who had chewed their food the regulation number of chews. She ended usually with a request for the ones who had washed their hands and faces before coming to school that morning. Throughout this daily procedure the Young Ben's arm would remain draped over the back of his seat, a source of irritation to the Ants, of whom he was a nominal member.

One morning early in January, a morning when Brian had managed to get past his mother and his grandmother without having his unwashed hands and face detected, he automatically put up his hand when Miss MacDonald asked how many had washed their hands.

Almost immediately he realized his mistake, but as he went to take down his hand, he saw that Miss MacDonald was looking directly at him, hesitated, then felt that it was too late to do so.

In red chalk Miss MacDonald marked down the Gophers' score. She turned from the board, and as she looked at Brian, he wished that he had taken his hand down. He went up to the front with the Grade Ones for their reading lesson, usually taken in a half-circle of apple-box seats that Mr. Briggs had made. As Brian opened his reader and looked up, he saw that Miss MacDonald's pale eyes were fixed upon his hands. They were unclean hands, particularly soiled between the fingers where sweat and dirt had congealed.

Miss MacDonald had taken off her glasses and was swinging them idly in a slow circle. Her face was intent, unpleasantly so. "Brian."

"Yes, Miss MacDonald."

"Did you say that you had washed your hands this morning?"

Brian felt a sudden flutter of panic at his heart.

"I have your name down on my list of those who washed their hands."

He wished that he had taken his hand down.

"Let me see them."

He held them out.

"Did you wash those this morning?"

"No," he said weakly.

"You said that you had."

"I didn't mean to, Miss MacDonald."

"Why did you put up your hand, then?"

"It — it just sort of went up."

She snorted. "Come up here." She rose from her desk and led him to the center of the room before the class, then turned to the other children with their expectant faces looking up to her.

"Here is a little boy who didn't wash his hands this morning." She paused. "That isn't so bad — sometimes all of us forget. But when it's — when we are asked whether or not we washed our hands, none of us" — She paused — "*lie* about it."

The sibilance of pencils hissing over paper, the snuffling, the whispering, the shuffling of feet, were stilled. Someone giggled shrilly; Brian recognized that it was Mariel Abercrombie.

"This boy did *not* wash his hands, and he *did* lie about it," said Miss MacDonald. Brian looked down at the floor.

"Brian!"

He looked up to see that she was smiling. "Will you hold up your *washed* hands for the class to see?"

He looked down at the floor; she hated him, he supposed dully.

"Hold them up, Brian."

Head tilted forward, he raised his arms slowly, shoulder high, palms in. Miss MacDonald stepped before him and turned the palms out to face the class. As she stepped back, he missed the shielding of her body, and stood, a small and abject soldier in the attitude of surrender with thirty pair of eyes upon him.

"We'll just have you stand like that," said Miss MacDonald in a kindly voice, "with your washed hands for all the class to see. We don't want to have you think—it isn't punishment," she hastened to say. "The Lord punishes little boys who don't wash their hands and then say that they did."

She returned to her desk and took up the Grade One reading class again.

His head bowed, his face burning, filled with utter shame, Brian stood with his arms up and the offending hands turned out to the class. He raised his head and saw that every eye was upon him —the Young Ben's too. He saw several children lean forward to whisper. Many of them were grinning. The Young Ben was not; it was difficult to say what the expression was upon the Young Ben's angular face. He had laid down the knife with which he had been whittling the end of a ruler; he was leaning slightly forward in his seat, his eyes flicking from Brian to Miss MacDonald and back again. He was frowning slightly, almost as though he were puzzled. As Miss MacDonald sent the Grade Ones back to their seats and crossed the room to take up arithmetic with the Grade Threes, stepping carefully around Brian, the look of puzzlement in the Young Ben's face gave way to resentment.

It was not just the children who were watching him, Brian felt; he was aware of a vague knotting at the back of his head, as though an unseen watcher was looking on. He closed his hands to ease the strain—opened them again. He swallowed to rid himself of the bitter dryness in his mouth. He had to keep blinking his eyes to save himself from the complete disgrace of crying in front of them all.

Miss MacDonald had looked secretly at Brian several times, and once she had wished that she could think of an excuse to let him sit down. But seeing him stand there, a seeming stoic with unconcern in his posture, she had hardened. She was an efficient woman who looked for results; a strapping was fruitless, she felt, unless a child broke down and stood red and sodden-eyed before her; the more hiccoughs and tears, the more effective the punishment. The year before, the Young Ben had silently endured sixty strokes of the strap before she had given up and sent him in to Mr. Digby.

The Young Ben was uneasy in his seat now; he shifted his

position often; he picked up his knife from the desk top, laid it down, and picked it up again. Brian's arms were heavy. The muscles under them were painful. Over the tops of his shoulders they were almost unendurable. His chest ached.

The classroom was hot. A conscientious janitor, Mr. Briggs made the flames in the school furnace leap high on winter days. To Brian, wishing that he could get away from his own arms, that they were not part of him, the room seemed to be lifting and drifting. The faces in the front row were suddenly clearer. The faces in the front row receded. The Lord's anger must be a fearful thing.

"You may sit down, Brian."

He began to walk to his seat, then remembered his upraised arms; he looked questioningly to Miss MacDonald; she nodded; he let them drop to his sides. They fell heavily and hung leaden with pins and needles in them, as though he had slept on them for a long time. His knees trembled as he went slowly down the aisle. Just before his seat, he felt them melt under him; he dropped to the floor.

With panic in her face, Miss MacDonald rose from her desk, upsetting her chair with a clatter. By the time she reached the aisle, the Young Ben had leaped from his seat. He picked up Brian, stood a moment with him in his arms, then placed him gently in his seat. He turned to face Miss MacDonald, and as he did, his hand dropped to the knife on the top of his desk. Miss MacDonald reached out her hand to Brian with his head back over the seat. She saw the ugliness in the Young Ben's eyes; she saw the knife in his brown hand; she did the most sensible thing she had done in her life —asked Charles Funder to get water from Mr. Briggs, then turned back down the aisle.

Brian spent recess in the boys' toilet, hidden in one of the cubicles; when the end-of-recess bell rang, he wiped his face of sweat and tears; he avoided Artie and Forbsie as he hurried up the stairs.

He waited in his seat till the rest had left at noon.

As he walked home he raised his eyes only once from the sullied snow underfoot; that was when the flat mill dray, with its bobsled runners and eighteen setters loping ahead, behind, and on either side, passed him a block from MacTaggart's Corner. He came to an empty lot and saw that the spread purity of snow there had been trampled with the clock design of a fox-and-goose game. He was still faint and weak, and when he felt an arm slide around his waist, he welcomed it. With the wind ominous in the telephone wires, sending wisping snow-smoke over the walk ahead, the Young Ben walked the rest of the way to Brian's house with him. He left Brian as silently as he had come to him.

Brian ate his lunch in silence under his mother's questioning glances.

By the time that school was over that afternoon, the wind swept down upon the town, throating wildly, tossing the black branches of bare poplars, lifting the loose snow and driving it into the children's faces, stinging their eyes and noses above the scarves tied round their mouths. Brian tasted the coldness of it with each breath, a clinging sensation at the back of his throat and in his nostrils — like the touch of an icicle on a bare hand.

He was unable to eat his dinner that night, and when his mother gently asked him what was wrong, he burst into tears. He could not bring himself to tell her about the lie.

He listened to a rising wind that night as he lay in bed with Bobbie. The brass weather stripping on the doors of the house vibrated mournfully through the darkness again and again. Brian lay wide-eyed, filled with awful guilt, and — much worse than that — with the fear of promised punishment.

He felt a gathering Presence in his room as the wind lifted high, and higher still, keening and keening again, to die away and be born once more while the sad hum of the weather stripping lingered on in the silence. Fearful — avenging — was the gathering wrath about to strike down Brian Sean MacMurray O'Connal, the terror-stricken Brian O'Connal, who had lied about his hands. He dared not move. He dared not lie still. He dared not cry out. He dared not stay silent. Taking its rhythm from the wild wind, panic lifted within him, subsided, rose again and washed over him till he trembled unmercifully and sweat started out over his entire body.

Nearer and nearer the Presence drew. The house moved. A giant hand began to shake the bed. Brian cried out, and once he had

94

done that, the screams came again and again and again. Bobbie, wakened, added his shrill voice to Brian's.

Light flooded the room. Maggie O'Connal stood above her sons. She looked into Brian's wild eyes. He put his arms up to her. She left Bobbie for his father to calm down, and carried Brian in her arms from the room.

After he had told her of what had happened at school, and after he had fallen asleep in her arms, she lay awake with her eyes against the dark for a long time.

Maggie O'Connal sat sideways on one of the front seats in Miss MacDonald's room; her smallness made it seem quite natural. Upon her dark face there was a puzzled look.

"You don't — there's no reason that you should dislike my son, is there, Miss MacDonald?"

"Why — no — there isn't." Miss MacDonald was slightly embarrassed. Brian's mother had just told her why Brian had not been to school for the past two days.

"He is just a child," Maggie O'Connal said. "He's only six." Her brown eyes looked at Miss MacDonald steadily, searchingly. "I'm still unable to understand why you — "

"He lied to me," said Miss MacDonald simply. "The boy had not washed his hands — "

"Yes, I know," said Brian's mother. "And of course you didn't know why he — just what made him do it — but — do you *like* children, Miss MacDonald?"

"Yes — of course — I like them." There was a slight note of irritation in the teacher's voice; that had been an unfair question.

"To be a teacher — a person should. I think it would help a lot." Maggie O'Connal was silent, and Miss MacDonald had the feeling that she was expected to say something. She was not sure what she was expected to say. "I — I don't see why you should threaten him with God's punishment."

"He lied to me," said Miss MacDonald again. "He hadn't washed — "

"I suppose you didn't realize what it involved — "

"I didn't think that it would hurt his health."

"It hasn't. We have him pretty well calmed down now, but I still don't understand — "

"He had it coming to him." Miss MacDonald was beginning to resent the interview. "I don't think I can be held responsible for — if your son is high-strung — nervous — he had it coming — "

"But not that," said Mrs. O'Connal. "No child has that — "

"I feel that I was quite right," said Miss MacDonald positively; she was not a woman afraid to back her conviction; at the school before this one she had told the board exactly what she thought of them.

Maggie O'Connal got up.

"You've never been wrong, have you, Miss MacDonald?"

"Why — certainly — I — "

"No . . . You must be an unhappy woman."

"I — "

"I am a woman of some restraint — Scottish — you will appreciate that it's difficult for me to say what I'm going to say. I have few friends or acquaintances — instead, I have my husband and two sons. Brian is mine. I bore him. In doing so I got hurt — slightly. Since the first nine months, he has been outside me, and I suppose I have regretted that ever since. Perhaps," she said quietly and with a look almost of compassion in her dark eyes, "if you were to have a child you might be a happier and a better teacher."

Miss MacDonald's mouth opened as though she were about to blurt something. It closed and opened again foolishly. A stricken look appeared in her eyes.

"I — I'm sorry, Miss MacDonald."

Maggie O'Connal left the room.

ELEVEN

The firelight winked and blinked up the walls of the room; it fell on the grandmother's face, highlighting the bridge of her aquiline nose, reflecting from the surfaces of her glasses, giving to her thin, down-curving mouth an unrelenting look. She sat perfectly straight in her wing chair with her rheumatic leg stretched out in its brace. Bobbie slept on his father's lap. Brian lay at the foot of his mother's chair, full length on the floor before the fireplace. His eyes transfixed, he watched the bluing flames lap like little waves over the orange coals. Here and there a large flame broke itself off and vanished; part of the fire's body fell, and a shower of sparks rained up to melt in the higher darkness of the fireplace.

Several times, after the night his mother had taken him in with her, Brian's terror had returned to him; the following day his mother had taken his temperature and had sent for Dr. Svarich. He had slept with his mother the next night, and she had told him again that God was a kindly being uninterested in frightening little boys; but it was not until he had looked from the breakfast room window to a yard covered with freshly fallen snow, and to rimed trees and hedges twinkling in the sunlight, that the frightening conception of an avenging God had been replaced by a friendlier image borrowing its physical features from Santa Claus, its spiritual gentleness from his father.

Bobbie moaned slightly in his sleep. He lay with his head in his father's neck, one arm outflung; the eyelashes curving down his fat cheek were gilded in the firelight. Brian saw that his grandmother's mouth had fallen open to make a small, dark hole in her face. He wondered why people slept.

"Why do people sleep, Dad?"

Gerald O'Connal pursed his lips. "Habit."

"What's that?"

"Doing something over and over."

"Well — why do you sleep over and over?"

"You just do — while you sleep, you rest."

"Can't a person rest without sleeping?"

"Not as well," his father said. "When you sleep you rest better." Brian returned his attention to the fire.

"I've seen the Young Ben around the front of the house a couple of times," remarked O'Connal. "What's he up to, do you suppose?"

"He wants to know am I all right," Brian answered with his eyes still on the fire.

"All right?"

98

Maggie O'Connal looked up from her knitting; she glanced quickly at her husband, then at her son's head by her foot.

God could be like a flame, Brian was thinking, not a real flame, but like a flame. Perhaps He was a great person made entirely of flame—with a flame beard and flame lips licking out to change the shape of His mouth. For a moment he thought that the old terror was going to wash over him. He should not have thought that.

"I'm not sure that he"—Brian's father looked over to his wife — "he's a suitable companion."

Maggie O'Connal's eyes were filled with speculation. "I don't know," she said. "I don't know what to think. But—somehow I feel that it's all right."

His mother had said that God was a spirit; one couldn't see a spirit. Flames could be seen. God wasn't flames. He could walk through a door or a wall—he could walk along the ceiling like a fly. "Does God sleep?"

"I — He — I don't think so." Gerald O'Connal's voice was startled.

"Doesn't *He* need a rest too?"

"He doesn't ever get tired. We can take that up tomorrow. To bed, Spalpeen."

"Don't forget the furnace, Gerald," Maggie O'Connal warned. "I'll take Bobbie." She lifted her voice. "Mother!" The grandmother stirred. "We're taking the children up!"

"I'll just sit here awhile," Mrs. MacMurray answered her.

"You can sleep with Bobbie tonight," Brian's mother told him.

"I'll be all right."

Alone in the darkened room, the grandmother sat in her chair, listening to the wind in the chimney flue; it had a deep and imperative sound that came again and again. Her old mind was filled with the winter prairie that must lie around the town. She thought of a homesteader's hut, of a woodbox and of a gaunt, dark man coming in the door to fill it. She saw his arms full of birch chunks; she saw the plump, cherry belly of a Quebec heater with a mica umbilicus, heard the slow sizzle of John's spit tobacco juice, then smelled the ripe-fig smell of it.

Her mind took out the sensory fragments, handled them briefly, then laid them away again. Beyond the emotional coloring that each had, they possessed no particular significance. Meaning was a tag that people tied to things, nothing more. Rheumatism had an importance of its own, of course; like a fly that bothered and bothered, it could not be denied.

She rose stiffly from her chair, reached behind her for her cane, then began her way toward the stairs.

Before the maple dresser opaled with little birds'-eyes Maggie O'Connal, with her dark head tilted as though in listening attitude, braided her hair for the night. It was like being on the other side of a fence. Other people, she decided, must feel the same about the bits that had broken away from their own bodies to live on the other side of the fence—to have lives of their own. *Dear God*, she wished fiercely, *make them turn out all right* — not just all right: world beaters — the best there was. She heard the cavern sounds of the coal shovel below. Like their father — that would be enough.

Like one of those damned icebergs, thought Gerald O'Connal as he slid the shovel under the coal. What was it? Two thirds under water, one third on top. *Did God sleep?* What had made him ask that? Did they say whatever came into their heads? Was it a carry-over from that affair at school?

Gerald clanged shut the furnace door, then laid the shovel in its place against the wall. This Young Ben thing — The boy's interest in his son was surprising in itself, for the Young Ben was a lone wolf. With those high cheekbones and the wedge shape of his face, he looked a little like a coyote. What could the two possibly have in common? His mind went back two years to the time he had buried the baby pigeon for Brian; there had been something even then.

At the head of the steep cellar stairs he paused; better take a

100

look at the thermometer. He went through the breakfast room and the short hallway to the living room with its dying fire, then to the front hallway hung with coats, its corner littered with overshoes; he opened the door to the chill freshness outside. He struck a match and held its light up to the thermometer hung on the porch wall. Twenty below . . . The sky possessed a dark, still clarity, unmarred by clouds, teeming with stars fiercely blue and red and white in the winter darkness.

Brian and Bobbie, he thought; they seemed to understand each other; perhaps it would last as it had with him and Sean. Sean, who had sent him money while he got his pharmacist's certificate in Toronto, from lumber camps in Pennsylvania, Quebec, Washington; Sean, who made as much work of writing his name as he did of stooking a forty-acre field. He had paid the money back. Thank God for the dry years that had made Sean so bitter; at least they had made the money mean as much to Sean as it had meant to him.

Marrying — raising a family — business — you drifted apart. Hell, they were brothers, weren't they? Perhaps he could tell Sean there was still a couple of hundred owing—that would finance the irrigation project he had his heart set on for next spring. Sean would believe that the money was still owing; he was careless about money — marking his accounts down on a barn door with a nail. He must get out to see Sean.

The naked branches of the poplar were transfigured with the light from the bedroom window above. Maggie had not gone to bed yet. He turned back to the enclosing warmth of the house.

TWELVE

Spring came to the prairie with the suddenness of a meadow lark's song. Overnight the sky traded its winter tang for softness; the snow, already honeycombed with the growing heat of a closer sun, melted — first from the steaming fallow fields, then from the stubble stretches, shrinking finally to uneven patches of white lingering in the barrow pits. Here and there meadow larks were suddenly upon straw stacks, telephone wires, fence posts, their song clear with ineffable exuberance that startled and deepened the prairie silence — each quick and impudent climax of notes leaving behind it a vaster, emptier prairie world. The sky was ideal blue. Crows called; farmers, impatient as though it were the only spring left in the world to them, burning with the hope that this one would not be another dry year, walked out to their implements, looked them over, and planned their seeding — barley here, oats there, wheat there, summer fallow there.

In town the branches of trees fattened into sticky buds. Geese flew overhead at night in wavering vee's, their far-off calls drifting down. Mariel Abercrombie brought in the first crocus to Miss MacDonald. Forbsie Hoffman announced the first gopher. Miss MacDonald marked the information down on a chart for spring, drawn on the board; she had one for fall too. As she did each spring, Mrs. Funder added a baby to her family, the ninth; Dr. Svarich delivered it on an April night. Calving and lambing came and went. Mrs. Abercrombie and Mr. Powelly, the minister who had taken Mr. Hislop's place, began a campaign of Personal Visitation to Bring Souls to the Mercy Seat. An iron-willed man, Mr. Powelly got on well with Mrs. Abercrombie; it was a case of like calling to like, perhaps.

The Young Ben was truant for three weeks; it was an absence that Miss MacDonald did not bring to Mr. Digby's attention until well on in the second week. Miss MacDonald had never forgotten the look in the Young Ben's eyes as she had faced him in the aisle the day that Brian had fainted. Several times throughout the winter term she'd spent uncomfortably sleepless nights seeing in her mind a lean, brown hand clenching an exquisitely honed hunting knife.

As the term wore on, she found herself more and more nervous, more and more reluctant to turn her back on the class. She had developed a nervous ticlike twitch of her neck muscle, an uncontrollable little explosion that jerked the cord and moved her shoulder muscle visibly under her dress. By Easter she was sure that she needed a change of school.

That spring the Ben moved his still in from the prairie. The Ben was an artist in one respect, the hiding of his still. Perhaps the term "still" flattered the great granite pot to which he had haywired a length of copper coil; but there was no doubt that his lavish imagination truly created when it combined his everyday, commonplace still with an equally everyday, commonplace hiding place.

For years he had been content to follow the usual technique of hiding the thing in a cave some distance from his shack and covering it with squares of prairie sod and brush. Determined this spring to be more than a blind technician, the Ben secreted his still in his well. A month later, in April, the mash boiled over and inebriated a Dominicker hen, two Barred Rock roosters, and a mostly Holstein cow. He knew then that he had to move his still again — not because he feared chronic alcoholism among the inhabitants of the barnyard, but because a staggering cow or a weaving rooster argued the existence of a still.

Since the evening that Allie Gatenby and Joe Pivott had confronted him on the trail home, the Ben had dug no graves. He had no money for beer, for "eating" tobacco, or for grain and kerosene for his still. He insisted that he suffered from rheumatism and that he couldn't bend over with a shovel.

He turned finally to eggs for money. Whenever opportunity presented itself—usually when the Mrs. Ben was answering a call of nature at the back—the Ben would sneak down to the henhouse and steal two or three eggs at a time—never more, for he dared not let his wife know that the eggs were disappearing. With the eggs he was able to get ten or twenty cents at Blaine's General Store. Then he would repair to the Royal Hotel. He needed the wherewithal to buy only the first beer; his yarns bought him the rest.

Unfortunately for the Ben, egg financing came to an end in May. Then Mrs. Ben caught him with six eggs in his smock pockets and threatened to inform on him to Jake Harris; the Ben was forced to seek some other method of getting money and to find a safe place for his still.

That spring Barney Hepworth, janitor of the Presbyterian church, refused to take Dr. Svarich's advice and go to bed with what he was sure was only a spring cold; he died of pneumonia.

104

The Ben went straightway to Mr. Powelly and acquainted him with a moving desire to make personal confession of a newly discovered faith. It was in the midst of the revival campaign and Mr. Powelly welcomed the offer of the Ben's soul; later in the evening as he sat in the manse study, it suddenly occurred to him that the Ben would be just the man to fill the position of janitor recently vacated by Barney Hepworth.

The date of the Ben's reception into the congregation was set for the third Sunday in May. He began his janitorial duties immediately. A week later he moved his still into the basement of the church. It was an ideal hiding place; no one but the Ben ever entered the coal room, where the still and its kerosene burner rested on a dark shelf of earth just inside the building foundation; the telltale fumes of the mash were quickly absorbed by the manure pile thrown up behind Mr. Thorborn's dray and livery barn at the back of the church. Without fear of detection, the Ben could visit the still, fill the burner with kerosene, the coil bed with ice, the pot with mash, and himself with brew.

The Sunday that the Ben was received into Knox congregation was in a way a turning point in Brian O'Connal's spiritual life too.

As he usually did on Sunday mornings, he awoke long before the others in the household; he tiptoed into his mother's and father's room, his grandmother's, gathering up best shoes. The polishing of the family shoes was his weekly chore, a job important and satisfying to his six-year-old heart.

Shoe polish, he thought, had a dark smell like ink; this kind did; it went on with a brush — a daub of a brush that had the top of the bottle on the end of its twisted wire handle. He loved the way it smoothed its liquid black over the toes of the shoes, around the eyeholes, jetting the squared edges of the soles, and leaving the shoes slippery looking at first, then dulling slowly. He always did his own first, laying them carefully on a sheet of newspaper in the breakfast room; then Bobbie's with their square toes, his father's and mother's next. His grandmother's were last, with their high tops limp and a hole in one heel where the brace went through.

Sunday was different, he decided. It gave one a strange feeling of set-apartness. Until *they* came down he would be all alone with the cuckoo clock ticking loud in the living room beyond the hall, ticking loud like an old man limping along. He'd better put the shoe polish in its drawer before it got tipped over on the floor. That had happened once.

Past the gleam of polished table tops in the living room he went to the window in his father's den. He looked out to the empty porch, its trellis thick with Virginia creeper. He stood there a moment, then turned away with a sudden feeling of restlessness, a hungering dissatisfaction that descended upon him without warning. The front door swooshed behind him as he went out to the Sunday morning serenely still.

For a long time he sat on the porch steps with his chin in his hands. The Catholic church bell began slowly and majestically to tongue the silence. Like on a lawn, he thought, with the inarticulate yearning in him deepening, a kid turning slow somersaults over a lawn — looking up with his head, then ducking it to take another slow turn completely over on the lawn. When the bell stopped, the morning stillness seemed to have a quality of numbness. Sunday was different. Sunday was very Sabbath.

A twinkling of light caught his eye; and he turned his head to see that the new, flake leaves of the spirea were starred in the sunshine — on every leaf were drops that had gathered during the night. He got up. They lay limpid, cradled in the curve of the leaves, each with a dark lip of shadow under its curving side and a star's cold light in its pure heart. As he bent more closely over one, he saw the veins of the leaf magnified under the perfect crystal curve of the drop. The barest breath of a wind stirred at his face, and its caress was part of the strange enchantment too.

Within him something was opening, releasing shyly as the petals of a flower open, with such gradualness that he was hardly aware of it. But it was happening: an alchemy imperceptible as the morning wind, a growing elation of such fleeting delicacy and poignancy that he dared not turn his mind to it for fear that he might spoil it, that it might be carried away as lightly as one strand of spider web on a sigh of wind. He was filled with breathlessness

106

and expectancy, as though he were going to be given something, as though he were about to find something.

"Breakfast, Spalpeen."

The feeling broke; it broke as a bubble breaks. Once it had been there; and then, with a blink, it broke.

Bobbie sat at the kitchen table, a brown ring of peanut butter around his mouth. The crisp smell of toast was in the room as Brian began to eat his oatmeal. It was lumpy. His father always made it lumpy. "It's lumpy, Dad."

Bobbie said, "He isn't a very good porridge maker, is he, Brian?"

"Eat it up. It's just once a week."

"It's just once a week," Bobbie said.

"I heard him," Brian said. "I'm not deaf."

Bobbie wiped part of the peanut butter from his mouth with the back of his hand, leaving a smear that stretched to one ear. He slid from his chair. "I got to go to the toilet."

"Just go," his father said. "Need any help?"

"No, I don't. Just later — my shoes — Mama does them."

When Bobbie had left them, Brian's father said, "Shall we take her breakfast up to her?"

"Sure!" That was part of Sunday, taking a tray up to his mother. He began to eat his porridge hastily.

Maggie O'Connal lay with her thick braids dark against the pillow's whiteness, her eyebrows straight over eyes slightly oblique, intensely brown; it was a boy's face actually when one ignored the softness of the eyes and the hair.

"Breakfast in bed!" she exclaimed as she sat up. "How nice!" She never disappointed them by not saying, "How nice!"

There came a rushing sound of water running; it gargled lustily, was about to die, gained new strength and came again.

Brian's father sat down on the edge of the bed.

"Careful, Gerald!" Maggie O'Connal clutched at the tray.

The sound of water came again and then again.

"Four times," said Brian. "Gramma up?"

"I heard her a moment ago on the stairs," said his mother.

He supposed that he had better bring her shoes up to her, thought Brian. She liked to put the Sunday ones on as soon as she got up, so that she would not have to insert the brace twice. The swift sound of water came again.

"Five times," said Brian. "Is he going to flush it right till church time?"

"Break me with the water bill — Bobbie!"

The gurgling came once more, with less fervency and with a touch of finality about it.

Bobbie entered the room, rather heroic looking even with the flap of his sleepers down. "I went." He climbed up beside his mother. "It's lumpy. He made it lumpy this morning. Last week it was salty. It was salty and — "

"All right," his father said. "All right."

The door opened, and the grandmother appeared with her shoulder poked up by the crutch that she sometimes used around the house. "Who was last in there?"

"Bobbie, I believe," said Gerald O'Connal. "What seems to be — "

"Does he have to wad it full with paper each time?"

"Bobbie!"

But Bobbie was no longer in the room.

Gerald O'Connal turned to his wife. "Oh — well." He got off the edge of the bed. "When do you expect Sean?"

"Sometime after church. Dinner's at two — that should give him plenty of time to get in."

"Is Uncle Sean going to have dinner with us?"

"Yes," Brian's mother said. Her face did not show Brian's excitement over the prospect of Sean's coming. It was not that she wasn't fond of Sean; she could not help but be, when she saw in him the same easygoing generosity that was his brother's; all the same — Sean's language around her boys!

As they walked to church, the grandmother and Gerald ahead, Brian with his mother, Bobbie now with one, now with another, Brian thought of the drop of water on the leaf. His mind lingered over the memory of it, trying to recapture the exaltation of that moment when he had looked down upon it. A sudden aching gripped him by the throat. The Catholic church bell deliberately took up its brazen sound again. Over a lawn, over a lawn, and over a lawn, thought Brian.

Just before the church, Maggie O'Connal bent down, straightened Brian's hair with a few deft flicks, then turned to Bobbie with his face patiently up. Perhaps the feeling would come to him again in Church. He would make it come, thought Brian as the family walked through the vestibule and into the main body of the church. Surely it would come, he told himself while they were led to their pew by Judge Mortimer.

With one part of his mind he was aware of his grandmother beside him, arranging her purse, her cane, her hymnbook, her purse again as she took her handkerchief out. He looked past her to where Bobbie's feet hung in mid-air; by stretching he could make his own touch the floor. He shifted his gaze to Mr. Harris's neck before him, and noted that it bulged over his collar, showing pink through the bristle of gray hair. It would have a rubbery give, he thought, if he pushed it with his finger.

He saw two blue-black heads in the front row — the China Kids; they sat always in the front row, so they weren't heathen Chinee. Perhaps Old Wong was a heathen; he never came to church with the children. Their mother was dead, and Wong never came to church at all. Then it was that Brian saw the strange heads in the row behind the China kids: one gray and tufted, the other equally wild and untidy, but buckskin in color. The Ben and the Young Ben had come to their church! With a thrill of excitement, Brian leaned forward in his seat the better to see them; he felt his grandmother's restraining hand on his arm.

His attention shifted to the choir coming in, their black tassels swinging as they entered, clutching at their long gowns and half-wrapping them around themselves so that they wouldn't catch on the corner of the pulpit as they mounted to the choir loft. It seemed right to Brian that the men should go in the back with their deep voices. In the front row, next to Mrs. Tate, who played the organ, Mrs. Abercrombie's bolster bosom swelled under her choir gown.

Her eyes were immediately lost upwards as soon as she had settled herself. Brian wondered what she was thinking about — what they were all thinking about as they sat silently waiting. He wondered who rang the Catholic church bell.

Mr. Powelly was entering, his light, fawn hair brought carefully over the balding front of his head in thin strings that looked as though they had been glued to his pale scalp; his hands were swallowed to the finger tips in the sleeves of his gown, whose loose arc over his shoulders, as he turned to ascend to the pulpit, reminded Brian of the coloring on a magpie's back. It was an ascetic's face that turned to the congregation, spare and long-jawed; an absent-mindedly indulgent smile, lifting the corners of his wide and almost lipless mouth, made his sharp features speciously benign. Maybe God looked like Mr. Powelly, thought Brian.

The congregation rose. Holy holy holy, they sang. That meant unbelievably wonderful — like his raindrop — a holy holy holy drop lying holy on a leaf. It had a round sound; he could see Mrs. Abercrombie's small mouth round with it, a round little well, ready for her to blow a round holy bubble. The feeling he'd had was holy — a holy feeling that had come and broken like a bubble.

They were sitting down now in the House of the Lord, his father, his mother, his grandmother, Bobbie, the China Kids, the Bens, Mrs. Abercrombie — everybody sitting down; and it said *This Is the House of God and the Very Gate of Heaven* in tall and crooked letters of gold above Mr. Powelly's head.

Brian turned his head to see the stained-glass window where the blue-and-ruby Christ carried a lamb in His arms, His head turned tenderly down upon it.

"'What man of you,'" the minister read out, "'having an hundred sheep, if he lose one of them, doth not leave the ninety and nine in the wilderness, and go after that which is lost, until he find it? And when he hath found it, he layeth it on his shoulders, rejoicing.'"

He looked down to the second row, where the Ben and his son sat, the Ben bolt upright, his wild eyes staring up from their rims as red as meat, his gray hair in electric disorder.

110

"'And when he cometh home, he calleth together his friends and neighbors, saying unto them, Rejoice with me; for I have found my sheep which was lost.'"

The Ben's naked jaw moved gently, monotonously, back and forth. The Young Ben's gray eyes in his still face slid first to one side, then to the other: wary eyes, seeking out and measuring the people who hemmed him in.

Brian tried to imagine a Being in the darkness above the choir loft, egging on Mr. Powelly, telling him what to say next.

He felt a nudge and turned to take the peppermint his grandmother held out to him. Then his mind was on the sweetness of the candy cooling under his tongue. You couldn't get a feeling with a peppermint in your mouth, he thought. He looked across the aisle at the glossy, yellow pew end; just like a chick's head on a long neck. He drew the outline of the pew end with his finger. He felt his grandmother's chiding nudge again.

The Ben, in the second row, still had his baleful eyes upon Mr. Powelly. "We are glad to have you as a member of the congregation," the minister said. "Please step up to the front."

A startled look appeared on the Ben's creased and vein-netted face. His jaw ceased its motion; his hand went swiftly to his mouth. He got up.

Brian heard a gentle purring down the pew. His father had fallen to sleep. He'd get it when they got home.

" . . . the hand of fellowship," Mr. Powelly was saying. "Welcome to the fold."

The Ben, who had not been forewarned of this part of the ritual, took the minister's proffered hand reluctantly. Many are called, but few of those summoned come to the selecting with a partly chewed wad of Old Stag Tobacco secreted in the palms of their right hands.

Mr. Powelly deposited the cud surreptitiously in the pot of lilies of Jerusalem standing next to the pulpit.

THIRTEEN

Sean O'Connal was a bachelor, Maggie O'Connal had once said, because he preferred it that way; any woman who might have married him, she had gone on to say, would have preferred it that way too. In her own quiet manner Maggie O'Connal was fond of her husband's brother, but she was fonder of her children, and the nonchalance of his black language around them often made her wince.

When the O'Connal family returned from church, Sean was at the house. The boys said hello respectfully to him as soon as they saw him in the wing chair by the fireplace. Sean awed them as no other grownup could hope to; his deep and booming voice and the broad barn-door build of him were enough in themselves to inspire reverence. When one added to these his great, untidy red mustaches stained with tobacco juice, it was no wonder that the boys were held speechless by him. His language hypnotized, but not with the monotony that is in most men's swearing; Sean's flow was agile and expressive, particularly when he was angry.

He was angry now as he sat with his great, thick knees spread and his big-knuckled hands resting on his blue serge pants. Sean was dressed for Sunday dinner in town; above the collar that constricted his neck only on such special occasions, the cords stood out; his usually florid face flamed even more intensely. His eyes had a full look about them, the look of a man being slowly but efficiently choked to death. He was pipeless; his mustaches moved in and out with the breath that betrayed smoldering emotion.

"Have you got a smoke there?" he greeted his brother.

"Certainly, Sean." Gerald O'Connal took a cigar from his vest pocket. Sean spit the end of the cigar savagely to the carpet.

"Cannot find me goddam pipes, nor do I know what the hell's happened to a tin of Old Stag with six plugs in it yet!"

"What seems to be the trouble — "

"That stubble-jumpin', one-an'-a-half-step sod-buster callin' himself me hired man!" Sean exhaled a cloud of blue smoke. "Don't know why I keep the sorrowful barstard aroun' — he's a good worker, but —'Cure yer husbanda the goddam drink habit,' he reads in some slippy page magazine, an' the next thing I know, he's sneakin' somea the black stuff intuh me tea unbeknownst to me! Ain't it enough — the yearsa drought — the cutworm an' the hoppers an' hail — ain't it enough withouta — "

"Brian — Bobbie!" Maggie O'Connal said to her two open-mouthed boys. "Go and change your clothes!"

" — hired man all the time tryin' to save me black soul? An' there will be no wheat this year again! Baked hotter than the breath offa hell itself! If it isn't that, then it'll be the hail to knock the heads down—to dance an' jump like popcorn ona fryin' pan—hailstones the sizea both yer — "

"Brian — did you hear me!"

"To knock her down flatter'n a saucera sour cat — "

"Upstairs!"

In their bedroom on the third floor, as he changed his clothes and helped Bobbie to undress and dress again, Brian could hear his uncle's voice rumbling below, like thunder casual in the distance. As they came back down the stairs, he heard:

"If I could only get me hands on that one! Ab wouldn't be the only changed man aroun' these parts!" He referred to Elijah Mac-Cosham, the Christian Scot, who had converted Ab. Ever since that night in the Odd Fellows' Hall Ab had been a changed man; he smoked no tobacco, chewed no tobacco; when he came into town he stayed away from the Royal Hotel beer parlor; he gave the billiard hall a wide berth. It was a shame that Ab could not take his religion or leave it alone, that he thought it too good a thing to deny the man he worked for. If ever a man cursed, or smoked, or drank, it was Sean O'Connal; an oath, a pipe, or the rawness of liquor was constantly in his mouth.

But Sean had toned down considerably by the time that the boys had reached the bottom of the stairs, soothed by the blue and aromatic cigar smoke that wreathed his head. "Growin' up like stinkweed," he rumbled as the boys came to the center of the room. "Like goddam stinkweed."

"I'm a little prairie flower," said Bobbie.

"Are you now?" said Sean, circling the boy with one arm and drawing him to the chair.

Bobbie looked up at his uncle, drew away, and struck a pose.

"I'm a little prairie flower," he parroted, "growing wilder every hour—nobody cares to cultibate me—I'm as wild as ever."

Sean's roaring laughter filled the room. He slapped his knee. "I'm as wild as ever," he shouted. "That's goddam good—wild as ever!"

"It's supposed to go—'wild as I can be'," said Brian. He saw that his mother had come to the door from the breakfast room, drawn there by the sound of Sean's laughter.

114

"As wild as ever — who taught you that?"

"Gramma," said Bobbie.

"An' ye're as wild as ever?"

"Yes," said Bobbie, staring fascinated at his uncle, "I goddam am."

"Bobbie!" The exclamation came from Gerald O'Connal and from Maggie at the door to the breakfast room. "Outside!" she ordered. "And — and Brian too! Stay in the yard. We'll call you when dinner's ready."

As they left the house, Brian was wishing that he had been the one to say it.

Sean had quieted down by dinnertime; he was a man who loved food, and both Maggie O'Connal and her mother were good cooks. As with all Sunday dinners, they ate in the dining room off the living room, Brian's mother carrying the loaded dishes in from the breakfast room, the empty dishes out. They sat around the table after dinner was over. Gerald had given Sean another cigar. And now Sean was talking about his new cook.

"Beef to the heels like a finishin'-lot heifer — Annie's her name — cook — she kin cook! Pads aroun' that kitchen barefoot — her toes spreadin' like netted gem puhtatuhs — stuck on Ab — God knows why; so now I can't let him go without she goes with him, an' I wouldn't trade her for a little red wheelbarrah fulla dimonds." He looked down to the ash on his cigar; it reminded him again of what Ab had recently done. "That — that — that — Hayin' time — seedin' — harvest, he's at me! Like a goddam fly he is — buzzin' an' buzzin' till I'm twitchy as a cow at fly-time!"

"How is your irrigation project coming, Sean?" asked Maggie O'Connal ominously.

"Huh? Oh — that!" Sean's voice dropped to almost normal conversational level. "Got the dugout done an' the main ditch dug — she's right where the tilt of the land runs off the water." His voice had become gentle now. "Oh — I tell you she's gonna be lovely — tuh see the rows a carrots liftin' their feathery heads — the radishes an' the scallions. There'll be head lettuce crisp an' green. I'm plantin' melons — they'll grow," he practically crooned, "ah — they'll grow prettier than all the scarlet-coated cardinals at Rome

— an' there'll be the sweet smell of water on the air above me green-garden, while"—his voice took a skip and a jump—"while the goddam wheat gits baked crisper than bacon fried in the firesa hell!"

And he's away again, thought Maggie O'Connal wearily. But as it always did, Sean's anger eventually burned itself out; his voice died down to the volume one expects from a man talking to another across the street, or over the sound of machinery, or to a horse at the other end of a barn. "Oh, I tell you it's enough to drive a man crazy. If it weren't for me garden, I'd be moving in next door to poor old Saint Sammy."

"Saint Sammy!" ejaculated Brian's father. "That's a new one, isn't it?"

"Saint Sammy-in-the-pianah-box?" said Sean. "Have you never hearda him? Sammy Belterlaben—used to farm the old Horn place—livin' on Magnus Petersen's now."

"His hired man?" asked Gerald O'Connal.

"No. Got him a pianah box, stuck a stove in front of her, built on a poplar pole c'rral, an' there he is. Magnus lets the old man live there—he's harmless—him an' his horses. Ah—there's some grand horses for you—pure-bred Clydes an' not a onea them broke."

"But what does he keep them for?" Brian's father wondered.

"To pat an' pay pasture for. Yearsa gittin' rusted out an' saw flied out an' cutwormed out an' 'hoppered out an' hailed out an' droughted out an' rusted out an' smutted out; he up an' got good an' goddam tired out. Crazier'n a cut calf. Got all sortsa names outa the Bible for his critters."

"Poor man," said Maggie O'Connal. "I don't envy him living alone on the prairie."

"Bent Candy envies him."

"Why, Sean?" asked Brian's father.

"Wanted them horses for years—got his dirty han's on damn near a townshipa land—scratchin' her up with his goddam tractors—"

"But—he doesn't use a horse to work his land—what's he want with Saint Sammy's—?"

116

"Greedy," said Sean. "Plumb greedy—or maybe it's the only good spot the man has in him—fussy about horses. Funny—guess it's the only good thing you can say for him—fussy about horses—them Clydes anyways." For a moment Sean was silent as he thought of Bent Candy, the caterpillar man. Candy had prospered during the dry years, spreading his crops over land wherever discouraged farmers had left; he put in acre after acre of wheat, his overhead was low, he could show a profit on only ten bushels' return to the acre. He had been lucky too; if rain fell, it fell on Candy's land; hail had stripped down both sides and around his crops but never on them.

"Deacona the Baptist church," Sean was muttering. "I guess he'd do anythin' to git them horses." He looked reflectively at his cigar. "I would meself."

"But—what about last winter?" said Brian's father. "We had fifty-below weather for quite a stretch. That was a terrific blizzard early in January. Do you mean to say he's out in a piano box—"

"Got a sort of a nest," explained Sean, "made from binder-twine bits an' raw sheep's-wool. He burrows into it like a gopher set for winter. Says he doesn't mind the cold in winter half as much as the flies in summer."

"Well," said Gerald O'Connal, "the prairie has some queer ones."

"The Lord looks after His own," said the grandmother, who had contributed little to the conversation up to this point.

"We had one in church this morning," said Brian's father. "The Ben has joined the church. He's to be the new janitor."

"The hell you say!" Sean jolted upright in his chair. "The Ben! Joined the church! No!"

Brian's father nodded.

"Wouldn't that scare a kiyoot from a dead steer now! Wouldn't it! 'Tisn't catching—like the plague through the jacks—every seven years—"

"It won't get far," said Brian's mother. "When the epidemic gets to you, Sean, it'll be stopped dead in its tracks."

Sean put his red head back and laughed.

Brian's mother bit her lip.

And Sean, looking at her, felt a slight stir of uneasiness; he respected his brother's wife. Women were funny.

That night before he dropped off to sleep, Brian thought of the Bens, who had been in church that morning; he thought of the Saint Sammy his uncle had talked about; he thought of Sean's hired man, Ab. As he lay in bed with Bobbie soundly asleep beside him, the memory of the drop he had seen on the spirea leaf came suddenly to him. It was some time before the electric tingling, again returning to him, finally permitted him to go to sleep.

He dreamed that night that his Uncle Sean placed his hand on Saint Sammy's head, called for the Young Ben to sweep out a piano box; then told the Ben, in the next seat to Brian, to go to the head of the class, where Miss MacDonald was holding up her hands. The Young Ben was covered with shining drops.

In the living room below, Maggie O'Connal and her husband sat by the fireplace. The grandmother had gone to bed; Sean had left for the farm. There was a small wrinkle of intentness on her forehead as she knitted.

"The roast was good, Maggie," Gerald O'Connal ventured.

His wife counted stitches a moment before she looked up to her husband stretched out on the couch. "You fell asleep in church, Gerald."

He stirred guiltily. "Did I?"

"It happens too often. At Abercrombies' the other night —"

"I'm sorry, dear."

"It isn't as though you had been having late nights at the store. I'm so glad you've stopped that. Gerald, are you feeling well? There's no — I don't see why you have to fall off to sleep —"

"I'll try to stay awake," he promised.

"And I hate to say anything to you, but ... Sean — the way he ... his language!"

"Ummmmh."

"It isn't right for the boys. Look what Bobbie said this morning."

"Ummh-hummh."

118

She began to count stitches, her lips moving as she did. "Don't you think if you were to suggest to him —" She began to count again, came to the end, mentally tabulated the result. "You can do it, Gerald, better than I — you're close to him."

"Ummh."

"Never mind about the sleeping — it could be worse — your mouth doesn't drop open. If you could think a little more of me — forty isn't old enough to have your husband dropping off to sleep like that. It's — it's disconcerting, Gerald — to think of being married — that much time hasn't slipped by." Silence filled the room. A gentle hissing sound came, stopped, started again. "Gerald!"

His mouth had dropped open. It wasn't right that a person should drop off to sleep so often — so easily. She felt a sudden constriction around her heart.

Just the clock ticked on in the silence.

She began to count stitches again.

FOURTEEN

Brian's dog — a slender, red-and-white bundle of nerves, who declared immediate and vociferous war on anything that passed the house on wheels, runners, four or two legs — was not, in a social sense, a good dog. Jappy was a tramp — he was away from the O'Connal home frequently for days at a time, returning ripe with the smell of dead gopher; he was incontinent — three generations of his progeny were about the town, one line a startling adventure in canine miscegenation that had to be seen to be believed; it sprang from a casual springtime alliance with one of Joe Pivott's setters.

Between the dog and the boy there was an easy comradeship and a mutual respect, with now and then sudden flashes of downright love on Brian's part, for if Jappy was not a model dog in many ways, he was ideal in one: he was death on gophers. He had a nose unequalled by that of any other dog in town, including even Joe Pivott's highly sensitive setters, or Jappy's own partly Llewellyn grandchildren; at the mouth of a hole when a drowned gopher poked out its head he was quick and sure. And he always knew when a gopher-hunting expedition was under way.

Throughout the summer Brian found himself with a heightened eagerness to discover again the strange elation he had experienced early in the spring. He found that many simple and unrelated things could cause the same feeling to lift up and up within him till he was sure that he could not contain it. The wind could do this to him, when it washed through poplar leaves, when it set telephone wires humming and twanging down an empty prairie road, when it ruffled the feathers on one of Sherry's roosters standing forlorn in a bare yard, when it carried to him the Indian smell of a burning straw stack. Once the feeling had been caused by the sound of Gaffer Thomas's bucksaw wheehawing impatiently on the other side of the O'Connal back fence; another time, by a crow calling; still another, by the warm smell of bread baking. A tiny garden toad became suddenly magic for him one summer day — the smell of leaf mold, and clover, and wolf willow. Always, he noted, the feeling was most exquisite upon the prairie or when the wind blew.

There had been the day, well on in summer, that he and Forbsie Hoffman, now called "Fat" by one of the mutations common to boyhood, and Art Sherry had gone out drowning gophers. Bobbie had tagged along with them.

Out Sixth Street toward the spreading prairie they walked, Brian and Fat carrying between them Art's mother's washtub. Each carried in addition a red lard pail; Bobbie's bumped awkwardly against his fat legs as he alternately trotted and walked to keep up with the older boys. Once upon the prairie they turned east toward Haggerty's Coulee, where they had heard there were many gophers. While Fat's dog and Jappy ran ahead, the boys wandered in leisurely fashion, their conversation rambling as it usually did, until it arrived at the question of what a gopher did when he was being drowned out.

"Sometimes," Fat said, "you get three washtubs down their hole, and the water stays there quite a while, and you think he ain't ever comin' up, and then all of a sudden she goes down."

"She goes down." Bobbie always echoed the conversation of the other boys, who paid little attention to him.

"They back into the hole an' plug her up," Art explained, his face, as always, grimacing behind the thick spectacles that rode his nose. "When he unplugs, then the water comes down."

"The water comes down."

"You take the end of the washtub now," Brian said to Art.

"Not yet. I'll carry after Haggerty's Coulee."

"You never carry," Brian accused him.

"He never carries." Bobbie echoed his brother's speech most often.

"I do so," said Art. His glasses twitched; he put out his foot and tripped Bobbie to his face. Bobbie got up unconcernedly with his pants and shirt covered with spear grass, as were the clothes of all of them. At the edge of the prairie they'd had a spear grass fight, pulling the barbed hairs from their stalks and throwing them at each other; it was a good game.

"That is a ant," Bobbie pointed out.

"Anybody can see that," said Art.

"I can see that," said Bobbie. "I saw a girl one once."

"Look!" Fat cried and pointed to the dogs in scurrying chase over the prairie ahead. "They found one!"

"I don't see any!"

"Where?" yelled Art.

"A girl gopher," said Bobbie mildly. "I knew — "

"There it is!" Brian caught a glimpse of a brown back rolling in frantic gallop, saw the flirt of a tail as the gopher, inches from Jappy's eager nose, was swallowed down a hole. "He's down the hole!"

Both dogs were at the opening. Jappy ecstatically threw the dirt behind him—stopped to insert his nose right to the eyes—took it out — began to dig again. Fat's dog circled anxiously.

"You an' Fat fill the tub!" directed Art. "I'll watch."

"I'll watch too," said Bobbie as Brian and Fat ran off toward the river, the tub between them, the lard pails swinging in their free hands.

They brought back two tubs of water, tipped them carefully down the hole, after each one, watched eagerly for the gopher to come out. Jappy sat with his ears cocked, his head solicitously on one side; he made anxious sounds in the back of his throat.

"Maybe he's got him a back door," suggested Fat after the second tub. "Maybe he's went out the back door — "

"The dogs would of seen him go," said Art. "He hasn't got any back door—more water is what he—look! She's going down now!" One great bubble burst itself on the surface of the water filling the hole; it was followed by many little ones wobbling to the top. "He's took his ass outa the hole, an' he's comin' up now!" shouted Art with excitement. "Git ready!"

The gopher's flat head broke the surface of the water; just out of reach in the throat of his burrow, he crouched with his head barely above water, his almond eyes looking up at the boys and the dogs. Out of the corner of his eye, Brian could see Jappy's tapered body quivering.

"More water!" shrieked Art. "All he wants is more water! Halfa lard pail an' he'll come all the way out!" Ike rushed to the tub himself, tilted it over the lard pail, ran back, and soused the contents down on the waiting gopher. It came out in a lunging rush, its fawn hair dark with water, plastered wet against its skin. The dogs darted for it. Jappy got it by the scruff of the neck, shook his head, and threw it over his back. The gopher hurtled through the air to land near Art; it lay still upon the prairie. Art ran to it. He picked up the wet, tan body. It began to kick. "He's still alive!"

"He'll bite," said Fat fearfully. "They kin bite!"

"No, he won't. I got him round the belly. He isn't biting anybody. All he kin do is squeak."

It was squeaking now; the thin and frantic sound threaded

from Art's closed hand. Brian looked away. He saw with a start that the Young Ben was standing there; he had come upon them without a sound, and was staring at them with his pale, gray eyes under hair the color of the prairie itself. He was barefooted, and as he turned toward Art, Brian saw the beginning of the crease of his bare bottom through the tear hanging open in the seat of his faded overall pants held round his middle by several frayed strands of binder twine.

"I'm gonna take the tail offa him," said Art, with the gopher still struggling and squeaking in his hand.

"I knew a girl gopher once," said Bobbie.

Art saw the Young Ben then. "I'm gonna rip the tail off of him," he said again.

"She cut off her sister's finger an' it grew back on."

"Their tails grow back on if you let 'em go." Art was speaking to the Young Ben.

"An' she cut off her head an' it grew back on an' she cut off her legs an' they grew back on," chanted Bobbie.

Brian stared at the high and circling cheekbones under the tanned skin, at the freckles under the gray eyes. He looks like a coyote, thought Brian, like a watching coyote. He realized with a start that an excitement, akin to the feeling that had moved him so often, was beginning to tremble within him. His knees felt weak with it; the Young Ben could cause it too. The Young Ben was part of it. He's something I *know*, thought Brian.

Art had taken the gopher by the tip of its tail and was holding it head down by his thumb and forefinger. He raised his arm above his head and began to swing the gopher in a large circle. "Hold yer dogs back!" he cried. He snapped his arm. The tail remained in his hand.

"They all grow back on," said Bobbie sadly as the gopher thudded to the prairie sod.

Now to one side, now to the other, the gopher ran in squeaking, erratic course, both dogs after it. The Young Ben leaped. He passed the dogs, threw himself full length upon the tailless gopher. He lay there with the squeaking under him. While the boys watched open-mouthed, he reached under himself. With one mer-

126

ciful squeeze he choked the life from the animal. As he stood up he dropped it to the ground. He began to walk toward Art.

Fierce exultation gripped Brian as he realized what was about to happen. Face twitching nervously, Art backed away. He knew that something was wrong. Just as he had thrown himself upon the gopher, the Young Ben leaped at Art, who fell backward under his attacker's weight. The Young Ben fought as the boys had never seen anyone fight before. He was a clawing, wild thing on top of Art. He gouged Art's eyes, from which the glasses had fallen; blood sprang in long tracks as he drew his crooked fingers again and again and again down Art's face. He pounded him about the head, the throat, the ribs. He stood up and kicked Art rolling helpless on the prairie. When he stopped, one felt that he had done so simply because he was exhausted. He looked at the terror on Fat's face, at Bobbie sobbing, then for long and level moments at Brian.

Brian returned his gaze and watched him wheel and begin to run in the direction of Haggerty's Coulee. In his heart Brian ran with the Young Ben—running with an easy lope each step of which smoothed into the other like the ripples of a broad stream flowing. When he had ceased watching the Young Ben, he saw that Fat had gone to get a lard pail of water from the river. He made no move to help as Fat soaked his shirt, and washed the blood and dirt from Art's face. His clothes unbelievably ripped, Art had a dazed look upon his sharp face, the look that one expects to see upon the face of a man whose home has just been levelled by a prairie tornado. "I didn't do anything to *him*," he said tearfully over and over again.

And Brian, quite without any desire to alleviate Art's suffering, shaken by his discovery that the Young Ben was linked in some indefinable way with the magic that visited him often now, was filled with a sense of the justness, the rightness, the completeness of what the Young Ben had done — what he himself would like to have done.

Art had to be led home like a blind boy; he was unable to see a foot in front of himself without his thick glasses.

Brian thought often of the prairie incident, always with the same thrill of excitement. He would remember the feeling of revulsion that had gripped him when Art had jerked the tail from the gopher. He would wander out to Haggerty's Coulee, hoping that he would run across the Young Ben, his whole being tingling with expectation. He would return disconsolately home.

On one such occasion he was accompanied by Bobbie and Jappy. As the boys walked, the dog ran ahead of them, to come back and jump up on their legs, then run out again. Suddenly he stopped at a wild rose bush ahead, his nose to the ground, tenseness in every line of his lean and quivering body. Brian and Bobbie went up to see what he had found.

The tailless gopher lay upon an ant pile, strangely still with the black bits of ants active over it. A cloud of flies lifted from it, dispersed, then came together again as at a command. Brian stared down at the two rodent teeth, the blood that had run down the nose and crusted there; he saw a short stump of tail skeleton with a ragged tab of skin that had stayed with the body when Art had ripped away the tail. It was difficult to believe that this thing had once been a gopher that ran and squeaked over the prairie. It was difficult to believe that this was anything but dirt.

Bobbie began to cry. He turned away from the still body over the coning ant hill. He pulled on Brian's arm. The feeling was in Brian now, fierce — uncontrollably so, with wild and unbidden power, with a new, frightening quality.

"I don't like it!" Bobbie cried. "I want to go home—I want to go home — I want to go home!"

Prairie's awful, thought Brian, and in his mind there loomed vaguely fearful images of a still and brooding spirit, a quiescent power unsmiling from everlasting to everlasting to which the coming and passing of the prairie's creatures was but incidental. He looked out over the spreading land under intensely blue sky. The Young Ben was part of all this.

"I want to go home, Brian!"

Brian put his arm protectively around his brother's shoulder, and the two began to walk back across the prairie to the town.

The Bens no longer sat in the second row of Knox church; any ties that might have bound them were rudely severed three weeks after the Ben's formal reception into the fold. "The Lost Sheep", that Sunday's delicately balanced sermon pointing out the church's newest member, had been followed the next Sunday by a Sermon built around "The Parable of the Lost Penny", and the one after that by "The Prodigal's Return". The next Sunday the Ben's still in the church basement blew up.

Ignited by the yellow, moth-wing flame of the kerosene burner, which the Ben had left turned too high, it exploded between the announcing of the Ladies' Auxiliary chicken dinner to be held the following Tuesday at the home of Mrs. Abercrombie, and the passing of the collection plate. It detonated with a thud that was felt rather than heard by every member of the congregation. Later, at home, Brian's grandmother spoke of the scares she had had as a girl when Fenian raids had threatened. Brian, who had been mentally defying the Lord's lightning in church, had turned a startling white. In the absolute silence that had settled down, there could be heard from below the clanging of metal objects dropping one after another. The Ben sprang from his seat and hurried from the church.

Seeing him go, and thinking that whatever was the matter it could be attended to by the Ben, Mr. Powelly went on with his sermon.

The church was heated by a system of hot air vents placed conveniently along its sides, and leading to the furnace room where the accident had occurred. From these, soon after, there stole a yeasty breath that blossomed into sweet fumes of ferment hanging oppressively.

Meanwhile, the Ben below feverishly collected parts of his still from far corners, the copper coil which was still in one piece and such bits of the granite pot as had not been imbedded in the rafters of the Sunday school room or various chairs there. It was lucky that it was an evening service when the still exploded. Throughout the rest of the church service, the Ben shuttled frantically between the cellar and Thorborn's Livery Barn, where he secreted the evidence of his brewing activities in the harness room.

Summoned tardily the next day, Jake Harris told Mr. Powelly that there was not enough evidence to prosecute the Ben. The minister was aware of an undying, Old Testament thirst for revenge — a thirst, he resolved fiercely, which should have its full slaking one day.

FIFTEEN

Fall held a pleasant surprise for Brian— a new teacher. Several weeks before school opened, the children had known that Miss MacDonald was not coming back. Art had told them; his father was a member of the school board now, Mr. Thorborn still its chairman.

Just before fall registration Mr. Digby made an appointment to meet Miss Thompson, the new teacher, and to go over with her the plans for the term work. He met a young woman with quick and definite features. Her bluing-black hair, cut short, seemed even blacker against her very white skin. She had the sort of dark eyes that seem all pupil, so deep is the brownness of the iris; it was the eyes that kept her face from being bland. Quizzical, decided Digby. She was living with Miss Taylor from the telephone office and Miss James of Blaine's store, she told the schoolmaster; Digby knew the brown cottage she described, on the other side of the creek. When he said that he hoped she would like her new school, she assured him that she would; the sudden expressiveness of her face, the girlish quality of excitement in her, attracted Digby immediately.

"And you were at Westward," he said, referring to her last school.

"Three years," she said; "before that — Azure."

"Azure," mused Digby. "Seems to be . . . Oh, yes — Svarich . . . Didn't Peter Svarich have a practice in Azure before he came here?"

"Yes," said Miss Thompson quickly. "Dr. Svarich was in Azure."

Digby looked at her sharply. Something wrong; her mobile features were quite free of expression—deliberately so, he thought. "I — I suppose you know one another?"

"We do," said Miss Thompson.

Also determined, decided Digby, for all the cameo quality of her pale, small face. He brushed back the lock of sandy hair that insisted upon falling over his forehead; as he did, he saw that his shirt cuff was showing a good inch below his sleeve. It was frayed. "How long were you there?" As he asked the question he felt a twinge of annoyance with himself; it was none of his business.

"Five years," Miss Thompson told him. "It was my first school — one room."

Probably attended normal school at eighteen; if she had taught eight years, that made her twenty-six or seven. Twenty-six — seven — from thirty-eight, he calculated — twelve. With a slight frown on his rocky features, he got up from the desk. "Let's take a look at your room, shall we?" Most women would be attracted to Svarich, he thought, as he held his office door open for her. He

132

wished that he had changed his shirt that morning. She would have been five when he got his first school.

When he had shown her around, and had given her the forms she must fill out for the first of the term, he said, "I'm going downtown. Perhaps I can show you some of it, if you're headed that way."

He pointed out the power house to the south and east of the school, and explained to her that the river and the railroad ran past it to cross First Street behind the *Times* building. Three blocks before First Street they passed the Presbyterian church, turned and walked by Thorborn's livery barn.

"You've met him," said Digby, "our school board chairman?"

Miss Thompson nodded.

"Most of the members have their businesses down this next street—Mr. Parsons, Hardware—Johnson, Men's Clothing. Mr. Gillis, the town secretary, is also school board secretary—his office is in the town hall three streets over to the west."

As they walked down the street that ran before the post office and to the bank corner marking the beginning of the main business district, Digby showed Miss Thompson Cobb's Plumbing Shop, Milt Palmer's Shoe and Harness Shop. Once on First Street, he explained to her that Sherry's Mill, the Jenkins Dairy, and the MacDougall Implement Company had their buildings along the railroad tracks to the west of First Street. In the second block of First Street, he showed her O'Connal's Drugstore, Nelson's Bakery, and across the street, the Hi-Art Theatre, Temple of Refined Entertainment and Education. They passed the Bluebird Café, run by Wong, came to Funder's Meat Market, and then a large sandstone building on the corner of Railroad Avenue and First Street. "This is our one hotel," said Digby, "the Royal. There are spittoons in the lobby of the Royal — the Pool Hall — Judge Mortimer's office. The spittoon is the distinguishing badge of the town's three dissipations—beer drinking, snookering, and penny ante."

They had stopped before the lilac and honeysuckle bushes on either side of the *Times* building; from within could be heard a persistent, metallic clatter. "Thursday," Digby explained. "Mr. Stickle brings the *Times* out tomorrow — four pages — you'll be able to get it at O'Connal's, the Royal lobby, or the post office." He looked down at Miss Thompson. "I guess I leave you here. I — I hope you like us. It's a good town."

"Oh, I'm sure I will," said Miss Thompson, and Digby again felt the inner lift that the clear, young quality of her voice had given him before. He began to walk back down First Street in the direction they had come.

Miss Thompson stood alone before the *Times* building. A round little man with his bare arms inked and broad suspenders running up and over his sloping shoulders, came to the open doorway. He nodded to her. Mr. Stickle, she thought as she started on her way.

She crossed the railroad tracks, looked down them to the seven grain elevators, then began to cross the wooden bridge that spanned the river. So her cottage was on the *wrong* side of town; it must be, if that sprawl of tar-papered shacks was German Town. The outhouses there showed that the homes lacked plumbing; the foot of each was banked with dirt. Fierce-mustached men lived there, men with black-burning roll-your-own cigarettes permanently in the corner of the mouth, necessary men — the laborers on the C.P.R., on highway maintenance, and on sewer work for the town: Polish, Austrian, Bohemian, Ruthenian, Hungarian, Galician, not-yet-Canadian.

She stopped at the end of the bridge and rested her chin in her hands while she looked down at the slow flow of the thin creek. Peter's people. Digby had not pointed out Dr. Svarich's office; there had been no need of that; she had seen his sign, PETER R. SVARICH, PHYSICIAN AND SURGEON, on the new, low building next to Funder's Meat Market. She looked at the woman bent over a washtub in one of the back yards, and her mental picture of Peter's mother was renewed — a nut-brown woman with unbelievably lined face, a dark kerchief over her head, a dark skirt blooming from her full middle. Unlike Peter's clever hands, his mother's had been fat-muscled, with blunt finger tips. Mrs. Svarich had been silent in the presence of Peter's father, a man whose face suggested

134

a Notre Dame cathedral imp, ever so slightly aristocratic, ever so slightly goatish. He had been a continually smiling little man with twinkling eyes.

She supposed that Peter's eyes must have been like that at one time, before she had known him. She knew now what she could not have been expected to know earlier — that Peter was ashamed of his foreign birth. As she turned from the end of the bridge, she felt a ripple of contrition pass through her. She began to walk swiftly toward her new home.

A careless man about his clothes, Digby would ordinarily have put off having his shoes attended to until the lifts were almost gone and the nails thus freed made every step painful; but after he had left Miss Thompson he felt moved to atone for the frayed and dirty shirt in which he had received her. Upon impulse then, he directed his way to Milt Palmer's Shoe and Harness Shop. Digby owned only one pair of shoes, so that whenever he visited the shoemaker's shop he was forced to sit on the bench behind the counter while Mr. Palmer fixed his shoes. He did not mind this; it gave him an excuse to talk with Milt Palmer, and there under sheets of leather and hung rawhide saddletrees, where the aroma of the Ben's brew mixed with the richness of leather smell, he could exercise a natural talent for dialectic which had been neglected much since his old friend Hislop had left the town.

Usually when he called upon the shoemaker he brought an armful of books and took an armful away. Mr. Palmer was a philosopher. A small man with black and almond-shaped eyes, his gray hair in tight ringlets close to his small, round head, he made Digby think of a clown without grease paint. His nose flared out at each side so that there were three distinct parts to it; it was as though a stalkless strawberry had been placed under the eyebrows kiting up in perpetual surprise.

A jug of the Ben's brew inhabited a spot under the counter; Mr. Palmer spent his nights there; if you leaned down, you could often see the corner of a gray blanket trailing.

The bell above the shop door tinkled as the schoolmaster entered; Mr. Palmer got up from his last. His eyebrows flew higher at the sight of Digby. "Gone agin! You had another month yet!" His voice suggested that his pharynx was of metal.

"Lot of walking," said Digby. "The heels aren't really gone this time." He lifted a section of the counter and walked around to sit on the bench.

Milt Palmer reached under the counter; his arm came out with a demijohn; it gurgled a moment in the V of his arm. He held it out to Digby, who shook his head and leaned down to untie his laces.

"Who you got this time?"

"I didn't bring anything," said Digby.

"Oh." Milt turned back to his last. He turned around again. "You kin leave Thomas Aquinas home next time."

Digby turned his face up, rather flushed from bending down. "What's wrong with Thomas?"

"Ain't fussy about him. Matter of fact I ain't so fussy about any of 'em any more." He took the shoe that Digby handed him. "Lotta crap."

"Crap?"

"Thinkin'. Gonna give her up. Gonna quit. No point in her."

Digby handed him the other shoe. "That's nice. Why?"

"I was lookin' at a tree the other day—Ain't much left besides the tops on these shoes."

"What about the tree?"

"It was doin' all right."

"Without thinking," primed Digby.

"Without thinkin'. I said to myself, 'That there tree is doin' all right, an' it's doin' it without thinkin'. Me—I think—I'm havin' one hell of a time.'"

"Are you?"

"Yep. I'm givin' it up."

"Thinking?"

"Thinkin'."

"Can you do it?"

"I kin try. May come hard at first, but I kin try. I'll take a good run at her—maybe make a better man."

"Well—just what do you mean—a man?"

"Animal—two legs—right number of guts—right kind."

136

"So's a chicken."

"I can't lay eggs."

"Then you're a two-legged animal that doesn't lay eggs?"

"That's right."

"You make shoes and harness."

"That's right."

"Have to think to do that, don't you?"

"Some."

"So you're not a tree—a tree can be a tree without thinking—it's a good tree when it's growing without thinking. A shoemaker, on the other hand, is an animal—uh—with the right number and kind of guts — that has to think some to be a shoemaker; if he doesn't think, he's not a good man or a shoemaker."

Mr. Palmer looked down at the shoes in his hands. "Maybe you're right." He lifted his little black eyes, with their astonishing eyebrows, to Digby. "But I still wish to hell I was a tree." He turned away, then back again. "But most of all I wish I wasn't a man."

"Why?"

"Means I'm a critter like the Reverend Powelly. Had him in here yesterday, suckin' aroun' tryin' to find out did I know where the Ben had his still hid. Had quite a talk with him. We talked about God."

"Did you?" said Digby.

"Yep." Milt sat down at his last and began paring with a curved knife on the leather remnants on one of the shoe heels. "Won't be so fussy about comin' in again."

"Why not?"

Milt spat on the floor. "Him an' God didn't do so good." He turned to face Digby. "I sure wisht I was a tree. I figger they got somethin' we haven't got."

"What have they got?"

"Don't make no mistakes."

"Perhaps that's part of being a man."

"Hell — that don't help me none — I'd settle for a spriga pigweed. The way I see it — there's two kindsa reality — "

"Then you're a dualist."

"I'm Milt Palmer — the pie-eyed harnessmaker — I — I ain't

137

nothin'. There's two kinds — real an' what a fella figgers is real. They ain't a bit alike."

"But — they must be — "

"Not a goddam bit."

The bell tinkled above the door, and Bobbie O'Connal entered. He came in on his red wagon, steered it for the opening in the counter, and came to a stop by the last.

"I ain't makin' anything today," Milt Palmer said to him. "Jist fixin' the schoolmaster's shoes. Come back tomorrow."

"What are you making tomorrow?" asked Bobbie.

"Double team harness," Milt told him.

"Who for?"

"Joe Pivott."

"With tassels?"

Milt nodded. Bobbie turned the tongue of his wagon and went out again.

"Sure it is. What's real. I'll tell you — the beginnin' — that's gettin' born; the end—that's gittin' dead . . . Both of them is real— good an' real."

The bell tinkled again, and Brian O'Connal stood by the counter. Milt paid no attention to him. "In between there's hunger an' there's sleepin' an' wakin' an' there's wimmen an' this here brew at the Ben's. Them things is real. Along comes Powelly or your friend got diddled outa his church — whatta they do? Somebody dies, they're right handy with the Heavenly Land on High an' a shiny box an' flowers an' a lotta things ain't got nothin' whatsoever to do with bein' dead. You know what death is? Rotting— stink— dust— an' you're back to the prairie again. Take birth — what's that? Sprinkling with water? Announcement cards? Seegars? Hospital ward? Hell no! Blood an' water an' somethin' new for a while— mebbe a shoemaker that wishes he was a tree."

"Have you seen my brother?" asked Brian.

"They're all a-scairt of reality unless they thought her up. Scairt silly; so they pretty her up—'cept one of 'em. God—I wish I was a tree!"

Brian on tiptoe at the counter stared at Mr. Palmer. He saw

138

Mr. Digby in his stocking feet with an intent look upon his face. "You forgot thinking, Milt."

"No—I didn't forget her—but I'll throw her in jist to please you — 'tain't worth a damn. Death — birth — love — hunger — wakin' — sleepin' — drinkin' . . . That's reality — not what you think about them."

"There's one Book I've got to bring to you," said Digby.

"What one?"

"The Bible."

"What for?"

"Ecclesiastes."

"Has Bobbie been in here, Mr. Palmer?"

"No—yes—he went out jist a minute ago." Milt jerked back his head and filled his mouth with tacks. "I doubt it," he said to Digby.

"I don't," said Digby. "I'll bring it."

Mr. Digby, thought Brian as he went out the door, has a hole in his sock.

SIXTEEN

Miss Thompson's children found her refreshing after Miss MacDonald. The first day of school she told them that they would not have to stand up by their seats to recite; she seemed to have a faculty for infecting them with enthusiasm in their work. Several thought of her respect for individuality as weakness; but that was changed after Fat, in a burst of high spirits, threw a blackboard eraser across the room to hit Stevie Botton on the back of the head.

Fat, who wept easily, returned from the cloakroom dry-eyed. He was reluctant at recess to show his hands to Brian and others who asked to see them. Two of them pushed him down, sat on him, got a look at his palms. There was not the slightest blush of red there. They let him up in disgust. Fat confided in Brian a week later, making him promise first not to tell. Miss Thompson had bent him over an old desk in the cloakroom; Fat had been too indignant to cry, and for days after, he nursed a resentment toward her. He had been cheated; at least one ought to be able to stand in an awed circle of children and show them red or welted hands. The way she had done it, a person couldn't show anything—not even talk about it.

Though she gave the children more freedom than they had enjoyed before, Miss Thompson expected a great deal of them. Except toward the China Kids, she showed no favoritism; with Tang and Vooie she seemed to have an extra brightness in her voice; in games the Chinese children were selected for coveted positions a little more often. No one resented this, except perhaps Mariel Abercrombie. In the years they had attended school, Tang and Vooie had been subjected to periodic ostracism, a mild form of persecution usually started by Mariel, a full-faced little sadist of ten years. It was she who started the whispering that rippled along the rows, like wrinkles spreading over a pond, breaking into tight and hurried little excitements that spilled into recesses—when the girls would walk each other off with arms about each other's waists, while Mi Tang was left to sit stolidly at her desk, un-whispered-to, un-walked-off-with. There had been for instance the time during the Grade Three wedding project when Tang had informed the class that her mother, who was now dead, had been bought by her father for a lot of money. Mariel had touched off the class's shrill tittering; isolation had followed at recess.

In her first fall, Miss Thompson was startled several times by Ach Vooie, who was in Brian's class. During a Grade Two reading lesson the second month of the fall term she had waited for Vooie to read the yellow chalk legend, "The man has a dog. The dog runs."

"Your turn, Vooie," she had said.

He sat staunchly enthroned in his seat.

"Vooie."

His eyes were fixed carefully on the corner of her desk.

"Don't you want to read, Vooie?"

The broad nostrils of his snub nose flattened imperceptibly more.

"If you don't try, you won't be able to read like Tang."

The flat, tan lids flickered down to show her momentarily the cameo clarity of their edges. Then:

"He don't wanna little blue star for the little book. He want no money — heaven beyond his power."

It was one of the many proverbs with which Old Wong spoke to his children, and in itself it explained the decline of the Bluebird Café after the death of his wife. Since that event, he had turned to a Stoicism that told him the world was upsetting and could take from him; he had retired to the tranquillity of his dark kitchen to sit for long, lonely periods of time, his red toque a bright spot in the shadows.

His business had suffered; tables stood bare; counters disgorged themselves of cent candy and celluloid combs and tobacco; the café itself became indescribably dirty; a patina of dirt and grease grew over everything. Children and parents alike often told each other with the same delicious thrill that Old Wong was an opium eater.

Near the end of October, Miss Thompson noticed a listlessness in the China Kids, so she sent them down to Dr. Svarich; then with the resolution of one who knows that some things are inevitable and that putting them off simply increases their awkwardness, she went down to the doctor's office herself.

Svarich's office building stood next to Funder's Meat Market; the only new building on the business street, it was of rough brick with its entrance door between two windows, their broad panes sliced with Venetian blinds. Miss Thompson hesitated a moment, then opened the door. Except for an overalled man with a bandage around his head and one ear, the waiting room was empty. The teacher stood just inside the door, her eyes on the metal-tubed

142

furniture with its red and blue leather upholstery. It was what he would pick, thought Miss Thompson—not old-fashioned, but of this day — stark to the point of no individuality. It demanded attention but no ridicule. It was Peter's furniture.

The door with frosted glass opened at the back, and Peter Svarich stood there. He glanced impersonally at Miss Thompson, then beckoned to the bandaged man with a nod of his head. The man got up; the door closed behind him. Miss Thompson sat down in a red leathered chair as artistic as a theorem.

She had wondered what it would be like, to see him again. Now she had. He had changed little in appearance; his face still had its satyrlike conformation, the V-peak of crisp, black hair salted slightly with gray; the deep creases bracketing his long mouth had deepened. And in her heart, she was asking herself, hadn't there been a hint of the familiar flutter, a suggestion of the breathlessness that had always possessed her when she was about to see him?

The bandaged man emerged from the door; he went to the chair upon which he'd left his cap; Peter Svarich gave Miss Thompson exactly the same nod he had given the patient who was leaving. The teacher entered the office.

"Peter—I—I—" She found it difficult to express what she was feeling as she looked at the discontent in the lines at his mouth. "You must understand that I didn't know you were here when I came — when I applied—"

"I believe you," Svarich said. "About these children . . . "

"Oh, Peter—is there any reason that we have to be unkind to each—"

"They're suffering from malnutrition," he said in his dry voice. "What the hell do you care?"

Miss Thompson in spite of herself felt a stir of the old resentment. "I care," she said in a voice that matched the impersonality of his. "They're my children."

"Not yours," he said. "You didn't conceive them — bear them." If he had thought to shock her, he was disappointed.

"I said they were my children," she said simply. "They are Chinese, and they are my children, though I have not slept with any

Chinese recently." She looked at him steadily with her intense brown eyes large in her pale face. "They would be mine," she said, "if they were Ukrainian."

The lines of bitterness almost forgot themselves on Svarich's face. "I believe they would," he said softly. "I believe they would—and they might have been."

A faint flush colored Miss Thompson's face. She moistened her lips with the tip of her tongue, and with a quick motion of her hand that Svarich remembered as characteristic of her when she was moved, she brushed at her hair. "It would have been a bad bargain for both of us — you know — "

"I suppose," he said; "and as you say, there's no point in being unkind. I'm sorry. Now — about these children — they're not getting enough to eat. If you're interested, I'd advise you to go and see their father. See what the situation is." He looked at Miss Thompson a moment. "Same face," he observed; "same heart. I— I'm glad to see you again, Ruth."

Ruth Thompson held out her hand. Svarich took it with the look of a man about to do something that he knows perfectly well is not good for him.

Miss Thompson walked quickly from the office to the Bluebird Café, and as she walked she wondered why most people were fooled by Peter Svarich, why they went no further than his outer defense of irony, assuming that there was no further to go. She wondered if she had ever unconsciously done him that injustice; it seemed to her that she had always known his bitterness was not selfish — that he was not shallow.

Brittle — that had been Peter, unable to adapt. The course of love had not run smoothly; there had been too much of emotion, of irritation growing into sarcasm calling out recrimination, and that in turn bringing flaming anger. She had told him finally that they could not have a smooth marriage out of it—not possibly. He had listened to her almost as though he had expected it all along; that had sent her off the deep end again. They had not been able even to end it with restraint.

She found Wong in the back of the café; he came to meet her as she entered the kitchen door. He had been feeding the children mush three times a day. He had just enough oatmeal left for one more day. Miss Thompson left the café and walked swiftly in the direction she had come from Svarich's office, till she came to the sign that said, "Your Tonsorial Requirements Looked After." She walked in without hesitation.

"Mr. Neally."

His Worship the Mayor, owner of the town's two-chair barbershop, turned to her, leaving his hand to continue by itself smoothing the lather on the face of the man tilted back beside him. Even across the shop, Miss Thompson could hear Mr. Neally's breathing, harsh and labored like that of a Boston terrier.

"An' how's the demigong today?" he said heartily. Mr. Neally always said everything heartily.

"I've just come from Wong's."

"Anythin' I kin do fer you?"

"Yes, there is. Those children are not doing very well."

"Ain't they?" With his forefinger he tilted up the nose of the shavee and bent over.

"What has the council done about those — about seeing that those children get food?"

Mr. Neally wiped the razor on a square of paper and laid the result upon the customer's chest. "We're considerin' the matter. We're considerin' it," he said heartily.

"But — this must have been going on for some time — is anything going to be done about it?"

When he answered her the jovial quality of his voice was a bit strained; this was a political matter. "I'm jist the Mayor, you know — ain't the ee-lectors; an' them Chinese ain't the only ones needin' relief — got a lotta families on relief — got a lot of 'em on relief. We ain't so sure the Wongs is the town's responsibility — that's got to be looked into — there's wheels inside of wheels — there's wheels — "

"But — those children are starving — "

"We sort of figgered to leave her at the status of quo — we figgered to leave her there. They're Chinese an' them folks got their own way to take care of the indigement. They got tongs, ain't they?"

145

Miss Thompson did not answer him; she had left the shop.

"What you thinka that?" Mr. Neally said to the man in the chair, a touch of querulousness in his voice. "Tryin' to run things already." He bent down and pumped the chair upright. "Ain't bin in the town two months an' she's tryin' to run things. Next thing she'll be decidin' your cases for you, Judge."

Judge Mortimer spat through his ragged gray mustache and unerringly into the spittoon. "Nup," he said, "she wun't."

"Hair trim?"

"Yup."

That evening Miss Thompson called upon Digby at his boardinghouse. She told him about the China Kids and her visit to Mr. Neally's barbershop; she asked him if he couldn't get some action. He assured her that he would do his best and insisted upon sharing half the Wong grocery bill with her. After that had been agreed to, Digby took down cups and teapot from the curtained shelves at one end of his room. When Digby filled his pipe, she took a packet of tobacco from her jacket pocket, spilled a pile into the palm of her hand, and rolled a cigarette. As she looked up from licking the paper, she saw his eyes on her.

"I always have," she said. She brushed the tobacco crumbs from her lap. "I can also drive a binder, and break a horse."

"That's nice," said Digby. "You can teach too."

"Thank you," said Miss Thompson.

When she had left, Digby's room seemed somehow much emptier to him.

At the end of the month, Digby and Miss Thompson found that Peter Svarich had taken care of the Wongs' grocery account at Blaine's Store.

The China Kids were not the only unfortunates who benefited by Miss Thompson's active sense of justice and her understanding. Very soon after she had come to the school she had surprised upon the Young Ben's face a look that returned to her again and again in the days that followed, a look haunting in its intensity and disturbing in its strange appeal. She found herself, during classes, looking over to the boy where he sat beside Brian O'Connal and the other

146

Grade Two pupils, whom he dwarfed. She tried to name for herself the expression that was in his triangular face; thought of a person caught naked in a public assembly—looked into the narrow, gray eyes, and suddenly knew—it was the look that lies in the eyes of a caught thing. She changed his seat to a back one among the Grade Four students; there he sat uneasily, lifting his thin shoulders almost a foot above the younger children. It was the best that Miss Thompson could do.

The Young Ben played no games with the other children; he did not bother with agates in marble season, and would take no part in organized team games. He could run with the swiftness of a prairie chicken, Miss Thompson found out from Brian O'Connal; he could jump like an antelope; but he could not be interested in races or Field Day competitions. School was an intolerable incarceration for him, made bearable only by flights of freedom which totaled up to almost the same number as the days he attended. In a tacit understanding with Digby, the new teacher made no official mention of the Young Ben's truancy.

She sought to ease the boy's tension by assigning him numerous tasks; she asked the Young Ben often to post letters for her; if she wanted a window opened, she let the Young Ben do it. Almost daily he took messages down to Mr. Briggs in the basement. Mr. Digby noted all this; he blessed the chance that had sent Miss Thompson to his school.

Digby had changed. In November he bought a new suit at Blaine's—a rough, herringbone tweed, coarse and wiry—a cloth that stubbornly resisted Mrs. Geddes's repeated attempts with an iron to put a crease in the trousers, which had as much personality as gunny-sacking. In spite of his morning and noon efforts, the sandy lock of hair continued to spring down over his forehead. He no longer wore the black, knitted ties he had before, but instead, brightly striped and cross-hatched cravats equaled in brilliance only by his socks. That Christmas he gave Miss Thompson a present — a five-pound tin of roll-your-own tobacco.

The Ben had not changed. He had no worries now that his still was secreted beneath three feet of manure in the cow barn. The cave there had a square, well-like lid filled with the stuff and fitting perfectly into place. Since the Ben's brief career as janitor, Mr. Powelly had nursed scalding bitterness in his heart. Deliberately he had arranged personal encounters with Jake Harris, bidding him do his duty. He made passionate exhortations to the police department at town council meetings; as time went on without the Ben's being brought to justice, he delivered pointed sermons from the pulpit, criticizing the garbage department ("Community Cleanliness Next to Community Godliness"), bristling with illustrative reference to the fire department ("Flames of Hell Are Ready for the Unready Fireman"). It was of no avail.

The Ben had solved his financial difficulties; although he had on occasion before sold liquor, he now made a regular business of selling the gray, cloudy liquid that dripped from the end of the copper coil. His more regular customers included Joe Pivott, Sean O'Connal, Peter Svarich, and more often than any of these, Milt Palmer, the town shoemaker.

The spring after the Ben's still blew up in Knox church, Mr. Powelly was slightly mollified when, through Jake Harris's efforts, Milt Palmer was fined twenty-five dollars and costs by Judge Mortimer for being in possession of a three-quarter-filled jug of the Ben's brew. Very soon after that, the Ben added Judge Mortimer himself to his list of customers.

SEVENTEEN

In the O'Connal family, Christmas began
as a rule early in December, when the boys started to decide what
presents they would like. In Brian's second year of school,
Christmas was called earlier to the parents' attention because with
the beginning of winter Brian asked for skates.

Maggie's first response was unbelief; it was difficult for her to
think that one of her boys was old enough to want skates. She

reminded him that he was just past seven and that Forbsie Hoffman did not have skates yet. Brian replied that Art Sherry had them. Art, who was a year and a half older than Brian, had inherited a pair from an older sister; their high tops had been cut down; they had to be worn with three pairs of woolen socks so that Art's feet would not slide around in the shoes — but to Brian, skateless, they were things whose beauty would endure forever.

Skates became a frequent topic of conversation at meals. At length the grandmother said she was sick of hearing about them; would it not be possible to get the child a pair so that he could break his neck and give them a few peaceful meals? Maggie forbade Brian to mention skates at the table again.

The day that he saw the new tube skates in the hardware store window, Brian called on his father at work.

"Why can't I have them, Dad?"

"Because your mother says you're too young for them."

"But I'm not — I'm — "

"Seven's pretty young for skates."

"I was seven a long time ago—in the fall—I'm past seven!"

"You're still too young — when you're older — next year, perhaps."

"I'll be older at Christmas. That's a long ways away. May I have them for Christmas?"

"I don't think so, Spalpeen."

After Brian had left, Gerald felt a pang of remorse; it was difficult to see why the boy could not have skates. That night he had a talk with Maggie.

"Perhaps by Christmas time?" he asked her. "He'll be almost seven and a half then."

His wife looked at him a long time before answering him. "You know—I love him too, Gerald. I hate to deny them things as much as you. It's just that he seems so — do you think he's old enough? Do you — honestly?"

"I think so, Maggie."

"It isn't because he wants them so badly?"

"Well — he's old enough — let him skate."

After a decent interval Brian was told that he might possibly get skates for Christmas. Bobbie then insisted that he should get skates too, but he finally settled for a hockey stick and a puck.

Brian looked forward with eagerness to the promised skates. He thought of them often — during school hours — whenever the boys gathered after school with worn, sliver-thin sticks to play a sort of hockey between tin-can goal posts and with a blob of frozen horse manure for a puck. The more he thought of them, the less envious he was of Art with his "wimmen skates". There would be nothing feminine about *his*; they would be sturdy tubes with thick, felt tongues.

The night before Christmas he was almost sick with excitement and anticipation as he lay in his bed with Bobbie beside him. He could see the skates clearly with their frosted tubing and the clear runners that would cling to his thumb when he ran it along them to test their sharpness. He could see himself gliding over the river, alone on shining ice. With a twist and a lean — a shower of ice-snow — he came to a breath-taking stop.

Bobbie stirred in his sleep.

"You awake, Bobbie?"

Bobbie did not answer him.

Perhaps there would be straps over the ankles; not that he would need them, for his ankles were strong. His feet wouldn't slop. He flexed them beneath the covers — stronger than anything. Maybe they were too strong, and when he pushed, he would push the ice clean full of cracks.

He closed his eyes tightly. If only he could get to sleep the time would pass more quickly. When one slept it was nothing — swift as a person on skates — swift as the wind . . .

"He came, Brian! He came!"

Bobbie was jumping on the bed, his hair bright in the winter sunshine that filled the room.

Brian jumped from bed. "C'mon!"

Their stockings, lumpy with oranges, each with a colored cardboard clown protruding from its top, hung from the mantel of the fireplace. Bobbie's sleigh that could be steered was before the tree. Bobbie threw himself upon the parcels.

"Wait a minute!" cried Brian. "They're not all yours — just with your name!"

He began to sort out the presents upon which Maggie the night before had printed in the large block letters that Brian could easily read.

Anxiously Brian watched the growing pile of parcels beside him. He opened a deep box to find it full of colored cars and an engine, in little compartments. He opened another — a mechanical affair which when wound caused two long black men to dance, all the while turning around. Slippers were in one promising-looking parcel. As he opened the last of his parcels he was filled with the horrible conviction that something was wrong.

Then he saw a parcel behind the Christmas tree. His name was on it. He opened it. They were not tube skates; they were not single-runnered skates; they were bob-skates, double-runnered affairs with curving toe-cleats and a half-bucket arrangement to catch the heel of the shoe.

For a swift moment Brian's heart was filled with mixed feeling; disappointment bitter and blinding was there, but with it a half-dazed feeling of inner release and relief that he had got skates. They were skates, he told himself as he turned them over in his hands.

"What's the matter, Brian?" Bobbie had looked up from his fire engine.

Brian got up and went into the living room; he sat on the window seat next to the shamrock plant, the bob-skates upon his knees. When Bobbie came through a while later clutching a hockey stick a foot longer than himself, Brian paid no attention to him.

Throughout dinner he spoke only when spoken to. When his father and uncle were seated in the living room with lighted cigars and his mother and grandmother were in the kitchen, washing the dinner dishes, he went unnoticed to the hallway, put on his coat and toque, and with the bob-skates went out.

He passed other children as he walked, pulling Christmas sleighs and Christmas toboggans, some with gleaming Christmas skates slung over their shoulders. Through the fiercely tinseled snow sparkling unbearably in the sunlight he walked, not toward the downtown bridge where children and adults swooped over cleared ice, but toward the powerhouse and the small footbridge. There he sat near a clump of willow, fitted the skates to his feet, buckled the straps over his insteps, and went knee-deep through the snow on the riverbank to the ice.

Once on the ice he stood for a moment on trembling legs. He pushed with one foot; it skidded sideways; the other went suddenly from under him, and he came down with a bump that snatched his breath. He got carefully up and stood uncertainly. He pushed a tentative skate ahead, then another. He stood still with knees half-bent. He gave a push with one skate preparatory to swooping over the ice. He fell flat on his face. He got up.

He began a slow forward sliding across the ice — painfully — noncommittal steps of a stroke victim just risen from bed. He was not skating, he was walking with an overwhelming feeling of frustration that reminded him of dreams in which he ran with all his might, but stayed only in one spot. He fell again, and felt his elbow go numb. He sat on the ice, looking at his own feet ahead of him.

He began to cry.

Brian's parents, his grandmother, and his uncle were seated in the living room when he got back to the house. He was carrying the bob-skates as he came out of the hallway.

"Been skatin'?" asked Sean.

Brian did not answer him. "Uncle Sean asked you a question, Son," said Maggie.

Sean's big, freckled hand reached out to take one of the bob-skates. "Damn fool question," said Sean. "Fella doesn't skate with bob-skates. Had somebody pullin' you, did you?"

Brian shook his head.

"What's wrong, Spalpeen?" Brian's father was looking at his tear-stained face.

Brian rushed from the room.

"What do you mean?" Maggie turned to Sean. "What's wrong with his skates? What did you mean —"

"They call 'em skates," said Sean. "Can't skate with 'em. Just teaches kids a healthy respect fer ice, that's all. Got no grip at all—skid like hell. Never forget the first time I took Gerald on ice with a pair—'bout the same age as Brian. He had one hell of a time—ended up hangin' onto me coattails whilst I pulled him around."

"But—then that means that Brian—he's—" Maggie got up and went swiftly from the room.

She found Brian at the kitchen window.

"Don't they work, Son?"

Still looking out the window, Brian shook his head.

"Aren't they what you wanted?"

"Tubes," he got out with difficulty. "Like in Harris's."

"I'm sorry, Brian." Maggie watched his shoulders moving. She turned his face around to her. "Don't—please don't! I'll fix it!"

She went to the phone.

"Mr. Harris? Have you a pair of—of tube skates left? Small size? I wonder if we—if you could come down to the store with me—my son—will you—will—"

That night Maggie O'Connal stood at her children's bedside. With her white nightgown almost to her heels, her hair in two black braids, she looked like a little girl in the dimness of the room.

A glinting caught her eye, and she saw a length of leather lace hanging down the side of the bed. Brian slept with his hand clenched around the runner of one tube skate, his nose almost inside the boot. Maggie reached out one hand and laid it lightly upon Brian's cheek; she kept it there for a long time. Then she gently took the skate from his hand.

She turned and with the flat, soft steps of the barefooted went from the room.

154

EIGHTEEN

In his seat, under the yellow chicks and white rabbits alternating around the top border of the blackboard, Fat Hoffman twirled a ruler on the point of his pencil. Seeing the look on his friend's face and watching him shifting his seat, Brian O'Connal wondered what had excited Fat. He must have something to tell; he had been late that morning.

The recess bell rang; Fat's ruler dropped with a clatter; Mariel

Abercrombie, who had been leaning over so that her hair almost hid her face as she whispered to Eileen Gatenby, straightened up. Mariel was in the midst of another whispering campaign against the Wongs. Today was Mi Tang's birthday; there was to be a party over the Bluebird Café — just for girls. Miss Thompson had announced that she would like Mariel to stay at recess, and now as the others filed out, Mariel remained seated. Brian, looking back over his shoulder, saw her there; she was in for it; snooty, he thought, as he took Fat by the arm in the hall.

"I got rabbits!" said Fat excitedly.

In the bright light of the schoolyard, Brian stared at Fat. "Live rabbits!"

"One is gray — it is the Belgium rabbit. They were hopping around the front room like anything this morning. They were there when I came down!"

"Were they!"

"You can help me—build a pen—you use wire—old screen— a person can build a pen out of old screen!" Fat's full cheeks shook as he talked; his snub nose was peeling from the year's first sunburn. It was a nose which had caused him extreme shame and embarrassment throughout his school days; the lightest blow could cause it to spout blood. Even had he not been the timid soul that he was, Fat could never have won a schoolyard fight, for it was understood that such contests were automatically ended with the bleeding of a nose.

"What out of old screen?" Art stood in front of Fat. Ten now, Art played more often with Pinky Funder than he did with Fat or Brian. It was Pinky who was sneaking up behind Fat now.

"I got two rabbits for Easter," Fat was explaining. "One of them has pink eyes and the other is a Belgium rabbit. He is gray."

Art's mouth was open in his sharp face; interest was alive in the startling eyes behind his thick glasses. "What about rabbit pens?"

"You come after four—you and Brian. Nobody else though."

"I know where we could get boards," said Art, his glasses hopping again and again with his excitement. "Gaffer Thomas." Pinky Funder got up, looking disgustedly at Art, who had ignored

156

him kneeling and waiting for the unsuspecting Fat to be pushed over. "Behind Brian's hedge—a whole pile. I got nails!" He put his arm over Fat's shoulder and began to walk him off while Brian tagged eagerly along to pick up more details about the rabbits.

Miss Thompson, meanwhile, sat at her desk and looked thoughtfully at Mariel Abercrombie standing before her. As she did, she thought of what she had overheard in the cloakroom that morning just before school had started. She heard again the girls' shrill voices.

"Nobody's going to her party anyway." That had been Mariel.

"I'm not going — Gracie's not going — nobody's going but you," said Helen Roberts.

"I know a riddle!" cried Mariel. "She's in Grade Three—she's got a nice blue bow in her hair — her name starts with an 'E'."

"Eileen Gatenby!" the others chorused.

"An' another: She's in Grade Four — she has black hair that isn't curly—it is straight and it is stringy and kind of greasy! She is yellow and has slanty eyes!"

"Tang!"

With an effort, Miss Thompson brought her attention back to Mariel standing stolidly before her. The child had chops like her mother.

"Tang is having a birthday party today," said Miss Thompson.

Mariel looked at her.

"She has invited me," said Miss Thompson.

"It's Parent-Teachers day," said Mariel with the same flatness in her voice that was in her father's.

"I think I can manage it for a minute before the meeting. Are you going?"

Mariel did not answer her.

"Are you going to Tang's party, Mariel?"

The child looked over her shoulder at several pupils who had entered the room.

"Mariel!"

Mariel's head swung round, the hair flying out at the sides of her face. "No," she said. "Mother says not!" The answer was triumphant.

For the rest of the school day Miss Thompson's troubled mind was only partly concerned with her classes; she was just vaguely aware of the yeasting excitement around her, of the higher pitch in classroom noises, the extra foot scrapings, going-to-the-basements, and pencil sharpenings. It was with relief that she heard the four o'clock bell.

After the children had left, she sat quite still, staring past the straight edge of her desk to the smaller one below where a lump of yellow plasticine had been impaled on two pencils and an angled twig of willow softly budded with grey. Where her blue-black hair line was definite against the paleness of her face, her fist had made two small wrinkles; her brown eyes were softer still with a remote and absent look. Her gaze left the misshapen pencil holder; she opened her desk drawer and took out a tobacco package with a folder of papers tucked in its top. She rolled a cigarette while her eyes lost themselves in the moted bar of sunlight dropping from the window.

The mothers of her children were good women, she thought, as her deft fingers rolled the paper around the tobacco — good cooks and good women. She ran her tongue along the gummed edge of the paper. They organized countless chicken dinners; they went each Sunday to the Baptist, the Catholic, or the Anglican church, sat in Knox's glossy, pine-yellow pews or in the choir loft under the stained Jesus with a long-legged lamb in his arms. . . .

Just outside the window a meadow lark sang. . . . She could speak to Mrs. Abercrombie at the Parent-Teachers meeting, but no doubt the woman's response would be unfortunate. She was too much like her daughter; listening to Mrs. Bowdage's paper, she would have Mariel's same slightly stunned look of inattention — hers, to Democracy; Mariel's, to the decimal point. It would do no good — speaking to all the mothers would do no good; the thing was too terribly involved. Her gaze followed the pink picked out in the eyes and ears of the rabbits, each pursuing his own pollen-yellow chick along the side blackboard. She could imagine no greater feeling of futility if she were asked to pull rabbits from a hat. Magic was needed.

A crow was calling urgently outside, and as she watched, it lifted over the schoolyard, the tip feathers of its wings showing separate like black fingers against the prairie sky. "One crow, sorrow—two crows, joy," the old saying went through her mind. Still calling, it went over the houses that marked the careless edge of the town; for moments it hung above the thin horizon — one dark and silent speck.

The meadow lark sang again. Her mind returned to the empty classroom dry with the smell of chalk and dust; she wondered that, without its placid sea of expectant faces looking up, the room could still suggest children; it was as though it retained a pervading afterwarmth of their bodies. The nail of her finger tapped sharply against the desk top. From the room beyond came the dull, bumping sounds of Mr. Briggs "redding up". Miss Thompson pinched the end from her cigarette. She stood up, glanced at her watch, looked about the room. She picked up the pile of exercise books from her desk. As the door closed behind her the meadow lark sang again.

On her way downtown she passed Hoffman's yard, where Brian and Fat and Art and Bobbie bent over the rabbits; Brian had his arm tight around Jappy, who struggled vainly to get at the rabbits. The white one's eyes were marooning pink; they were glassy; red veins traced the insides of its long ears. The other was a race horse of a rabbit with a ridged nose; as Fat put it down, it slowly unwound in soft hops. "The Belgium one is the fattest," said Fat. "It bulges."

"If you feed the white one lots," Brian said, "it'll get fat too."

"I wish we had some," Bobbie said to his brother.

"Let's git goin' on them pens," said Art.

After putting Jappy in the barn, they set to work building a boxlike structure, one end of it a wire-covered frame hung on leather straps, the whole thing set up in the long, ribboning grass along the north side of Hoffman's barn.

While the boys worked on the rabbit pen, their teacher walked along the main street past the false-fronted stores and toward O'Connal's Drugstore. People greeted her; from across the street several of her children called out to her; at Funder's Meat Market, the Ben bowed low to her with the careful solemnity of drunkenness. She nodded to them all with a quiet friendliness that contradicted her state of mind and showed no distinction between parent, child, and town drunk. Stepping over one of Joe Pivott's setters, that slept with abandon in the spring sun, she turned in under the drugstore's ruby jar. When Brian's father came out to wait on her, she bought a small, carved bottle of twenty-five-cent perfume. She also bought a "Happy Birthday" card.

She came to the orange splash of potted geraniums behind the Bluebird's dusty windows, opened the door that was half glass, half cardboard, and went in. The swinging door at the back of the café opened; from the far darkness came the *slip-slip* of slippers sliding; in his red toque, with long and startling white hairs growing from the corners of his mouth, Old Wong appeared.

"Where are the children?" asked Miss Thompson in her clear, precise voice.

"He opstahs — he theah — he theah now." Old Wong spoke with a complete stopping and starting of each word, now and then the sudden singing of a long vowel. "You go — you see he some." He turned to push open the kitchen door again.

Two white decks of sandwiches rose from the wood-slabbed table; two large, chipped pots were on the long stove. She followed the bobbing, red toque up a steep stairway, at the top of which the Chinaman pointed out a doorway to her. He started back down. Miss Thompson opened the door.

They were in one corner of a tilting settee, quite close together; Tang had her arm around Vooie's neck; over the top of the stove with its elbowed pipe disappearing into one wall, Miss Thompson could just see the boy's black, chrysanthemum head. She stepped around the stove.

"Happy birthday, Tang."

The tan, flat planes of their faces tilted up to her; their dark eyes stared.

"Thank you." Miss Thompson barely heard the words.

160

She held out the bottle of perfume with the card tied to it, and with her arm still around her brother's neck, Tang took it. "Thank you," she whispered again. Her hand dropped to her lap.

The teacher looked down at them uncertainly. There was no doubt that they knew. She looked up to the pictures hung on the soiled wall above the settee, one of a Chinese woman with her straight hair drawn back and around, the other of a tendril-bearded Epicurean with relentlessly serene mouth; both pictures were so delicately colored as not to be colored at all. As well as she could, under the gaze of the two silent children, she turned from the room. The abrupt stairs urged her forward.

At the kitchen table Old Wong sliced still more birthday sandwiches. Birthday cocoa had begun to steam in the granite pots. Evidently he did not know yet. She hurried from the café.

In the sunlit street, the feeling of utter helplessness which had been leeching at her heart suddenly flooded her whole being. She thought again of Mariel's riddle. Mr. Funder's "Good day" to her went unnoticed. Surely the mothers could have helped! She stepped aside to allow a man and a woman, each holding one arm of a crucified child, to pass. She couldn't face them at the meeting. She couldn't!

She felt a hand upon her arm and looked up to see Peter beside her, his head dark and neat above the white of his jacket. His sensitive face was solicitous.

"Come in here," he said.

She went in.

"What is it?" he asked. "What's bothering you?"

"Oh, Peter — the world's an awful place!"

"And you're just finding out?"

"I — Tang and Vooie — "

"What is it?"

She told him.

And when she was through, he looked down at her with his face slightly wry and ever so slightly tender. "What did you expect? You don't expect to be taken seriously, do you? You're only a school teacher. You're not the Mayor — the banker — a businessman; you're not the wife even of a property owner. What you should do is pick a man of weight in the town—marry him—then go to work."

"They're all married."

He looked at her a long moment. "Not all of them."

Her face flushed. "You've changed some."

"Not much. I *could* be content with the crumbs from the feast," he declared drily.

"Sorry, Peter." And now he had the old look that suggested he was amused with himself, the look that meant he was hurt.

"Better get along to your meeting. Don't want them to have to hold up Democracy for you."

"I guess I can make it now. I feel better. Thanks, Peter."

As she walked to the Parent-Teachers meeting, to be held at Mrs. MacTaggart's, she reflected on what Peter had said, on what he had so carelessly suggested. It was his way of protecting himself, to make light of something about which he felt deeply. Poor Peter.

As she turned in at MacTaggart's Corner, she heard the discreet tinkle of china through the opened front door. Then Mrs. Bowdage had already given her paper. They had not held up Democracy for her.

NINETEEN

At first there had been only two rabbits in the pen by Hoffman's barn; now there were ten. The boys were elated at this something for nothing, and, although they had considered the possibility of increase, they had not hoped for it so soon. The bulging Belgian hare was the mother; Brian and Fat had witnessed the actual appearance of the baby rabbits.

"Gee, Fat," Brian had said, "they look funny — they haven't got any hair!"

"They will," promised Fat. "They'll grow up and get it."

"Then *they'll* have rabbits," Brian predicted, "and *they'll* grow up."

"And have rabbits too," supplied Fat.

"And they'll grow up and have rabbits."

"We'll have lots of rabbits," concluded Fat.

"What'll we do with 'em, Fat?"

"Sell 'em," Fat told him. "Dad paid fifty cents apiece for these. We'll sell 'em."

And so for two weeks they waited with impatience; Art had already called their attention to the interesting coincidence of bulge and new rabbits, a phenomenon they had not before associated with birth. At the end of a month, when no new rabbits had put in an appearance, Brian went to his father.

"Dad?"

"Yes, Spalpeen?"

"How do rabbits get started?"

From his leather chair in the den, Gerald O'Connal stared at his son, the lamp at his elbow glinting on his dark, red hair, the room silent except for the deliberate *bup-bup* of his pipe. For some two years now he had been expecting this. He must be frank and honest about the thing. "You know how a plant gets started?"

"How?"

"From a seed. You plant it in the ground, and it grows into a plant." He let his arm drop to scratch an ear of Jappy lying beside the chair.

"I know that."

"Know what?" asked Bobbie, who had entered the room.

"Something I'm explaining to Brian. With animals, it's the same."

"Is it?"

"What is?" asked Bobbie.

"Babies," said Brian. "He's telling me."

"You remember asking me about pigeons — a long time — about four years — ago?"

"No," said Brian.

"I told you then that the pigeon grows inside the egg — inside — the egg is inside the mother pigeon until it hatches out. All the

164

time that she is hatching the egg, the baby pigeon is growing there. When it has grown enough, it comes out."

"They don't with rabbits," said Bobbie. "Brian saw them come right out — he said he saw them — "

"Rabbits are different. They don't have eggs. They simply grow inside the mother, and when it's time, they grow—they come out."

"They come out," said Bobbie.

Gerald O'Connal looked down at Brian's thoughtful face. Jappy rose and stretched himself with his head lined out and his hind legs oblique and tense. He trotted from the room. Evidently the explanation had been enough, Brian's father told himself. He picked up his *Regina Leader* again.

"Where does the seed come in?" asked Brian.

"That — oh — that's what the baby rabbit grows from inside the mother rabbit, Spalpeen."

"Is she full up with them?"

"Yes — she — in a way."

"You can't grow anything without seeds."

Gerald O'Connal laid down the paper. He looked at Bobbie with his chin in his fat hands, bent back at the wrists with their fingers curled against his plump cheeks, his blue eyes watching his father's face. "That's right. The father rabbit plants the seeds."

"Where'd *he* get them?"

"Why — they're in him."

"Why don't they grow up in him and come out of him then?" asked Brian relentlessly.

"Because they don't. They have to grow in the mother rabbit."

Brian was silent. He looked up thoughtfully to his father. "And like Art says — that's what he's doing when ... "

"Yes — that's what he's doing. He's — planting."

Brian's intense stare was disconcerting. "In a way," Mr. O'Connal finished up.

"Dad?" Bobbie lifted his chin from his hands. "Could he plant turnips into her?"

Brian looked at his brother with disgust.

The buck and the doe that Mr. Hoffman had brought home came of a particularly fertile strain, the boys found out during the

165

course of the summer; they were delighted as litter after litter made its appearance and the rabbit population of Hoffman's back yard increased by arithmetic progression. The increase soon became an alarming thing, however, as it became apparent that few of the progeny seemed inclined to death and that none seemed to have heard of the Malthusian theory. The boys began to have difficulty in finding food for the rabbits. Gaffer Thomas, after a short while, refused the boys cut grass from the lawns he mowed; he needed it for a compost heap he was making.

On in the summer, the boys turned to raiding gardens, dealing out their visits in such a way that there would be no great drain on any one plot. After Mrs. Abercrombie caught them carrot-handed, they had to give that up. They found it difficult to get wood for the increasing number of rabbit pens required; all the boxes and crates in their homes had been used up; they had worn out their welcome at the Sash and Door Factory. Pens lined the sides and one end of Hoffman's yard; there were old apple boxes, peach and pear crates; and in them all, rabbits crouched and hopped and sat up. There were gray rabbits, black, and white, and all the permutations and combinations of the three, with bucks and does at every period of growth.

Mr. Hoffman, who had tried in the beginning to segregate the sexes, was at a loss, for he was not accurately discerning in the matter of rabbit sex, and he was not home long enough between train runs to check his selection. There were rabbits nibbling, rabbits with their noses wobbling, rabbits industriously going over and over the little circular motions of face washing. Mr. Hoffman had the assurance of many townspeople that the rabbits could not continue to increase without new doe and buck stock to dilute the weaknesses of inbreeding, but the rabbits were not aware of that. There were rabbits with their ears laid along their backs, with ears bolt upright, with one ear flopped, with two ears flopped; there were rabbits in the very act of conception, of gestation, of giving birth and being given birth to. They were in Hoffman's yard in such numbers that one's mind ceased to think of them in terms of rabbits, slipped a notch and thought of them in terms of rabbit.

There were one hundred and twenty-three rabbits.

Fat had done what he could; in the beginning several had been

166

sold, but it was not very long till there were no buyers; he had tried giving them away, but that avenue was no longer open; the town had reached its saturation point. The suggestion had been made that the rabbits could be turned loose, but it was immediately decided that it would not be fair to neighboring gardeners. On one of his trips home, Mr. Hoffman had announced that they would have to do away with the rabbits; Fat's voice had been raised in shrill and immediate protest; and his mother, like Fat a tenderhearted soul, had agreed with her son that the rabbits must not be killed. Mr. Hoffman left on each train run with the prayer in his heart that some one of the rabbit diseases would strike the lot; he returned only to find more rabbits.

Early in September he went into O'Connal's Drugstore on his way from the station, and engaged Brian's father in earnest conversation in the dispensary at the back of the store. His step was noticeably lighter when he came out and started for his home, carrying as he always did the little, black club bag that he took with him on train runs.

Late that night Joe Pivott's dray rolled into Hoffman's yard; Mr. Hoffman, Mr. O'Connal, and Joe worked swiftly and silently, filling sack after sack with kicking, grunting rabbits. Joe's setters quickly took care of the two which got away; the rest made a short trip to the river behind the *Times* building. Mr. Hoffman spent that night in deep sleep, broken only occasionally by the grinning image of one rabbit which might have been forgotten.

Fat was heartbroken; he pleaded with his mother for another pair, and when his father returned home, the boy asked him. Mr. Hoffman did not weaken; his hesitation was barely perceptible when Fat backed down to just *one* rabbit.

Brian was shocked, but not emotionally so as Fat was, by the blotting out of the rabbits. For several days after the event, he was filled with a feeling of uncertainty and uneasiness that recalled to him the Sunday morning over a year before, the day on the prairie when Art had torn the tail from the gopher. All summer, with a perseverance uncommon in a child of eight, he had set about a secret search for the significance of what he now called "the feeling". He often wondered if others — his father, his mother, his grandmother, Bobbie, Fat, or Art—suspected. Somehow, he felt, the thing would be spoiled if he were to let anyone know about it; he hoped with all his heart that this would not happen. He was afraid also that the other boys would laugh, though perhaps if he'd had an inkling that any one of them was experiencing the same thing, he might have confided in him. As it was, the Young Ben had once or twice occurred to him as the only right confidant; he had seen the Young Ben just four times during the summer holidays—at a distance.

Brian's father had left him only temporarily satisfied with his explanation in regard to rabbit birth. He went finally to his grandmother, who sat as she often did now in her room on the second floor of the house; it was a large sunny room, formerly the "spare" room, but now the grandmother's, since rheumatism had made it difficult for her to manage even the one flight of stairs. Brian stood by her high brass bed with its dinted knobs glinting in the sunlight; over the head of the bed hung two soapstone plaques —one of John Knox; the other Mary, Queen of Scots. On the wall near them and over the mahogany commode hung Brian's Grandfather John, a Lincolnish gentleman framed deep in an oval of gilt. Brian spoke to his grandmother in her rocker by the window; he told her what his father had said about rabbits. The old woman looked for a moment at the potted geranium with its leaves transparent green in the window's sunshine.

"Ye tryin' to tell me the facts of life, boy?" she said to him. "'Tis too bad ye're not a farm boy—there'd be no need then for this argy-bargyin'. What ye tell is the how—all right. The why— that's another thing. That's for the Lord." She rocked gently a moment, then looked up to Brian at her side. "Wherever ye find anything worth a whoop, ye'll find the Lord's got a hand in it."

"You mean that God—"

"He does—He always did—He always will . . . Look in the second drawer under the Flags of the Allies bedspread. There's a box of chocolates—mind ye don't muss things."

Brian bent down at the dresser drawer. He looked up with his hand on the carved walnut handles.

"God isn't very considerate—is He, Gramma?"

170

TWENTY

Fall brought another crop failure to the district; the land was dotted now with empty farmhouses, their blank windows staring out over the spreading prairie, their walls piled high with rippled banks of black dust; farmers and their families moved westward and northward to Alberta and the Peace River country. Freights were covered with unemployed, many of them young boys who had never had jobs in their lives—"gay cats"

and "scenery hogs", who had left the East to find work in the West, or the West to find work in the East.

The town showed the depression; houses needed paint; cars on First Street Saturday evenings were older models; plate-glass windows were empty where businesses had left; the MacDougall Implement Company was the only one of three implement firms remaining. The Sash and Door Factory closed down; Blaine's General Store failed. And for the first time in years, Sean O'Connal was almost happy; his garden irrigation project had worked wonderfully well. He set about trying to interest other farmers in the district in a plan he had to dam the river and irrigate larger areas of drought-baked land.

That fall, Brian's grandmother had a wicked cold that threatened to turn into pneumonia, but she managed to draw on reserves of Scotch stubbornness to throw it off. It was that fall too that Digby and Miss Thompson and Peter Svarich finally got action on the China Kids. After much deliberation, the town put the Chinese family on relief — a temporary measure until arrangements were completed for sending the children away; Tang to an uncle in Vancouver, Vooie to a home in Winnipeg. The taxes piled up on Wong's building were ignored. Two weeks after his son and daughter had left, Wong was discovered, still with his red toque on, swinging from a rafter in the dark kitchen; he had managed it by using a length of clothesline rope, by standing on one of the kitchen chairs and kicking it over. Jake Harris found no opium among his effects.

One Saturday late in September, Brian and Fat and Bobbie stood on the walk before the O'Connal house. In the dry boulevard Jappy was engaged in digging out an imaginary gopher. The dog's keen nose told him that there was nothing except grass roots and the twelve-hour-old scent of the Airedale down the street, but it was just as well to keep in practice, and there was no harm in this sort of thing if one didn't fool himself.

"What'll we do for fun?" Fat asked Brian.

"Art's won all the agates," Brian said. "Too cold for swimming — I dunno."

"Tom Mix is at the Hi-Art," suggested Bobbie. Bobbie had started to school that fall.

"It takes money," said Brian. "We'd need thirty cents."

"Where'd we get it?" asked Fat.

"Beer bottles," suggested Bobbie.

"Where?"

"Behind the Royal."

"Not this time of day," said Brian. "Not on a Saturday."

"Wouldn't hurt to look," said Fat.

"Let's go chew some tar," said Bobbie, "behind Jenkins's."

"Wouldn't do much good," said Brian in answer to Fat.

"Let's go to Sherry's mill and eat some bran," said Bobbie.

"It isn't good for you," Brian told him. "It makes you go."

"I don't care. I haven't went for a long time."

"Mother said not. We might as well go downtown."

"Get some wieners at Funder's," Bobbie suggested. "Can I come?" He knew very well that their mother had told Brian to keep an eye on his younger brother.

"Yes," said Brian, "you can come." Then, in case his brother might overestimate his generosity, "It won't be any fun."

At MacTaggart's Corner, the boys saw four loping setters down the street; a dray turned into view followed by eight more dogs with their heads lined out and their plumed tails curved slightly up. Jappy ran out barking to them.

"It's Joe!" cried Fat. The three raced to meet the dray.

Legs astride, Joe stood with the lines held loosely between his thumb and forefinger. Although he would be the last to admit it, Joe was almost as fond of children as he was of his dogs; in summer there were invariably several children standing beside him on the floor of the mill dray, in winter a chain of small sleighs trailing behind with children sitting or lying full length on them.

Brian and Fat climbed on to the back; Brian leaned down and pulled Bobbie up by the neck of his sweater, helped him to a position where he could hold on to the front of the dray for balance. On one side of Joe, Brian took up his position, emulating with careful unconcern the drayman's feet-astride stance. At a word from Joe the two grays speeded up the tipping of their hindquarters; the dray surged forward as the rumbling grind of wheels quickened. Brian, watching a Union Jack flutter from the peak of one of the horses' collars, felt the tremble of the dray floor in the soles of his feet, and up to his knees.

"Where yuh headed fer?" said Joe.

"Just ride around with you," Brian told him.

"Goin' tuh Harris's, then as fur as thuh mill." Joe slapped at the team's rumps with the lines.

He began to sing in a thin voice that slid as he willed it; then he did a little dance — first on one foot, then on the other, so that the flour came off his overalls in puffs; he whinnied and at the same time made the sound of a horse passing wind. The boys laughed, looking up into his powdered face with the cap that gave it a permanently slanted look in the way it hung rakishly over one ear.

"Wonder why a fella always has thoughts into his head?" wondered Joe.

"Is there?" said Fat.

"Yep — ain't ever empty — always thoughts into a fella's head."

"Not always," Fat said.

"Jist try an' not have any!" Joe invited him.

Brian had never thought of that; he'd never thought about thoughts before. Right now he wasn't thinking any thoughts; there wasn't any thinking going on in there. Yes, there was. He was thinking about not thinking, and he had just got done thinking about thinking about not thinking any thoughts, so he was thinking. Funny—boxes inside of boxes inside of boxes inside of boxes.

"Here she is, boys." Joe pulled the team up just short of the railroad tracks beside the elevator. The boys climbed down.

Balancing with arms out they walked the rails back towards the center of the town and past the grain elevators. They began to step out the ties.

"'Jenkins Dairy'," Fat read from the low, flat building on his left.

"'Coal and Wood — Rick Simpson'," Brian answered him.

"'The Home of Good Lumber—Taylor and Co., ell tee dee'," chanted Fat.

"'MacDougall Imp — Imp-ull-ment'," said Brian.

"What's 'ell tee dee'?" asked Bobbie.

"Search me," said Fat. "Let that alone," he admonished Bobbie, who had placed his hand on a railroad switch they had come to. It was not Fat's railroad, but after all his father was a conductor. "'Eye oof Hall'. My Dad's a Odd Fellow."

They had crossed First Street and passed the bridge. Fat suggested that they visit Thorborn's Livery Stable. They turned north, across an empty lot tall with dry grass that gave out a papery sound as it brushed their legs; Jappy was swallowed in it immediately, and their moving heads indicated his progress. Brian thought of Mr. Thorborn's horses, not the draught teams but the sleek, high-strung beasts that were the school board chairman's special pride; almost every day he could be seen sitting with his legs up and out on the shafts of a whispering-tired sulky as he exercised them, manes flying, forefeet flickering delicately in the out and out rhythm that belongs to pacers. Horses, Brian was thinking, were able to give him the feeling, almost every time. With the smell of fall wild on the wind that lifted carelessly now and again, with the clear air crisp and at the same time mellow, he was suddenly sad, his throat aching, his heart filled with unbearably sweet and maddening melancholy.

Three men lounged at the livery stable door; the boys heard one of them say, "Hearda them before — never figgered to see one."

"See what?" asked Bobbie.

"Has it got two hearts?" asked another.

"Don't think so," said the first. "How abouta beer?"

"What was he talking about — two hearts?" asked Fat.

"I dunno," said Brian.

"Calf," said the long-jawed man still leaning against the barn-door opening, his eyes on the dusty street where a dust-devil came whirling. "Brought a calf from southa town—got two heads ontuh it."

The boys dived into the barn's dusk, soothed with the richness of horse smell, dry with the sweetness of hay. There between the long lines of dropped tails, they waited for their eyes to become accustomed to the dimness. Here and there, Brian saw the turned head of a horse with white gleaming wild at the corner of its eyes; and as he stood he felt again the old lift of excitement, a bitter-sweet sensation rising within him and threatening to engulf him with its strangeness.

"I don't see anything," Bobbie complained.

"First box stall on yer left!" called out the man in the door-way.

They went in. They stood. Brian could hear the wind sighing at the chinking in the barn walls, could hear Fat's breath whistling gently through his nose, the regular grinding of horses at their oats, now and then the indifferent swish of a tail, the imperative knock of a hoof.

The calf was dead. It lay on the straw-littered floor. Its necks were like a slingshot—a willow slingshot with two arms Y-ing out. The feeling was fierce in Brian as he stared down; it possessed an uncertain and breathless quality; he felt as though he were on a tightrope high in the air. Silently he looked down at the two moist, black noses, the two sets of cupping ears, the twin foreheads with their identical diamonds of white, the hair in the center of each curling in twin whorls as though they had been combed by the same hand.

"It's funny!" said Bobbie.

"Gee!" Fat exclaimed. "I never seen anything like that before!"

One foreleg was folded into a cornered curve. Brian looked at the protruding hipbone, at the cleft, small hoof. It was a bull calf. To the shoulders an ordinary bull calf; from there it wasn't. Two heads; two where one should be. It was wrong!

"At Regina Fair they had a sheep," Fat was saying, "with an extra leg. It grew out the belly and it dangled."

Brian felt that he was staring at something he should not be staring at.

"Wonder how long it lived?" asked Fat.

176

This time, Brian was thinking, the feeling was different from what it had been other times: without the thrill that had attended the discovery of the dewdrop on the spirea leaf; with the thrill of uneasiness that had moved him when he had looked down upon the dead gopher.

"Would the both heads think?" wondered Fat.

"What if one wanted to go the one way," Bobbie suggested, "and the other wanted to go the other way?"

Brian was not so sure of the feeling this time; it lacked the sharper quality of the other times; he was not so sure, now, that it *was* the feeling. "Or if one wanted to eat and the other didn't want," said Fat. "Or if one wanted to drink an' the other didn't," said Bobbie. It isn't *right*, thought Brian.

"Let's get Art," said Fat.

When they told him, Art did not believe them, not until he had seen for himself. He believed them then. Vaguely aware of the others' voices, acutely conscious of his own thoughts, Brian wondered how there could be a calf with two heads. The more he thought, the more the futility welled up in him, urging him to forget the whole matter. He couldn't; he couldn't forget the calf that had lived for a few moments, lifting two heavy heads on its neck, only to die.

"I'll lend you shooters," Art was saying. "We can play for fun."

"The poison-holes over to Lord Roberts," Fat said.

Once at the schoolyard on the edge of the prairie, Fat and Art scooped out the "blow dirt" that had filled the marble holes dug along one side of the school building.

"I want to play," said Bobbie.

"You can't," Art said; "you hunch."

Bobbie did not argue; he did hunch.

Art won the first shot when they lagged for it; he hit the hole and ran up and back without a miss. In one more shot he would be poison.

Down on one knee, the tip of his tongue at the corner of his mouth, an intent frown on his forehead, Fat shot; he got as far as the third hole, his agate lying quite close to Art's.

"Your turn," Art said to Brian. "What's eatin' you?"

"Nothing," Brian said and knelt in the dust. Why did there have to be a two-headed calf? Now he was farther away from it than ever. He'd never know. There'd be no use in even trying to find out.

"Ring around it!" shouted Art, with his glasses moving as his face twitched.

"Black cat settin' in the center!" Stepping forward in his excitement, Fat nudged Brian's arm with his toe. The agate squirted from Brian's hand and went rolling wild of the first hole.

"Slips!" he cried and jumped forward on his hands and knees to recover the agate and try over again the shot that had gone wrong. As he lined up on the lip of the hole ahead, he saw in his mind the calf lying on the livery-barn floor, the calf that was a mistake. Slips!

In the days that followed, Brian was not visited with the feeling, and after a while he was not sure that he had experienced it as he stood in the livery stable, looking down upon the calf. The memory of the two-headed calf would not let him alone; in bed at night, before he dropped off to sleep, he remembered it; he thought of it often during school hours. He was thinking of it early in October as he walked home from school, the dead and yellowed leaves fallen from the poplars, sliding, at the bidding of the wind, along the walk ahead of him, their arched and brittle tips hissing slightly over the cement.

As he turned on to Sixth Street, he saw Jappy run out to meet Joe Pivott's dray passing in front of the O'Connal house, his red-and-white quicksilver body half-curved so that he could look up into the faces of the horses as he ran. Brian called to him. In that split second of distraction the dog was knocked off-balance by one of the horses' hoofs. The near horse veered at the scrabbling white thing under its feet, and pulled over its mate.

Brian saw his dog briefly through huge and hairy feet; he saw the metal-rimmed front wheels of the dray miss Jappy. The hind ones did not. A shrill and agonized cry arose, trembling on the fall afternoon, shearing the silence, going up and up and hanging there. As the wind carried the settling dust sideways, Brian saw Jappy lifting his shoulders and head in a vain attempt to rise, struggling, only to move in a futile circle with lifeless hindquarters for a pivot.

He ran to him. He took him in his lap. The cry went up again. It died down to a scarcely audible whimper deep in the dog's throat.

"Wasn't nothin' I could do, kid." Joe Pivott stood tall over him. "I didn't even see him."

Brian simply stared down at Jappy.

"I'm sorry, kid."

"It's all right."

"I didn't even see him. Is he hurt bad?"

Brian did not answer.

"Spine busted mebbe?" Joe's hand, its black hairs powdered pale with flour dust, reached for the small of Jappy's tapering back.

"You let him alone!"

"Okay." Joe straightened up. He stood uncomfortably. "I'm sorry."

"That's all right."

"Better not set here in the middla the road."

Jappy cried out again as Brian got up.

He was dead by the time that they got to the garage behind the house.

Gaffer Thomas lent him a garden fork. Brian returned to the garage, where he had left Jappy lying on some gunny sacking there. As he picked up the dog's body, he noticed that the head remained rigidly turned over one shoulder; the eyes were filmed with gray mucus. He went through the Caragana hedge, turned out on to the street, and started toward the prairie.

Halfway down the block his brother joined him. They walked in silence.

The prairie sod resisted the garden fork. A meadow lark sang twice as he struggled. The hardpan came away in flaking lumps to show glistening, riblike marks where the fork had been. A crow called, flew overhead, wheeled into the wind, and hung motionless a moment before allowing itself to be carried away. Moving clouds filled the limitless sky above.

"How did he die?" asked Bobbie.

Brian picked up the dog by the middle, still with its head turned relentlessly back over one shoulder. He placed it in the long hole with foxtails and spear grass tossing along its edges.

"I knew a girl that died."

The bent head rested on a shelf of earth halfway up the hole, and for a moment Brian expected to see the head move, to nudge as it did when Jappy laid his nose on his knee.

"She got drownded."

Brian straightened up and looked at Bobbie.

"She couldn't swim. That was how she got drownded."

Brian turned away and looked down at the raw hole with black earth heaped at its lip, the dog's red-and-white body still in its center.

"How did he die, Brian? What happened to him?"

Brian eased a forkful of dirt to the dog's body. The next were easier. He covered the head with its one red ear last.

"How did he — "

"Go on home," Brian said.

Bobbie looked at him.

"Go on home, will you, Bobbie?"

He looked as though he were going to cry. He turned away.

"I'll come later," Brian said.

He looked down at the grave, and it was hard for him to believe that Jappy was under it, that he wouldn't in a moment see the earth bulge up and the dog's head come out. Then he remembered the stiffness of the body, the turned head, the filmed eyes. He knew that a lifeless thing was under the earth. His dog was dead.

He heard a rustling in the grass and looked up to see the Young Ben with his pale hair on end in the wind and his disturbing, gray eyes steady upon him. The eyes left his face to rest on the grave, then back again. The Young Ben turned away; he came back stooping under the weight of a rock. He laid it on the grave, then went back for another. Brian joined him and together they carried enough rocks to cover the heap of loose dirt.

When they had finished, the Young Ben said, "Kiyoots can't git him now."

Somewhere within Brian something was gone; ever since the accident it had been leaving him as the sand of an hourglass threads away grain by tiny grain. Now there was an emptiness that wasn't to be believed.

PART THREE

TWENTY-ONE

Brian was called "Chirp" now, because he could make the sound of baby chicks cheeping. In the two years since his dog had been run over, he had grown little taller, still retaining the quiet poise of his mother, her quickness of movement, her dark hair and skin. Almost ten, he had passed into Mr. Digby's room; at the spring examinations he had been third in his class.

It was another dry year with crops brown before their time,

dust black against the sun sometimes for a week on end. Early in July the town lights had been turned on throughout the entire afternoon. Rain had followed, but it was too late to help the crops. And now, in the latter part of July, the hot winds breathed again, rising each evening at the end of still and burning days.

In the early afternoon of such a day, Brian sat on the porch of the O'Connal house, his dark eyes lost in reflection, aware only of little slapping sounds that came whenever a breeze off the prairie compelled the poplar's leaves slightly. For long periods of time they hung listless, then with the breath of a careless wind took up their tapping again. The air was hot and dry without a hint of rain in it, or in the sky decked with high puffs of cloud. Houses across the street were submarine in the distorting lift and tremble of rising heat.

He wondered why such days were called "the dog days"; because the dogs lay sprawled in the dust, perhaps, their long, wet tongues spilled from a corner of their mouths; or because the days themselves had the loose laziness of a hot and tired sheep dog. Dogs sweated through their tongues, he thought idly as he watched the black-and-white setter panting gently in the center of Sixth Street. Pull the tongue in; close the mouth; open; spill the tongue again, and pant some more. Pudding dogs, he decided, spotted pudding dogs, Joe's dogs.

A swim might be good, but he couldn't go swimming, for there was prairie itch in the low river now; it got between toes and fingers and somewhere else, raising tiny blisters. In any event walking to the river would be too great an undertaking for the lethargy within him. He imagined for himself the cool embrace of river water, felt the breathless, mid-air pause before enveloping chill, the transcendent peace of floating on his back. A small, green frog leaped to plop the stillness of his mind; just under the surface of his consciousness it swam in long glides with leaf-feet trailing. Its snout appeared, nudged the scum, and was still, two bump-eyes just showing. Through the dry afternoon he could almost smell the river now, its dampness stealing from it and giving life to the air around. He *could* smell it clear from the C.P.R. bridge and into town.

186

He heard the hiccoughing sound of pigeons on the porch roof above; he looked up to see them walk and stop and turn to walk again under the open window on the second floor. That was his grandmother's window. She sat by it now.

Mrs. MacMurray had got delicately old, her skin thin to transparency, her face letting its bone structure determine its character under white hair pulled severely back into a tight knot. From the blue-veined temples, on either side of her deeply recessed eyes, ran back a creaming streak almost egg-yellow in the white of her hair. Intentness lay on her forehead and in the two deep wrinkles at the bridge of her slightly hooking nose, as she listened to the August breeze in the poplar's leaves just outside the window.

Now that she was eighty, she knew her life for a firefly spark in much darkness; knowing this had made her eager for the little left to her.

She rocked gently, and as she rocked her mind went back to homesteading days; the richness of animal smell from sweating horses soothed her, the dryness of still prairie under summer sun came to her, and with it the sigh of wind bending long waves through prairie grass. The rum-colored carpet of her room in Gerald O'Connal's house became tan prairie circling wide to the horizon. Meadow larks startled the stillness. Beside her, John clucked to gently nodding horses. A red bandanna handkerchief, tied to the rim of the wheel by her side, rose and fell as the buckboard rolled. She counted the revolutions, each one bringing them closer to homestead stakes.

The fever of the Rebellion had cooled; Riel had been hanged in Regina. Quebec had turned Grit and stayed so ever since. John was alive. Maggie had not been born. It would not be long now; another good cold would do it; the last had been close.

The leaves of the poplar outside shook light from their dusty surfaces. The old woman heard a footstep outside her door.

On the porch below, Brian stared at the panting setter. Open the mouth; spill the tongue; close, open, close.

Hell!

As soon as he had thought it, he wished that he hadn't.

189

Sometimes thoughts could not be helped, for they were live and unpredictable things with hidden motivation of their own. *Damn* and *hell* were the livest of them all; they had a way of popping up full-blown and unbidden—not loud, but there in one's mind all the same. Art did not try to keep them down.

Down the street a door slammed; a woman's voice called. Brian's eyes lifted from the street with its houses, hedges, and lawns, leaving these solid things for the emptiness of the intensely blue sky. A dray rumbled down the street; a lawn mower began to chuckle urgently. The too familiar sounds filled him with a vague feeling of frustration, a feeling of loss and of not-succeeding, made all the more poignant by the stillness of the afternoon.

He stood up, eyeing the dog in the middle of the dusty road. He picked up a pebble from the side of the walk; it hit the dog with a thud. The dog looked over at him, then laid its head along its forelegs.

Oh well. See what Fat and Art were doing. As he turned out of the yard he looked up to his grandmother's window.

Bobbie stood by his grandmother's rocker. In spite of his eight years, he still kept his baby fatness; his tightly curled red hair had the lightness of color that was his Uncle Sean's; his blue eyes had faded to gray and, like his father's, possessed a fine, black rim around the iris.

"Anything else?" he said to his grandmother.

"Ye might lift my window a little higher," she said.

Bobbie went to the window, lifted it slightly higher, then turned around.

"The candy's in the second drawer."

He brought the chocolates to her, then stood patiently while she lifted the top of the box. The chocolates were gray with age; it was a box given her two Christmases before, and when it was done there were five more to go.

His head bent over the proffered candy, Bobbie stood undecided; he knew that she would allow him only one. He decided finally for a square chocolate of the chewy variety; they lasted longest. His grandmother picked a cream that would be kind to her gums.

Bobbie sat on the floor beside her rocker.

190

"Yer Grandfather John was a fine man," his grandmother said, "with a rabbit's-foot fob to his watch, a flair for the fiddle, and a way with horses."

"What about the bobcat, Gramma?"

"He could fiddle — don't chomp it, boy, suck — whenever there was a get-together in the early days yer grandfather was there with his fiddle under his chin. Lasts longer when ye suck. He'd fiddle high and he'd fiddle low — he'd fiddle the gut right off his bow." She went on in her low, deliberately accented voice to tell him that his grandfather could fiddle the squeak of a gopher, lost in wind whispering through prairie grass; crows calling; an anvil on a winter day; an ant pile broken open and the ants all scurrying round. She'd heard him fiddle jack rabbits bouncing off, a goshawk drifting high with a field mouse in its claws, a flock of geese and all their necks, a barn with its loft full of hay. "He fiddled to make folks laugh," the old woman said, "and he fiddled to make them cry." She stopped.

"What about the bobcat?" said Bobbie. "Tell about that one."

"All right," she said.

As she talked, the wind rose in the leaves of the poplar. It lifted the dust in the street along the front of the house; it whirled toward the center of the town in feverish little dust-devils. Thin clouds of dust hung tirelessly over the downtown streets where few people passed in front of the store buildings. In the door of the drugstore, Gerald O'Connal looked out. In the last two years there had come to be a full look about his eyes; slight, dark pouches were under them. Queer, he was thinking, this sleeping business; it had got worse in the last year. He could feel it slipping over him now, with the faint nausea that always attended it. A person never paid any attention to his body until it began to give him trouble. Better speak to Svarich again. He said it wasn't ulcers. What was it, then? Fresh air and rest, he'd said. How could a druggist rest?

"Hello, Mrs. Abercrombie."

"Grand day."

"Lovely."

Did the woman know that every crop in the country was . . . ? He hoped that neither of his boys were druggists. God, he felt awful. He turned back into the darkness of the store.

Down the street the door of the Royal Hotel beer parlor stood open, the interior yeastily kissing each passer-by. Within, a fifty-pound sack of feed on his head, the Ben stared at the beads threading to the collar of his beer, then up to the man across the table, a traveler for the MacDougall Implement Company, who had dropped in for a drink before going on to the next town, but who had stayed to listen to the Ben's stories.

"A owl has tuh light afore he comes tuh thuh groun'," the Ben said in his hoarse voice with his flaming eyes steady on the traveler's face. "He has tuh light; so I spread me some chicken guts over thuh groun', an' I look till I see me thuh poplar. That's her, I sez; if I was a goddam owl, that's where I'd light. I set one a thuh Young Ben's traps on toppa that poplar." He downed the rest of the beer, then looked again at the traveler. "Damn near lost a finger an' a eye. Christ, but them things kin scratch!" He looked at the empty glass, then at the implement salesman again. He cleared his throat. "Shore hot tuhday! Ever tell yuh 'bout thuh yella-beardy Hooterite caught his nackers in the thirty-six-inch thrashin' machine?"

The traveler mentally decided that he could stay overnight at the hotel instead of going on to the next town; he raised his hand with four fingers extended to the man at the beer pumps.

Outside, the wind stirred several tumbleweeds moored to the edge of the walk; it teased one out and sent it rolling jerkily down the street. It set the leaves in motion on the trees around the Presbyterian manse, where shades were drawn for coolness' sake. In the dimness of the study, Mr. Powelly's face was a pale oval.

"I am the vine, ye are the branches." He could use that; starting from there he could take it through "If a man abide not in me, he is cast forth as a branch, and is withered . . . " to—to "This is my commandment, That ye love one another . . . " He leaned back in the chair. To there; it would work in well with his theme, "The Vital Things". This was one of the vital things of the Gospel. That was it. Mr. Powelly leaned forward with his long, narrow face intent, and began to write swiftly over the sheet of paper that lay before him.

The wind could be heard in a more persistent song now, and out along the road separating the town from the prairie it fluted gently along the wires that ran down the highway. Brian and Fat and Art descended and went through the barrow pit filled with loose dust. Art shied a rock at a meadow lark. He missed it. Ahead of the boys, the long grass bent to the bidding of the wind, lay a moment, then sprang up again.

"Who has seen the wind?" Fat chanted.

"Neither you nor I," returned Brian.

"But when the trees bow down their heads —"

"Nobody gives a damn," Art finished up. Fat laughed.

The boys were walking out to see Saint Sammy, the old man who lived in a piano box on the prairie. The visit was Art's suggestion; he was the only one of the boys who had visited Sammy before.

Fat said, "How come he lives out here, Art?"

"He's crazy," Art told him, "crazy as a ground owl. Dad says the prairie sent him crazy. He went crazy from it."

"It's awful lonely out here," said Brian. "It would be easy for a fellow to go crazy out on prairie — all by himself."

"He's a bachelor," Art said. "He's a crazy —"

"*Peee-yew*!" Fat's snub nose was wrinkled.

The wind, which had shifted, was now blowing directly into the boys' faces, carrying to them a terrific stench of rotting flesh. "Somethin' died!" said Fat.

"Holy diddle!" Art's face writhed. "Where's it comin' from?"

"Over there," said Fat.

"Saint Sammy's," said Brian. "That's dead stink and it's terrible!"

"Maybe he died," said Fat, "an' that's him lyin' out on the prairie, smellin' like that! I never saw a dead man yet!"

"Oh — he ain't dead," said Art.

"How do you know he ain't? How do you —"

"Probably onea his cows — smells just like dead-cow stink to me," said Art knowingly, his face behind his thick glasses furious with twitchings.

"Or one of his horses," said Brian.

"Would a man stink as bad as a cow, Chirp?" asked Fat.

"Worse," said Art, "way worse."

"How do you know?"

"My Dad said. When he was in the war, he said they were way worse. He said you couldn't get your breath sometimes."

"Why does dead stuff stink?" wondered Brian.

"Because it's dead," said Art.

"But why?"

"Who cares?" Art said it as though he had a head cold; he was holding his nose.

"Maybe it's one of his horses," suggested Brian.

"No," Art contradicted. "I counted them away back."

"Let's go home," said Fat. "No fun seein' Saint Sammy with all stink all around. I ain't so fussy about dead stink!"

"You didn't want to see him anyways." Art turned on him. "You're scairt because he's crazy. You're scairt!"

"No, I ain't!"

"You sure are!"

"Wonder if a cow or a horse goes to heaven," said Brian.

"I'm going home."

"Go on home, then," Art said to Fat. "Who cares? Who cares if you're scairt of Saint Sammy?"

"I'm not!"

"Would they go to hell?" Brian persisted. "How would you know which horses went to hell?"

"The snuffy ones that messed the britchin'," said Art.

"He's just a crazy man!" Fat's voice was pitched high. "There's nothin' so wonderful about a crazy man!"

"Go on home then; we don't care."

"In hell they got to —" began Brian.

"—have the horses to haul the drays," Art finished up for him.

"So long, you fellows. I'm goin' home. I'm not —"

"To haul the coal," said Art in more detail, "for all them fires."

Fat had stopped, and as the others walked on he stood uncertainly with the wind washing through the prairie grasses high around him. Finally he turned and began to walk back to the town.

The smell grew stronger and stronger till it was a solid thing upon the air.

194

"There's where he lives," Art pointed out to Brian. "That's his piana box — an' there's his c'rral."

"But — where's *he*? I don't see him anywhere around."

"Probably inside, out of the flies," guessed Art.

"That smell's coming right from his place."

"Yeah, seems to be comin' from there."

As he neared the place, Brian felt a welling of uncertainty. "You sure, Art?"

"Sure—I'm sure." Art's voice lacked the clear ring of conviction it had when he argued with Fat.

"That stink's bad," said Brian dubiously. "I bet it's as bad as when your Dad — "

Art had bent down to his pant leg and seemed intent on picking spear grass from it. His voice was muffled. "Think we oughta get any closer?"

Brian looked back over the prairie to Fat's black, pigmy figure in the distance.

"We gotta go now." Art straightened up. "Or else we — what'll Fat say? He'll say we're scairt too."

"An' that — Hey, there he is — he ain't dead!"

"Like I said!" cried Art.

Brian saw the man ahead, walking over the prairie with a lilting lift as though he had a spring under one heel. One arm swung wide, and he carried his head to one side. The boys saw him stop, then slowly bring his arms above his head and just as slowly down.

"Come ontuh me where I dwell in thuh midsta my critters — come ontuh me with the jacks an' badgers an' weasel, an' skunk an' gophers too! Come ontuh me, boys!" he called out to them.

He was unbelievably whiskered, with a long and matted beard that grew in semicircles under his eyes, completely hiding his mouth except when it opened into a small dark well. Like his beard, the womanish hair that hung to his shoulders was gray. As he drew nearer with Art, Brian saw that the old man's eyes were water-blue with a staring fixity and an indefinable mixture of wildness and mildness. Perched on the very top of his head was a child's cap centered with a cloth button from which ran down quartering creases.

"Come ontuh me, boys, with the creepin' critter that hath life

195

an' the fowla thuh air an' thuh whole hosta them about me —
minus one — Lot's wife — she up an' died last month!"

The boys stared with mouths ajar.

"Lot knew her an' she was with calf an' she died an' the Lord
He visited me with a plaguea rheumatism, so I couldn't haul the
bresh to burn her there."

With his stomach delightfully anxious, Brian stared at Saint
Sammy. The old man walked a step away, then wheeled with his
long arm up.

"The Glorya the Lord come outa the East, an' His voice was
the wind in the smooth-on barley field! An' I called out to the Lord;
He answered me from the bellya the burnin' prairie. 'Bent Candy
won't git 'em,' He seth ontuh me. 'They shall be shod with silver
horseshoes — dimonds an' em'ralds shall be in their britchin', an'
their halter shanks shall be of purest gold! I say ontuh you, Saint
Sammy, don't sell them there horses ontuh Bent Candy!' "

His arm came down and he advanced upon the boys, who
drew back an involuntary step. "I gotta lotta blue labels now," he
said in a mild and confiding voice, "all offa underwear, an' I say
ontuh you 'tain't easy to git the red ones." He twitched around and
dived into his piano-box home.

Craning their necks, Brian and Art saw him plunge his hand
deep into the binder-twine bits and raw sheep's-wool that made up
his bed. He backed out, turned, and sat suddenly upon the prairie
with a battered tin box in his hand. He lifted the lid carefully,
looked up to the boys suspiciously, then down to the box again.
"Matchboxes," he said. "An' I say ontuh you I ain't got no new
matchboxes, whatsoever kin number the sandsa the sea — got any
red labels?"

They said that they had not.

"I saved them — labels an' matchboxes — saved the saved
matchboxes — saved the saved labels — the dropsa rain an' the
daysa eternity — saved, an' it come to pass that all was saved!
Sammy saved them all!"

A yellow butterfly flickered past; Sammy leaped to his feet,
whipping his cap from his head, letting the tin box fall to the
ground so that it spilled out its contents of labels and matchboxes,
bits of twig and stone, broken china, stove bolts, safety pins, pencil

196

stubs. In a broken run he followed the butterfly, then tossed his cap over it as it alighted. Carefully folding the edges of the cap in, he came dotting back. "Cigarette boxes? The Lord He created them. You ain't got no cigarette boxes?"

"We don't smoke," said Art righteously. "You save butterflies too?"

Saint Sammy slowly opened his cap, and took the fluttering butterfly out between his thumb and forefinger. "All kindsa yella ones over the breadtha the earth an' white ones an' the voicea the Lord come ontuh me sayin', 'Sammy, Sammy, save me the brown ones'—on'y there ain't but yella an' white ones an' they are round about me." He let the butterfly drop; it lay with futile wings on the grass.

"I have went an' rubbed the dust from off of its wings," said Sammy forlornly.

"What's heaven like?" asked Art. On the way out he had told Brian and Fat that Saint Sammy really got going when he talked about heaven and how God made the world.

"Wherefore it cannot fly no more."

"What's heaven like?" persisted Art.

"Sometimes nothin's not no good no more."

"Sammy, tell about when — "

Sammy's blue eyes stared at them. "He give them a few days an' accordin' to the Image an' His eyes on their hearts. Their eyes ain't seen the majesty of His glory ner yet the greatnessa His work, but their ways is before Him an' cannot be hid." Sammy's arm with its hand clawed, lifted, and pointed out the town low on the horizon. "Fer they have played the harlot an' the fornicator in the sighta the Lord!" His old voice trembled, thinned, and clutched at a higher pitch. "An' there is sorra an' sighin' over the facea the prairie—herb an' the seed thereoff thirsteth after the water which don't cometh! The cutworm cutteth — the rust rusteth an' the 'hopper hoppeth! Sadness hath come to pass an' they put no more little, red labels on the underwear—no more but the yella an' the white!" He shook his fists at the buildings dwarfed on the horizon. "He shall rain ontuh them fire an' brimstone — down on the bare-ass adulteresses—" His voice broke off and went ringing on in the boys' ears.

197

Looking into Saint Sammy's face, unexpectedly calm now after the squeezed intensity of the harangue, Brian felt stirring within him the familiar feeling, colored with sickening guilt.

"What's heaven like?" asked Art. "What's it like, Sammy?"

In a monotone, with the singsonging stress of a child's Christmas recitation, Saint Sammy began:

"To start with He give a flip to the fly-wheela thought, an' there was Heaven an' earth an' Him plumb in the middle. She had no shape ner nothin' on her. 'Let there be light,' He seth, an' there was some. 'Suits me fine,' He seth, 'an' I'm a-gonna call her night, an' I'm a-gonna call her day.' He took an' He gathered all the water together so the dry land stuck up; 'That there is dry earth,' He seth. 'Grass,' He seth, 'let her come.' An' she come. She jumped up green. He hung up the moon; he stuck up the sun; he pricked out the stars. He rigged out spring an' fall an' winter an' He done it. He made Him some fishes to use the sea fer swimmin' in—some fowls fer to use the air fer flyin' in.

"Next he made the critters.

"An' he got to thinkin', there ain't nobody fer to till this here soil, to one-way her, to drill her, ner to stook the crops, an' pitch the bundles, an' thrash her, when she's ripe fer thrashin', so He took Him some topsoil — made her into the shape of a man — breathed down into the nose with the breatha life.

"That was Adam. He was a man.

"He sat him down ontuh a section to the east in the districka Eden — good land — lotsa water.

"The Lord stood back, an' He looked at what He done insidea one week an' she suited Him fine.

"He laid off fer a few days whilst Adam named over the critters. Then He remembered.

"He took Him onea Adam's ribs — whittled him a wife.

"That was Eve. She was a woman."

Steadily sibilant the wind washed through the dry grasses all around, bending them, laying them low, their millions yearning all together.

"You better git, boys," said Sammy. "Tarry not, fer the Lord's a-waitin' on me." His arm went up and around, pointing out his horses: great, black beasts with their tails blown along their flanks, their thick necks arched and pointing out of the wind. "He waits fer Sammy in the east cornera the pasture — the Lord's corner." Without another word he turned and took up his spry way in that direction.

The boys walked back to the town. Down the ribbon of the road unrolling to the town, the wind sang a higher, shriller song; it whined and thinned along the pulsing wires strung down the marching poles growing smaller and smaller with distance—black, minute crosses where the town was. Art grabbed the corners of his jacket; he held them out at his sides and leaned back upon the bellying wings he'd made. He turned and walked backwards aslant against the solid wind.

It was dangerous to be a human being, Brian was thinking. How did a person get saved? What was a harlot?

"Art, what's a harlot?"

"A hoo-er," said Art. "They don't wear no pants. Fornicator's a new one on me. I didn't know there was any fornicators in our town."

It wouldn't be so bad, Brian thought, if a person knew, or even knew what it was that he wanted to know. Listening to Saint Sammy, he had been carried away by the fervor of his words; he had felt for a while that he was closer, but it couldn't be right. Saint Sammy was crazy, crazy as a cut calf, Uncle Sean had said. A thing couldn't come closer through a crazy man gone crazy from the prairie. Who cared about anybody living in a piano box on the bald-headed prairie?

And yet for breathless moments he had been alive as he had never been before, passionate for the thing that slipped through the grasp of his understanding and eluded him. If only he could throw his cap over it; if it were something that a person could trap. If he could lie outstretched on the prairie while he lifted one edge of his cap and peeked under to see. That was all he wanted — one look. More than anything!

TWENTY-TWO

STAY OUT UNLES YOU ARE ONE OF US

Between Brian and his younger brother
existed a casual relationship to which the older boy contributed a
careless patronage, and Bobbie, for the most part, an easygoing
fondness relieved now and then by sudden and deeper flashes of
feeling. Brian felt them too. The brothers were utterly loyal to each
other, but no more than to their other companions. The years of
childhood are long; the space between the two brothers was two

years wide. Both placed equally high value upon their father's attention and vied for it; for the mother there was respect, a recognition of the vein of iron in her will, and from time to time a warmer emotion which she looked for often but would not demand.

The grandmother's had become an extracurricular membership in the family, a majestic withdrawal now. Early in August, the warp of the O'Connal family life was changed. It happened on a day when Bobbie stood on the walk before the house, and, looking down the street, saw his brother and Art Sherry walking in the road by MacTaggart's Corner. He ran to catch up with them.

"Where are you going?" he asked.

"Nowhere," said Brian. "You needn't come."

Art kicked a lump of baked dirt along the road ahead of him; like Brian and Bobbie, he was barefooted.

"I'm coming," said Bobbie.

"We don't want you," Brian told him bluntly. "We're not going anywhere — just over to Fat's."

"I'm coming anyway."

"No, you ain't!" said Art. "Nobody invited you!"

Brian felt a faint lift of resentment toward Art; it was not *his* business what Brian's brother did.

"I'm not hurting anything," Bobbie said. "Mother said you got to look after — "

"You can't come," Brian said flatly.

"You're going over to the hut," said Bobbie. "That's why you don't want me — "

"We ain't goin' to any hut," said Art, though they were going.

"Yes, you are. That's why you won't let me come. You're going to smoke in there. That's why — "

"You shut up," said Art, "or I'll shut you up!"

"No, you won't." Resentment at Art's interference blossomed full in Brian. "You won't shut him up! You leave him alone!" He turned to Bobbie. "You can't come. We're not taking — "

"I'm going to tell, then," promised Bobbie. "I'll tell all about — "

"Don't you dare!"

"I told you to leave him alone, Art! He won't tell. I tell you what — you can come as far as Fat's. That's all."

Bobbie considered a moment. "All right," he said. He said it with the mental reservation that, once they had reached Fat's, he could win another argument just as easily. He had never been inside the hut that the boys had built in Campbell's vacant lot at the end of Sixth Street. He had looked often through the dusty window, and on one occasion had tried to pry off the padlock that hung on the door.

At the corner of Bison and Sixth, the boys came upon a man down on his knees; the wet, earth smell of cement stole from the square before him. He continued carefully to smooth the shining surface with his float. The custard look brought saliva to Brian's mouth. The man gave the square a last caress, straightened to his knees, looked at it, then turned and saw the boys.

"Git yer foot offa that two-be-four!"

Art stopped feeling along the edge with a curious toe.

"We ain't doin' nothin'," he said in an aggrieved tone of voice.

"An' you ain't gonna!" the man said. "Git!"

The dry grass off the boulevard rasped uncomfortably between Brian's toes. For three blocks Art kicked along a lump of dirt without breaking it or having to go back for it. He sang:

"The bear went over the mountain,
The bear went over the mountain,
To see what he could see.
On a sky of glass,
He skinned his — *Hey*!"

With his hip Brian had given Art a good hockey bunt into the road. Art regained his balance and put Brian down. Bobbie jumped immediately on Art's back, and for a few breathless minutes the boys rolled in the dust. Art gave in, and they continued on to Fat's.

"When I was young and had no sense,
I took my girl behind the fence,
An' gave her a kiss for fifty cents . . . "

sang Art.

Fat got up from the lawn of his yard as they came before his house. "Let's go," he said.

"We're not going," said Brian.

"What! We are so going —"

Brian jerked his head meaningfully in his brother's direction; Art led Fat off to whisper to him by the corner of the hedge. Brian lay back under the poplar with Bobbie on the grass beside him.

"I won't tell. I knew a long time about you smoking and I didn't tell yet," said Bobbie.

Brian felt a sudden rush of emotion toward his brother; it was not unmixed with a feeling of guilt.

"We got nothin' to do but kill time." Art had come back with Fat; he threw himself on the lawn and began to pick the yellow flowers from the Caragana and from a honeysuckle bush at his side.

Smoking wasn't any good anyway, thought Brian; it made you get all hot; Fat had been sick three times.

Somewhere a bee was making the quiet numb. Brian rolled over on his stomach; the sky was hazed and the sun simply a glowing spot with no distinct outline discernible. He saw the bee trying to get himself into one of the Canterbury bells along the hedge. He was a fat one.

"After they sting you, they go away to die," said Fat.

If a person had very small barber's clippers, thought Brian, he could trim a slew of black and yellow hairs from a bee.

"Wonder what Pinky's doin'," said Fat. Pinky Funder was a member of the hut.

"Home," said Art.

"Why?" asked Fat.

"Got a new kid last night."

"Did they?"

"I just said they did, didn't I?" Art put back his head and tossed a Caragana flower into the air; it lit in his mouth; he swallowed it with a triumphant flourish of his features.

"What was it?" asked Bobbie.

"How should I know?" said Art.

On the other side of the hedge, Mrs. Parsons called,

"Haaaaruld!" The boys mimicked her, stretching the name like an elastic band. Parsons's screen slapped indignantly at the afternoon silence.

"How come?" asked Bobbie.

"How come what?" said Fat.

"How come Pinky's folks get kids every year the way they do?"

"Why shouldn't they?" said Art.

"They got no gooseberry bushes."

As Art looked pityingly at Bobbie, Brian felt slightly ashamed of his brother. "You don't really believe that," said Art.

"Not really," admitted Bobbie. "That's just what they say — isn't it?"

"God sends them," Brian said to him.

Art threw a twig at the bumblebee, making it break off its hum and buzz puzzled above the flower. It lowered itself again. "That ain't right either," Art said. "That's dumber than gooseberry bushes. It's like sayin' the stork — "

"It is not!"

"Sure it is."

"I tell you it's n — "

"All right." Art began to pop Caragana flowers into his mouth.

"Who does send them?" asked Bobbie.

"Ask Chirp. He knows all about it." Art spoke with his tongue in the back of his throat so that his voice came out of his nose. Fat laughed.

"How do they come, Art?" Fat asked.

"Yer Ol' Man an' yer Ol' Lady," said Art.

"You're crazy!" Brian's voice cracked with feeling.

"Kids an' pups is the same," said Art relentlessly.

"Are they?" said Bobbie.

"That isn't true!" Brian was on his feet. "That isn't true, Art!"

"I know," Art said simply.

"Then — then – what's — "

"Just like dogs an' gophers an' — an' pigeons — "

"But I wasn't — "

"You," Art informed him, "come out the belly-button."

"I did not!"

"Yer Maw's belly-button," Art said in greater detail.

"I didn't come out of any belly-button!" He was shouting.

"Just the same — you did."

Brian looked down at the twitching grin on Art's face; he turned hesitantly and saw the bee climbing clumsily inside the Canterbury bell, gripping the flower with its working legs bulging fat and covered with dusty, yellow hairs. Under the bee's crawling weight the flower nodded gently acquiescent. Brian turned away.

Fat was grinning too. Brian felt ashamed and frightened. He wished that he didn't knock around with Fat and Art.

As he left the Hoffman yard he heard them laughing at him. Fat sang, "God sends 'em — God sends 'em — God sends the baybeeeeees!" Brian knew that he would never be even with Fat and Art.

"I don't believe them." It was Bobbie; his brother had come with him, thought Brian, warm with gratitude and a thankful rush of feeling that reminded him he had been mean to Bobbie earlier in the afternoon. "I know God sends 'em," said Bobbie. "Anybody knows that." He looked up to Brian's face with glowing confidence and faith.

"Do you, Bobbie?" said Brian gently.

"Sure I do."

"That's good," said Brian.

"You going over to the hut now?"

"You better go home," Brian told him.

As he had done two years before when he had left his brother alone with Jappy's grave on the prairie, Bobbie turned away without protest. Bobbie was all right.

The man who had been laying cement at the corner was gone; dark with dampness, gunny sacking lay over the new square. Brian lifted one corner of the sack. Clean and gray the fresh cement lay like pudding in the forms.

Brian placed his foot in the smooth center of the glistening square; he jammed it down hard. He did not bother to lay the sacking back into place.

It wasn't right, he told himself as he continued down the street; humans were different from dogs on a boulevard — from animals. It wasn't right, he told himself over and over again. He looked up to see the Young Ben across the street, leaning forward as he pulled a wagon piled high with washing. Art didn't have to go around telling stuff like that.

Brian stopped and stared across at the Young Ben; he never saw the other boy without excitement stirring within him; as ever it was a wordless attraction strengthening with each additional and fleeting glimpse he got of the Young Ben. He felt an impulse now to cross the street and walk along with the Young Ben, felt instinctively that somehow it would help him. But as he stood, the Young Ben turned the corner toward the downtown district; Brian walked on till he came to an empty lot lined with tall sunflowers. Through them he walked to the hut, a crazy, gray-boarded thing with rusted stovepipe angling from its roof.

"Stay out unless you are one of us," said the sign upon the door.

For a long time Brian sat on the battered wicker chair by the sewing machine that served as a table. He would never know now, he thought disconsolately. It had slipped completely and forever through his fingers, the thing that was hidden like a hazed sun; it had got away for good and never again would the feeling well up in him like water slowly rising in a hole dug near the bank of a river. Art had spoiled it. He had spoiled it!

And he did not want to know. He wanted never to know. Nothing was any good. The feeling had nothing to do with anything. It wasn't any good!

He stood up.

"Barstard!"

He said it loudly.

While Brian sat in the hut, the Young Ben stood before Harris's Hardware, the empty wagon beside him as he stared into the store window. A twenty-two rifle leaned against a washing machine with sunlight glinting from its metal fittings. Boxes of shells were next to the gun; one of them was opened on its side so that the shells were spilling out. The price tag, with its writing plainly visible from the street, said $8.95. Several gopher traps hung down along the back of the show window.

"Nice gun."

The Young Ben looked up to see Mr. Digby, ungainly and lean, his face in its angularity reminding one of rock in a pasture, his hair fallen over one eye in a straight lock. The Young Ben turned silently away pulling the wagon after himself.

The look that had been in the Young Ben's face stayed with Digby as he walked home; there was no doubt that the Young Ben wanted the gun badly, and the yearning that the Young Ben must feel found its match in the school principal. Digby also wanted something badly. He wanted Miss Thompson.

Just the night before in his room at Mrs. Geddes's, he had sat by the goosenecked lamp on his table, and he had thought the matter out. He was a teacher, a public-school teacher. He boasted no degree and could not look ahead to a possible high-school principalship. The best that could be hoped for was perhaps an inspectorship many years in the future. Actually he could offer her very little; one could hardly build up an estate on fourteen hundred a year. He could not give her even the dignity of a profession; ministers and teachers were not dignified—their work was not. A doctor, on the other hand—there was some distinction in being a doctor's wife. People looked up to such a person, but not to a schoolteacher's wife — certainly not.

He drew a plug of tobacco from his pocket and began carefully to shave it into his hand. To get away from four walls and a ceiling — the same room to be slept in, eaten, gone-away-from, come-back-to — same damn cage. He had something near four hundred in the bank now, he thought as he rubbed the tobacco shavings into shreds between his hands; that ought to get a person married. Then there would be somebody to tie down to, for good — somebody to depend on, somebody with whom there could be no—no . . . He cast about for the word. Not sham — barriers — someone to whom a person could be as honest as to one's self. He filled the bowl of his pipe and struck a match.

Svarich had everything to offer—security; not that he himself couldn't give that — security from actual want, but not security from the nagging little worries of not quite enough money. A chesterfield—how much did it cost? Dishes—they'd have to have dishes and something for the floor. That would do it.

It had worked itself out as easily as that the night before, but not so easily today, he thought as he walked home. He was afraid that he and the Young Ben were in the same boat. It was not likely that the Young Ben would get his gun.

As Digby turned into Mrs. Geddes's, Brian O'Connal walked slowly down Sixth Street, uninterested in the prospect of dinner. He found no one in the living room, and he noted that the metal cobs on the cuckoo clock hung down the full length of their chains. The first thing that Gerald O'Connal did, upon entering the house, was to pull up the weights that wound the clock. Under the carved fox's belly at the top of the clock, a small door opened; the red-beaked cuckoo popped out once; the door snapped shut with a clicket. Half-past. Brian did not notice the usual smells of dinner cooking. He was not hungry.

He heard movements upstairs, and as he turned by the stair banister, he saw Bobbie on the landing above. His brother had been crying.

"Daddy's turned all yellow," he announced.

Brian looked at him, trying to evaluate the statement.

"Really," Bobbie said. "Even his feet when they took his shoes off. Dr. Svarich was here."

"Was he!"

"It's his gald bladder," Bobbie told him. "The white parts of his eyes — they are yellow too, Brian. Brian — what's your gald bl — "

Brian started up the stairs two at a time; he met his grandmother in the hall. "Is he very sick, Gramma?"

"Ye'd best not go in to him," she advised. "Go wash yer hands whilst I get supper ready. 'Tis a relief to know what's been ailin' him. The jaundice never ran in the MacMurrays — "

"Where's Mother?"

"She'll be down. Get to yer hands and face now."

The memory of the afternoon was faint within him as he ate his meal, all that remained being an echoing feeling of nausea lost now in this new uncertainty. His grandmother had said it wasn't bad, but a person would have to be very sick to turn yellow. Would his father look like Old Wong? He was immediately ashamed that he had wondered that.

"Make out yer supper, boy."

"I don't feel like eating anything, Gramma."

"Try," she said.

When he tried to chew it, the food was suddenly a foreign substance in his mouth; he could not swallow. Opposite him Bobbie ate heartily. Bobbie had seen his father; it couldn't be so bad if Bobbie was stuffing himself.

When he had eaten, he went into the living room. Relentlessly the long-tipped autumn leaf of the cuckoo clock pendulum snicked back and forth.

Sick sick *sick* sick *sick*, it said.

He could hear movement upstairs—his mother, he supposed; from the breakfast room came the sound of dishes clinking. He ought to see his mother. He wanted to see his father. He got up.

In the upstairs hallway, his mother did not see him standing there, as she emerged from her room and turned to ease the door shut. Then she saw him, put her finger to her lips; Brian nodded. As they walked down the stairs together, he slid his arm around her waist. She laid hers over his shoulder.

He felt the deliberate and reassuring pressure of her hand, and with such suddenness that his heart almost stopped its beating, that his knees were weak under him, and his throat was aching with unbelievable hurt — the feeling was in him.

TWENTY-THREE

It was a mean gall bladder, Svarich told them; there would have to be a diet, a month around the house to rest and build up for an operation. He advised a trip to Rochester; Gerald O'Connal objected; Maggie O'Connal insisted. Leon, the clerk, could look after the store; Bobbie could stay with the grandmother in town; Brian, at his Uncle Sean's.

Maggie O'Connal had her reasons for not being terribly in

favor of the latter part of the arrangement. Like most others in the district, Sean's crop was a failure, and each time he looked at his wheat patched with brown and burnt along the edges, the acid of his anger ate deeper into his soul. His flourishing garden that summer no longer soothed him. He had met with little success in his attempts to interest other farmers in an irrigation scheme that would dam the river. There had been a final bid for aid from Bent Candy, the caterpillar man, deacon of the district's Baptist church and profaner of almost a township of flat loam.

"'Tain't no use in goin' to the bank," Sean had told him. "I figger if I was to get enough folks together was interested—enough machinery — we could put up a earth dam 'bout a mile westa Magnus Petersen's. She'd take time—a hell of a long time, but once the main ditch was dug — "

A red-faced man with beautifully white hair, Mr. Candy picked at his nose reflectively. "Ain't int'rested."

"But—man!" said Sean. "You gotta be! We all gotta be! Just because you bin lucky, you ain't always gonna be! Look at the garden I had—that wasn't luck—irrigation did it! An' if we got the whole district — if we did something — all of us — to help ourselves, mebbe we could *git* help! Irrigate fer wheat an' oats an' barley—irrigate the whole goddam works! The Gover'ment—the C.P.R. — "

"Ain't int'rested."

"Git 'em all goin' on garden irrigation an'—an' strip farmin' — leavin' the sod acrosst the prevailin' winds to keep her from driftin' — "

"Ain't int'rested."

"No, you ain't!" Sean's voice had the wild fervency of the wind. "Goddam rights you ain't!" he cried, with his pale red mustaches quivering in indignation. "All ye're int'rested in is the ten bushels to the acre that'll show ye a profit! Profit—profit—an' ye call yerself a religious man. Christian! Oh—I can show ye more religion up a gosh-hawk's — "

"Ain't int'rested."

"Black is yer soul, Bent Candy, blacker than all the dust yer heathen tractors raise! Goddam yer black soul—"

"Blaspheemy ain't gonna help you — "

"Goddam the hot bitch Goddessa profit ye worship whilst ye ride yer jigglin' little black tractor over the land, jigglin' yer little black soul for the rest of yer graspin' little black days, ye — "

"Git offa here!" cried Candy. "You ain't talkin' that way on my place! Git offa here with yer cursin' an' swearin'!"

"I'm gittin'," said Sean, "an I'll be seein' you in hell when that time comes."

He climbed into his old Ford.

"We'll both be there!" cried Sean as he started the car. "Ye will be there, bumpin' an' bouncin' an' jigglin' fer all eternity with a red-hot tractor seat to shrivel yer hide to everlastin'! We'll both be there!"

Mr. Candy had returned to his house to prepare for the prayer meeting that night and the board of deacons meeting after. They were to take up the matter of the new minister's insisting on using the Moffat translation. Mr. Candy had entered the house, to go over his text again — Luke, XXIII: 34.

Ever since that meeting Sean had given up hope of converting the farmers of the district. Of late the evangelism of Ab, Sean's hired man, had increased in fervor, so that now even the sole bright spot remaining to Sean, his cook, had dimmed. Annie, a big woman, whose bigness came not only of flesh but of frame as well, had stayed on with Sean in spite of his outbursts of temper, held by her fondness for Ab, burning in the Ural-Altaic blood that ran hot and slow in her veins.

The thought of Ab's pure and shining example convinced Maggie O'Connal finally that no great harm could come to Brian if he went to the farm; she realized too that her mother would have all she could manage with one child to take care of, in their absence. After all, it was not as though Sean was not a good man; he was not the Ben.

The Ben was undergoing medical treatment at the moment too. One month before he had subsided to a downtown curb, had been sick and, while snoring in the sun, had been visited by botflies. Eggs had hatched inside his right ear soon after, giving him exquisite torment. The man thought with his parasympathetic nervous system, Peter Svarich told Gerald O'Connal on one of his visits. The Ben's was the first case of its kind that he had treated.

Upon hearing of the Ben's misfortune, Mr. Powelly had expressed disgust; he had stopped Jake Harris in the street and reminded him that almost four years had passed without the Ben's being apprehended for his illegal brewing activities. And what, he had asked, was being done about the Young Ben? The boy had broken into Harris's Hardware to steal a twenty-two and five boxes of shells. When Jake told the minister that nothing had been done, since Digby had paid for both the shells and the gun, Mr. Powelly placed the teacher at the head of his call list.

The evening of the Presbyterian minister's visit was the end of a bad day in the romantic life of James Digby. He had spent the afternoon with Miss Thompson, had taken her in for tea to Nelson's Bakery. Past the soda fountain with its gleaming pumps and folded napkins stuck in glasses, he had steered her to one of the tables dotting the open space between the fountain and the pastry counter.

The fan directly above them turned leisurely, its breeze teasing out a wisp of Miss Thompson's black hair. The two were the only customers in the shop, and as they talked Digby felt, as he had a hundred times, the delight of just being with the woman. Just as simple as a drink of water on a hot day, except, he reflected, that the thirst was ineffable. Her gaze was so direct sometimes as almost to disconcert him; in her eyes now was a look that told him plainly she understood him, a look that established complete and intimate understanding.

He leaned suddenly forward. "I think," he said, "that we — could hit it off together, Ruth."

Miss Thompson looked at him, startled.

"I always thought people went about this sort of thing differently," Digby went on. "Why do they make jokes about — about proposals?"

The puzzlement on her face gave way to comprehension. "Jim

— you're not — asking me to marry you?"

"That's it," said Digby. He felt relief now. "I was always under the impression that these things just grew — that they required no formal — that people just took them for granted."

"Oh — Jim!"

"Think we — it might work out?"

Miss Thompson looked at him steadily for a long moment. "It's Peter and I, Jim. I'm sorry."

Digby was aware of a sudden and sinking sensation in the pit of his stomach. "Well—I—At least, you know my intentions were honorable." He felt her hand cool and gentle on the back of his. The look in her eyes was one of startled hurt.

"I'm very fond of you, Jim."

"Oh." Digby swallowed. He was aware of a stiffness and dryness in his throat, and felt his face flushing. "It's — that's all right."

"It isn't, Jim!"

"I ought to have known. It was stupid of me to think that you'd even — "

"It wasn't," she said quickly. "I'm fond of you. If it came down to a fine point — but — Well, I guess next to Peter, you come next."

Digby looked down at the white tablecloth. "It's all right," he said.

And that night as she lay in bed, Miss Thompson wondered why she had never thought of Digby in *that* way. With all her sympathetic heart she wished he had not asked her; and then, aware of a distinct tingling over her entire body, she wondered whether or not, if she and Peter had not finally made it up again, she would not have accepted Digby. She had thought that Digby understood, though she had told him nothing about her plans to marry Svarich when school was finished after this year. What would she have done if Peter had not entered her life again?

And yet she could not think of Digby as "poor Jim". Somehow a person did not think of the Principal with commiseration, not as with Peter. Digby could take care of himself. Peter needed her. That may have tipped the scales. Peter needed her.

214

That was the night that Mr. Powelly visited Digby. The schoolmaster answered the door himself. He took the minister through the dark, deep hall and to the room at the back of the house.

"I've come to see you about the boy who broke into the hardware store," said Powelly as soon as he was seated in the leather chair next to Digby's rumpled bed. Mr. Powelly was a man who prided himself on coming quickly to the point.

"Yes?" said Digby in the act of filling his pipe.

"I understand that you — paid the money for the articles he stole."

"He wanted a gun," said Digby.

"Do you think that with the unfortunate background he has — do you think you're doing him a favor?"

Digby looked down at the minister who had come to take the place of his friend, Hislop. He saw a rather earnest, long face under sparse fawn hair. "I thought a long time before I did it, Mr. Powelly. I'd welcome any help with the Young Ben that you — "

Mr. Powelly waved a long hand. "Far be it from me to tell you your job. It's just that when I heard today of what you'd done, I felt it my duty to call — to have a talk with you. That boy should have gone to reform school."

"Reform school!"

"Yes."

Digby exhaled smoke slowly, took his pipe from his mouth, and stared at the blue smoke threading from its bowl. "Why?"

"He's a bad lot. His father's a drunken old reprobate — "

"His father!"

"Yes. He's a profane, law-breaking — "

"'The fathers have eaten sour grapes, and the children's teeth are set on edge.'"

"Eh? Oh — no — No, that isn't it at all. I might find it hard to get an unbiased viewpoint of the father, but the boy — for the good of the town — "

"I don't think so." Digby moved with the quick awkwardness that was characteristic of him; he leaned against the bookcase by his desk; elbows on top, he examined his pipe intently. "I've known the Young Ben for several years."

"But for his own good, he ought not — he shouldn't be permitted — "

"If my life depended on it, I couldn't tell you what was for that boy's good — or for the good of this town. I'd like to be able to. What do you think good for the people who live in this town, Mr. Powelly?"

"Right now my concern is for the boy who — "

"Yes—I know. Let's consider a few generalities for a moment; emotion has a nasty way of clouding the issue when individual cases are considered. The human race itself — what do you think good for mankind, Mr. Powelly?"

"Why — I — it — "

"Is yours the Utilitarian viewpoint — the greatest happiness for the greatest number? Is it Stoic — the smallest? Do you follow Plato? Aristotle? Which side of the fence are you on? The empirical? The ideal? Do you perhaps sit on the top of it as a dualist? Do you feel that there is a continuous fence at all — pragmatist? Is Christ your — "

Mr. Powelly got up impatiently. "I've told you why I came! If you insist upon treating my visit as a joke — "

"A joke! Of course not!" Digby went to Powelly. "Please sit down. I'm interested — believe me."

Mr. Powelly sat down.

"I would not for one moment accuse you of — the trouble is that the Young Ben's a lone coyote, Mr. Powelly. You can't bring to bear on him experiences with others." Digby sat in the chair by his desk. "Because he is what he is, I don't think you have any need to worry about the good of our town. At no time has he ever threatened it. He has little or nothing to do with other boys. He won't go near them. He never has."

"But — that he should steal and then get off scot-free," protested the minister. "It would be through your—I'm sure it was with the best of intentions — your unthinking kindness. It can't help but create an unfortunate impression among other youngsters who may be so tempted."

"You overestimate the potency of the Young Ben's example. I can guarantee that his influence will be next to nothing."

216

"You don't intend to do anything, then—about a—about his correction?"

"Not much I can do."

"You could say that you had changed your mind about paying for the articles. The case could be reopened."

The pencil that Digby's hand had picked up from the desk was unconsciously drawing on a piece of paper by his side. "I don't think you really meant to make that suggestion," he said slowly to the minister. He looked at Mr. Powelly a moment, his hand continuing to draw. "The Young Ben wanted a gun. Now he has a gun."

Mr. Powelly got up. "I thought it would do no harm to call," he said stiffly. His face was slightly flushed.

"It was nice of you to come," said Digby with his eyes on the bookcase. "I've done what I think best."

"I'm sure you have," said Mr. Powelly. He turned toward the door. "That's what is going to make it more difficult to do what I shall have to do."

Digby's hand continued to draw after Mr. Powelly had left.

The man had been rationalizing; he had substituted a concern over the morals of the town youth for the real reason. He was blinded by his distaste for the Young Ben's father. And yet, thought Digby, he sincerely believed that he was doing right. Digby's eyes rested on the back of a book slightly out from the rest on the shelf: *Heart of Darkness*.

TWENTY-FOUR

After the Soo Line of the C.P.R. had disappeared into the prairie's flat emptiness, Brian drove out to the farm with his Uncle Sean. As the ancient Ford with a hissing plume of steam from its radiator cap bumped over the prairie trail, Sean cursed. He cursed the government which did nothing about such roads; he cursed the drouth that had roasted the crops. Where patches of bright mustard bloomed along the side of the road, he cursed that weed and continued on through leafy spurge, wild oats, wild buckwheat, pigweed, and stinkweed. He cursed the car when it blew a tire halfway to the farm; he cursed the jack when its old cogs slipped, the wrench when it skinned his knuckles. He cursed the eight miles to the farm, the brakes on the car when it went past the gate, the wire loop on the gatepost when it resisted him, its barb when it tore the shoulder of his coat as he leaned against it. He cursed Buck, the dog, who ran barking out to meet the car.

When he had come to a stop in front of the house, he sat for a few moments and cursed intransitively.

As Brian climbed down from the car, he saw the rising, falling figure of Ab going toward the hogpens; the hired man carried a bucket in each hand.

"Can I go see the pigs with Ab?" Brian asked his uncle.

Sean nodded.

Brian ran to catch up with Ab.

The man who had never given up trying to convert Sean — who had on one occasion hidden five of his pipes, broken a carefully colored meerschaum against the grindstone, and dropped five tins of Black Stag cut plug into what he sincerely believed the only proper place for tobacco—was an insect of a man with a wry, sad little face and a startling light in his eyes. The spiritual seed of Elijah MacCosham, the Christian Scot, had fallen upon fertile soil. When Ab greeted Brian, his voice had the sad whine of a mosquito's song.

Brian walked with him to the first pen, where a score of small pigs stood, all of them facing him, their noses turned up to him. Milk-bottle caps, thought Brian.

"They're looking," he said.

"That's because you're a stranger," said Ab in his high voice.

"Honest?" said Brian.

"Yep. Pigs is smart." Ab set the pails upon the ground.

"Can I come over too?"

Ab told him that he could. As Brian went to climb through, he bumped his knee on the bottom rail; with a *hoogh* the pigs scattered off. One of them still stood looking up to Brian. It must be sick, he thought as he watched its sides move spasmodically; it had difficulty in getting its breath; the ribs could be easily counted; it lacked a rump. "His tail hasn't got any twist, Ab."

"He's a runt," Ab explained.

Brian found the evenings on his uncle's farm strange. He was allowed to stay up until the flame flickered in the coal-oil lamp on the kitchen table. While Sean relaxed, big and silent in his chair with the spit gurgling in the heel of his pipe, Brian amused himself by tracing horses from the harness section of the Hudson's Bay catalogue.

Each night, after he had eaten a glum supper preceded always by the unintelligible and almost whimpering grace he recited, Ab would perch himself on the top of the woodbox to read the *Prairie Farm Review*. He returned again and again to the correspondence section, in which people asked for remedies for sick animals. Ab did this with Noreen in mind. Noreen was a contrary Holstein, who suffered from asthma; one could hear her labored breathing and her polite little coughs before entering the barn. Ab read the magazine each night, looking in vain for mention of a cow with asthma; not that he wanted to find a cure; nowhere in the world, he felt, was there a cow who could sneeze like Noreen; he would have been terribly disappointed if he had found an asthmatic cow in the columns of the *Prairie Farm Review*. He never did.

Annie sat each night with them in the kitchen, doing needlework on flour sacking, from time to time a slow smile lifting her long, tenting cheeks so that her eys were almost lost. One hardly noticed, then, the terrible cast in Annie's right eye.

At first Brian found the relationship between his uncle and the hired man a strange one. Sean never spoke to Ab — directly; he addressed all requests and observations to the air in front of himself, to the floor, to the wall, on one occasion to a newborn calf, on another to a manure fork leaning against the barn. Ab was expected to hear but in no way to shatter the illusion that he did not exist. Ab was the "He" in Sean's conversation.

The third evening of Brian's visit, Sean took his pipe from his mouth; he spoke to a moth fluttering vainly in the chimney of the lamp.

"That runt pig's not doin' so well, I see."

The moth was still a second.

"He should have taken care of it long before now."

The moth's wings were frantic for a moment, then stilled for good.

"'Twould be too much to expect him to take care of it in the mornin', I suppose."

Sean got up.

It was nice of Sean and Ab to take care of the runt pig, thought Brian, as he went to bed that night under the slant-ceiling of his upstairs room.

The next morning Brian followed Ab into the blacksmith shop; he watched him take down a hammer from the wall and began to follow him as he took up his rockering walk over the yard. "Better go play with the cats in the barn," Ab advised.

"I'd just as soon go wherever you're going, Ab."

"Nope," said Ab.

"Why?"

Ab did not answer him. He began to cross the yard again. Brian followed. Ab stopped.

"I told yuh to go play."

"But — why can't I come, Ab?"

"Because I said not — git!"

"I might," said Brian, "if you told me why."

"You wanta know," said Ab; "I'll tell yuh. I gotta knock that runt on the head."

"I thought you were going to take care — "

"That's right. You ain't gonna see. Go play with — "

"But — look, Ab, would — you wouldn't do that! You wouldn't hit him over the head — with a hammer!"

"She's gotta be did. I ain't fussy about it." He started for the pens again.

"Ab!"

"You'll git a great kick outa them cats!" he called back over his shoulder.

"You can't kill my runty pig!"

"Don't tickle me none. Gotta be did."

"Ab — please! Tell Uncle Sean you did, but don't!"

221

"I gotta," said Ab stubbornly. "I'm gonna."

"All right, Ab!" Brian drew a deep breath. "Go right ahead and kill that goddam pig!"

Ab stopped so quickly he teetered. He turned. "As the twig is bent, so the tree groweth! I sure hate tuh think what's gonna happen to you if I ever hear you talkin' like that agin!"

"Hit that pig with that goddam hammer, and you'll really hear me cuss!" Brian surprised himself with his fluency. In two canting strides Ab reached him, and upended him where he stood by the stock trough. When he had let Brian go, the boy saw that the chicken coop, the hogpens, and the barn were spangled. "That ain't a patch on what you'll git if I ever hear them words outa you agin!"

What difference now? thought Brian. "Two million, five hundred thousand goddams!" he called out.

It surprised him that Ab could run as fast as he did with his game leg; even with the rocker arrangement, Ab had greater speed than Brian by virtue of his longer legs, but he lacked maneuverability. The two covered the yard, one corner of the south pasture, and part of the garden. There they stopped, one at each end of a row of raspberry bushes. Brian could see Ab trembling in the afternoon heat; the whole garden was steeping hot and still, oppressively so.

Annie came from the house with a slop pail in each hand. Along a feathered row of carrots to his left, Brian saw a strutting Rhode Island Red rooster with his head jerking as though yanked along by an invisible string.

"I'll give you ten to come get what you got comin'!" shrieked Ab.

"Catch me!" called Brian.

They took up the chase again and ended it one at each end of a beet row. Brian could hear Ab puffing, and realized with some surprise that he had been enjoying himself. He didn't care if they stayed in the garden all day. Perhaps they would have, if Sean had not come out. Annie had got him.

"'Bout time you took a look at this here kid!" Ab called to him.

"What the hell's he bellyachin' about now?" Sean inquired of the beet row.

"Swearin' an' cursin' like a Irish thrasher — that's all!"

"Don't come any closer," Brian warned his uncle, but Sean did not stop. The boy began to swear, with a slight hardness to his *r*'s and a touch of the lilt that was in Sean's own voice.

Sean stopped in the middle of the beet row. "Holy — "

"Cut her out!" shrilled Ab. "Ain't yuh done enough without makin' her worse?"

"What coz dis trobble?" asked Annie.

"He don't want me to knock the runt on the head."

"Does he want him to die slow?" asked Sean. "It's a favor we're doin' him."

"Killin' a thing's no favor!"

"Leave him to me," said Sean.

"Mother will be glad to hear the new words I've — "

"God — "

"Hold her!"

"You get baby t'ing for bowtell," said Annie.

"I will not! I'll be good and — "

"Oh, yes you will," contradicted Ab. "You git that there nipple so's the kid kin feed the pig hisself."

Brian found that his Uncle Sean's hand was as heavy as Ab's.

In the days that followed he spent more and more time with Annie; both Ab and Sean preserved silence in his presence. Ab's was a sad, accusing one; Sean's, ominous. As prairie people often refer to a certain year as "the hail year", or "the rust year", Sean was heard to mutter several times about the "goddam gall-bladder year"; he did not do so in Ab's hearing.

And in his closer association with Annie, Brian came to know the depth of her fondness for Ab; she showed the boy the cowhide chest in her room where she had laid away pillow slips and table runners and dishcloths, all stitched bright with flowers: crocuses, buffalo beans, tiger lilies, and flax flowers. Annie's conversations were simple ones, consisting largely of the same question rephrased again and again: "You t'ink Ab marry sometimes?" "You t'ink Ab like to be my hoseban'?" Brian, filled with gratitude for what she had done in saving his runt pig, assured her that Ab had love in his heart.

Two weeks and five catalogue horses after the pig episode, Brian sat in the evening silence of the kitchen with his eyes on Annie bent over needlework. Ab was reading his *Prairie Farm Review*; Sean was puffing in his chair. Brian turned a page of the catalogue to the Optical Department ad. He looked for a minute at the clear-eyed woman in spectacles, surrounded by glasses of various styles; he thought of Art with his thick-lensed spectacles.

The next morning he said to Annie when they were alone in the kitchen:

"You got me my runty pig, Annie. I'm going to help you."

"Me — I don' need halp."

"With Ab — you got to have glasses, Annie."

"But — I can't read some."

"Not for reading — to fix up your eye."

"Feex my eye?"

"Sure — all we got to do is write away to — "

The kitchen door screen banged as Ab entered, a black cloud of flies about his head and shoulders. He greeted Annie, but not Brian, put a handful of oatmeal into the jug he carried, dippered it full of water, then went out.

Brian sent Annie's letter away the next day, and each time that he thought of the glasses after that, it was as if he had a stomach full of grasshoppers. The glasses did not come, however; Brian stood in the shelter of the windbreak and read to her the letter that came in their place. Annie must go to Regina to have her eyes tested. She told him that she could not go; Brian explained that if she told Sean she had a stomach-ache and must see a doctor, it could be arranged. He himself had once managed a difficult arithmetic exam in that way.

Dr. Svarich in the town, Sean told them, was just as good as any Regina doctor when it came to stomach-aches. Annie would then have been content to forget the whole matter, but Sean would not listen to her. He left the house to get the car.

224

Brian went into town with them.

Sean told Annie that he would take the eggs in to the store and get some gopher poison he needed while she saw Dr. Svarich. He looked at her as she stood in the middle of First Street, undecided. "What the hell's keepin' you?" he asked.

Annie started down the street in her long and lumbering canter. She stopped before the square, white Bank building. Inside, she went past Mr. Abercrombie's office and to the paying teller's window.

"I want feevty dollar now."

"Make out a withdrawal slip, please."

"I don' know — you make," Annie said to the teller.

He made.

They met Sean just as he came from the Royal Hotel. Anybody knew they didn't sell gopher poison in there, thought Brian.

"An' what has Svarich told you?" asked Sean.

"I take holy-day," said Annie. "T'ree-day holy-day."

Sean cursed helplessly as he and Brian drove to the O'Connal house to visit the grandmother and Bobbie; he continued to curse on the way back to the farm.

In Annie's absence, Sean himself did the cooking. He knew three dishes: fried eggs, oatmeal, and tapioca. He used one utensil: the frying pan. Ab, who in his doleful way had appreciated Annie's cooking, several times called attention to the indigestibility and monotony of Sean's cooking. Sean chose at first to ignore the criticism; the fourth time he addressed himself to the stove damper, saying that it was not his fault the "goddam cook took it into her goddam head to take a goddam holiday for no goddam reason at all." Ab finished his tapioca on the back stoop.

Both Sean and Ab felt that Brian had something to do with Annie's leaving. The boy found them often looking at him intently, and upon one occasion Sean appeared on the point of saying something to him, but seemed to change his mind. Brian knew when he wasn't appreciated; homesick for his mother and brother and father, he turned more and more to the runt pig for companionship.

With Sean and Ab, he went into town to meet Annie the day

225

that she returned; he stood excitedly on the station platform, scarcely able to contain himself when he heard the train whoop far-off to the prairie stillness. Ab said:

"She's passin' Magnus Petersen's now." Later, "There she is — beyond the roundhouse!" His shrill whistle carried a note of excitement too.

The train was sliding its cowcatcher along the tracks; and in the coaches slipping past, people faced each other solemnly; up by the engine the train let two tinging sighs from beneath itself. It stopped. Brian began to feel himself drifting sideways.

Annie got down two cars away; sunlight stabbed out from her new glasses. Brian ran to her.

Ab came up.

He came the closest then to swearing that he had ever done since he had stepped out of the Odd Fellows' hall eight years before.

"Christmas!"

Annie's right eye was perfectly straight behind the powerful lens of her glasses.

On the way to the farm Ab was silent, and in the days that followed, he observed a strange coolness toward Annie; it was as though she had been stricken with some terribly contagious disease as deadly as the sleeping sickness that had gone through the horses in the district the previous summer. And Brian, who had persuaded her to go away and get the glasses, felt that he was responsible for Ab's attitude.

An evening after Annie's return, he went out to the barn in search of Ab; as he stepped inside he heard the singsonging of milk into the pail; then he saw Ab at Noreen.

"Ab."

"Yeah?"

"Ab — what do you think of Annie's — glasses?"

The milk continued to hum *some-fun, some-fun.* "Fixed her up fine," said Ab.

"You going to marry Annie?"

"I was." *Fun-fun-fun*, said the milk as he stripped Noreen. The cow sneezed twice. "I ain't now."

"Why, Ab?"

226

"Jist ain't. All there is to her."

"But — why, Ab?"

"I dunno," said Ab. The milk took up its drumming again.

By the back porch where the runt pig lived in its apple-box home, Brian looked down. It would always be a runt, he decided, a shivery runt. It had no twist to its tail; it never would have. The world was a funny place. He loved his runt pig that wasn't any good for anything. Ab was fussy about Noreen, the snuffiest cow in the herd, with her wheezing and sneezing and coughing. Before Annie's eyes had been straightened he had . . .

Brian knew then. He ran to the house to tell Annie.

TWENTY-FIVE

Country was much stiller than town was; the clear, fall afternoons lay over the farmyard like something measured out; the sounds could not have been more distinct if they had been dropped down a deep well. From the blacksmith shop where Ab repaired a fork came a *tang — tang*. A bee droomed lazily. Annie sang in her kitchen. Duke and Empress, still hitched to the rack that Ab had left standing half-filled with manure, tossed their heads again and again at the flies; as they did the traces, the halter shanks, made impatient, little clinking sounds. *Tang — tang — ting — tang — tang*, went Ab's hammer on the anvil.

"We have hord a joyful sohnd,
  Jesus seves! Jesus seves!
Spread t' glednoss oll arohnd;
  Jesus seves! Jesus seves!"

Annie was happy. After harvest she and Ab would be married. Sean was giving them the upstairs of the house for their own. Soon there would be eight or nine threshers to cook for.

If he were in town now, thought Brian as he stood on the back stoop, he could be playing around with Fat or Art or Pinky, not hanging around with nothing to do. He wished he were Bobbie; a farm was all right only for a while. He stared discontentedly at the team harnessed to the rack, standing there with the lines looped about the post, waiting for someone to drive them. High on Duke's shoulder a patch of hide shrugged itself — like Art's face; Empress stamped one foot. Sometime, without anyone standing beside him, decided Brian, he was going to drive them alone. He would like to drive Duke and Empress hitched up to the big, gray rack bowing in its middle. He began to walk toward the horses.

It was an old rack, unbelievably haywired; pieces of board were missing from its floor; one hind corner hung low. He put his hands on one side and lifted himself up to stand with legs apart. Joe Pivott had let him drive in town, he remembered, as he looked down on the horses' rumps. He loosened the reins and held them between his thumb and forefinger as he had seen Ab and Joe do. His uncle Sean was nowhere around; Ab was still in the blacksmith shop. He tried a tentative cluck with his tongue.

Duke, a high-strung horse just broken the spring before, lunged into his collar; Empress followed. Majestically swaying, the rack creaked into motion. Brian slapped the reins at the horses' rumps. He would drive them just around the yard a little; it wouldn't hurt anything. He was driving them all alone, he thought with excitement.

With their broad hindquarters tilting regularly, their heads tossing again and again at the flies, the horses moved toward the barn. Brian slapped the reins again. Duke jumped nervously ahead

229

and fell back just as Empress leaped; both of them were trotting with their heads up and fighting at the bits. They were going somewhat faster than Joe Pivott's horses, thought Brian. He pulled on the reins; but the shoulders and rumps continued to rise and fall — faster if anything. The barn loomed.

He pulled on one rein hard; the horses responded immediately, veering to the left in a full gallop. As the wheels rubbed against the floor of the rack, they gave out an alarming, scraping sound; the rack tipped sickeningly, spilling part of its load of manure, righted itself, hung over on the other side to tilt off more manure, then settled down to bounce and slap under Brian with such violence that he had to clutch at the front for balance. With one hand he tried to pull back on the reins, but was forced to let them go so that he might hold the rack for greater security. The horses galloped free of all restraint, running blind, the rack clattering behind them — the haystack, water wagon, windmill, hogpens, chicken coop, blacksmith shop, and outhouse sailing past.

Jounced to his knees, Brian crawled to the side, clutching the edge where blurring ground slipped dizzying by. The rack canted. He'd have to jump. The rack tilted again, and he felt himself going; in the long, hung moment just before he was jolted loose, he saw Ab's grasshopper figure leave the blacksmith shop and come dipping over the yard.

Brian landed in long grass, sprawling with his arms out as though to welcome the dirt that shoved itself abruptly into his face. He was not hurt. As he sat up he saw Ab vault to the side of the rack he had headed off at the gate. The rack hit the set post of the gate, glancing as it did; then, like a horse loosed into pasture after oats, it threw up its hind end; the year-old and rotten reach broke, clung for a moment, held by haywire. And then the rack was out on the road, no longer a broken-backed thing, but a square-fronted, two-wheeled chariot drawn by horses with manes flying while Ab stood in wild dignity, sawing them from side to side in a vain effort to stop them.

Ab returned half an hour later with the team still hitched to the front half of the rack. He walked beside them, talking to them and leaning back against the lines; the horses' sides gleamed dark with sweat and strung with foam; Ab himself breathed heavily. Watch-

230

ing the return, through the kitchen window, Brian was thankful that Sean was not around. He watched Ab talk with Annie, who had gone out to meet him, and then, with a flutter of anxiousness, he saw Annie leave Ab and walk toward the house.

It wasn't his fault. He supposed he shouldn't have tried to drive the horses, but how was he to know they would run away?

"Ab wont to see you."

Brian went out with Annie.

"What you tryin' tuh pull off here?" Ab's voice thinned even more with anger.

Annie's broad face held a look of shocked disapproval.

"You know better'n tuh fiddle with them horses! We needed that there rack fer thrashin' — gonna take a coupla weeks tuh git that team quieted down!"

"I don't know," said Brian. "I just thought I'd like to drive—"

"You thought! Christmas — that's the trouble — you don't think. Ever sence you come out here she's bin one thing after another!"

"I'm sorry, Ab. I didn't know they'd run a — "

"Sorry! That's gonna do a lotta good now — ain't it?"

"Dat woz bad t'ing," said Annie sadly. "You coz Ab trobble — mebbe got hort."

"Wisht he'd bust his head wide open!" said Ab with a vehemence unusual with him. "Mebbe learn him tuh — tuh — " He expelled his breath with a *whoosh*.

Brian felt as though he were going to cry. He hadn't meant to hurt anything. How was he to know what was going to happen? He felt Annie's hand gentle on his shoulder; he pushed it aside.

Ab left with the team for the barn; Annie stood looking down at Brian. He turned away and began to walk across the yard, wishing that he were at home with his own people and not with *them*. They didn't give a whoop about him. By the gate two tipped-up hens were clucking absent-mindedly as they pecked in the bare dirt. He'd go home. He wasn't staying around them any more. He'd go home.

Delicious self-pity flooded his whole being as he walked down the road stretching and thinning ahead of him, the spidering telephone wires reaching to the far horizon. He'd go home and

231

leave them; pretty soon they'd be running all over the farm, trying to find out what had happened to him. They'd look in the irrigation dugout for his body. They would be very sorry for the way they had treated him.

At a crossroad culvert he sat down and watched a gopher's brown back roll. He could see a dark blob against the yellow distance ahead of him. It got bigger and clearer as it moved nearer. Up and down—up and down—pick them up and set them together —up and down again—then lay them against the others. The little black man looked carefully silly as he went down the long rows, making order out of disordered sheaves the binder had dropped. He could go home and be with Bobbie and his grandmother, he thought with a sudden and overwhelming rush of affection for them; she could cook his meals for him; he'd make his own bed until his father and mother got back. He didn't have to stay out at anybody's where they tried to boss him around. He wished now that he hadn't told Annie about smashing her glasses so that Ab would ask her to marry him. They killed things on farms.

What had been an insect down the road was a toy wagon now, drawn by toy horses. As he watched it draw near, Brian suddenly wondered if it might be Ab or his Uncle Sean coming to bring him back on the farm. He dived into the rank grass in the barrow pit.

When he could hear the rumble of wheels, he looked out over the grass. As though eager for something, a man sat hunched forward on the top of a spreading grain box; he was not Sean or Ab. Brian felt disappointed. Through the revolving spokes of the wheels, he could see a dog's feet moving; then, when the wagon had passed by, he saw that it was an old farm dog, its fawn coat matted and caught with burrs. He watched the wagon shrink down the road, and he thought of Jappy, who had been run over two years ago.

A meadow lark sang, and the prairie was a suddenly vaster place. There must be lots of miles left for him to go yet, he thought, for he could see no sign of the town. He was having difficulty in keeping alive within himself the resentment that had urged him from the farm; it was fast fading, till now it seemed to him a pitiful thing in the prairie's stillness. As the stook shadows lengthened in the fields, his loneliness drove him more and more into his mind,

232

there to seek the company of his thoughts and reassure himself in the face of all the frightening emptiness outside.

A strange lightness was in him, as though he were separated from himself and could see himself walking down the prairie trail. It was as though he watched an ant crawling up a stem, or a fly moving over a broad ceiling. It had been a long time since noon.

The sunlight bathed the prairie's stooks, haystacks, and fields with subtle light; gray clouds blackened; those near the prairie's edge blushed pink, salmon, rose. A titaree-ing killdeer called in the dusk. . . .

The night wind had two voices: one that keened along the pulsing wires, the prairie one that throated long and deep. Brian could feel its chill reaching for the very center of him and he hunched his shoulders as he felt the wincing of his very core against it.

Here and there a farm dog barked; farmhouse windows burned yellow in the night; and, seeing them, the boy felt still more lost and lonely. He thought of people sheltered in the four-walled wells of houses, content and warm by fizzing gasoline or flickering oil-lamp flames.

To his right a coning, dark shape loomed; he left the road, stumbled blindly down into the barrow pit and up again. Away from the road he was free of the wind's high whine and had instead the fierce, deep prairie voice of it.

He reached the straw stack and felt it clammy with night dampness. He began to dig, and when he had a hole cleared out, climbed in and pulled the straw about himself. Lying there he looked up to the dark face of the sky pricked out with stars. He was filled now with a feeling of nakedness and vulnerability that terrified him. As the wind mounted in intensity, so too the feeling of defenselessness rose in him. It was as though he listened to the drearing wind and in the spread darkness of the prairie night was being drained of his very self. He was trying to hold together something within himself, that the wind demanded and was relentlessly leaching from him. His fingers were aching with the cold; he slid his hands between his thighs for warmth.

From the darkness of sleep there came a tickling sensation, a pin

233

point of irritation that grew. Part of his mind, submerged in sleep, responded to the cold, the stiffness in his joints, while the rest of it slept on. The tickling reached him; he sneezed violently and was awake.

It was a gray world breathless and transfigured with the thin morning light. He climbed out of the straw stack. His arms and legs were not his own. When he swallowed, his mouth had a bitter taste; his throat was tacky so that his tongue stuck unpleasantly to the roof of his mouth. He wanted water. And he was hungry with a raging hunger that took his mind from the chill of the morning and would not let him be conscious of any other thing. His stomach was a live thing that he had not known to be in him before, eager with a fierceness that could not be denied, greedy as a calf nudging at its mother's bag, anxious as pigs running to a trough, standing in their feed, and sloshing it while it dripped from the sides of their jaws, impatient as a horse pawing at the floor of its stall. He knew now that he had never been truly hungry in his life before.

And there was more than the trembling weakness of his hunger; there was an experience of apartness much more vivid than that of the afternoon before — a singing return of the feeling that had possessed him so many times in the past.

His knees almost gave out under him as he walked away from the straw stack in which he had spent the night. Just as he reached the road the sun exploded softly over the prairie's eastern edge, its long, red fingers discovering the clouds curved down the prairie sky. He began to walk along the road, at the end of which he could now see the sloping shoulders of the town's grain elevators.

He heard a wagon on the road behind him, but he did not hide as he had done the day before. It was Ab. He stopped the team and sat silently, a high and waiting grasshopper upon the wagon seat. Brian's legs refused to lift him. Still holding the reins in one hand, Ab leaned forward and Brian felt the pull of him as he helped him up.

Ab did not start the horses. Upon his wry little face lay an expression as gentle as a benediction. He cleared his throat.

"Yer Paw," he said. "Telegraft lady phoned us last night, kid. Yer Paw down to Rochester — he went an' died."

TWENTY-SIX

The house was filled with the smell of them, a following sweetness that grew stronger and stronger as Brian neared the back porch. There they were banked, wreath against tilting wreath, in ovals, circles, half-circles, cross, and harp shapes. Upon each was sheening white satin and a card with someone's name; silver foil was wrapped around the stems. The artificial palm fronds, stiff and fluted things, reminded him of feathers on the ends of arrows. There were lilies with their tall stamens sticky, curving out in lipped cups, blood-red carnations sending out their spice so that the house was filled with the all-pervading flower smell.

All blinds were drawn and in every room a strange half-dusk had settled down; the outer world of brightness seemed to withdraw itself and to leave the house and its occupants in hushed intimacy. The voices of Maggie O'Connal and her mother and their visitors had a squashed quality, as though they were coming from under something. It was seldom that Brian's mother spoke, and when she did, it was in a low, toneless voice. For the most part she sat quietly with her hands in her lap, tenseness in her small dark face and a look of unbelief in her eyes. Brian had not seen her cry.

He himself had not cried yet. His father was dead, but Brian did not feel like crying. He did not feel happy, but he did not feel like crying.

In the dining room, where the carved, black casket with its gleaming handles stood by the sideboard, an errant beam of sunlight had escaped between the blind and the window edge; it lay long across the floor. Brian pulled aside the heavy drapes.

Sherry's windows were just ordinary, he thought; they didn't have their blinds drawn — just ordinary windows the same as always because Mr. Sherry hadn't died. No people visited *them* with pale handkerchiefs in their hands. He wondered if Art would have cried had it been his father.

The people who called had cried: Mrs. Harris, Mrs. Parsons, Mrs. Funder, and the others; all of them had cried. They placed their hands on his head and told him that he would have to be a brave boy now.

It was his father's gall bladder that had made him die; he had been very sick; he had turned yellow. He was a big man like Uncle Sean, only no mustaches and gentler. He wore gold cuff links. His whiskers gritted. He recited "Casey at the Bat". Once he'd helped to bury a baby pigeon on the prairie. He had a gold tooth in front. He brought stuff home from the store, once a fan with a Japanese girl on it. She had her hair piled high. It had been made of stretched silk.

238

He was a fine man. Mrs. Abercrombie had said that, sitting large and full-blown on the couch with its curved back, her small eyes red with weeping, the corners of her little mouth trembling. Others had said that it was hard to realize. It was a shame, they said; it didn't seem possible. From time to time a silence would settle down over the living room, and they would stare ahead of themselves; Mrs. Gatenby with her eyes on a point just under the chandelier, Mrs. Williamson with hers on the autumn leaf clicking back and forth under the carved cuckoo clock, Brian's grandmother's on the arthritic knuckles and bluing veins of the hands nerveless in her lap. Looking at his grandmother Brian felt a little like crying.

He rose from the window seat, looked for a moment at the shamrock plant in its red clay pot. He might as well go outside; Fat or Art might be around. He stood hesitant, filled with a feeling new to him, a listlessness and a waiting for someone to tell him what to do next; it was as though he had lost forever the privilege of inner spontaneity. There was longing sadness too.

Fat stood under the poplar at the corner of the front walk, kicking at the cog-head of a dandelion; round disks of light hung over his face, dancing there.

"Hello, Chirp."

Brian said hello to him in a subdued voice. Fat became engrossed in tearing the small leaves from a sprig of Caragana.

"You gotta go back?"

"No."

"Go over to the hut?"

"I don't care."

They walked down Sixth Street in silence. At the empty lot where tall sunflowers turned down empty pads to them, they turned and began to walk through the high weeds to the hut.

The damp smell of earth closed around them as they entered. Fat sat down in the wicker chair at one end of the sewing machine with its green cloth thrown over it; as he did, the chair exploded under him with a series of poppings and cracklings. Brian drew up a dented cream can. There was a new sign upon the wall, No Spiting on the Floor.

Fat breathed audibly, resting his chin on his hand, and tapping with a hollow sound against his teeth. He got up, crossed the dirt floor of the hut, came back with a deck of cards.

"Wanta play some cards?"

"I don't care."

"Rummy?"

"All right."

They played silently and seriously a game that usually went with shouts and slapping down of cards. When they came to the end of the deck, Fat laid down his hand. The king of hearts, for which Brian had been waiting, was not there.

"Where's the king of hearts, Fat?"

"Must of been played."

"No. I been waiting for it from the start. I needed it."

"It ain't there now. It's gone then. You won. It's your game."

"No, it isn't —"

"Sure—the king of hearts would of put you out—it would of—"

"Maybe it wouldn't —"

"It's your game, if there'd been a king of hearts. Let's play 'I Betcha'. Don't need any king of hearts for —"

"I don't feel like it, Fat."

"Okay," said Fat. He began to gather up the cards.

Brian stared at the gray blanket hung across the hut, the "perdition". "He was a fine man, Fat."

Fat stopped shuffling the cards.

"He died."

Fat stared at the floor.

"They're all at our house, and they're crying like anything. I haven't."

"Haven't what?"

"Cried."

"Haven't you?"

"I can't, Fat. I tried it but I can't. It's just like—nothing was any different."

"You bawled after your dog got run over, didn't you?"

240

"Some. But — they got the house filled up with flowers, and he's dead now. I'm s'posed to. A person ought to."

"I'd sure bawl if my Dad was dead."

"Maybe you wouldn't."

"I know I would."

"Well — I haven't."

"Where's the — " Fat got up. "Maybe you'll bawl at the funeral."

"Maybe," said Brian.

"I guess I better be getting home."

Brian got up. Outside, Fat said: "Where they got — where is he?"

"My Dad? In the dining room — by the sideboard. It's closed."

"The dining room?"

"No," Brian said.

"I always — Does he — I sort of wondered if . . . " Fat's voice trailed off.

"What, Fat?"

"Nothing."

"I don't think you would cry either, Fat."

"Maybe."

Brian said good-by to Fat, then turned into his house.

Mr. Digby leaned over the counter of Harris's Hardware. "Just what did he want, Ed?"

"Claimed it wasn't fair to the kid," said Mr. Harris. "Said I hadn't done the right thing lettin' you pay for the gun and the shells. I want to do the right thing."

"What else?"

"Wanted to know was there anything else missin' after the Young Ben bust in."

"Was there?"

"I don't think so. Told him I'd try and check up."

"If there is, you let me know, will you, Ed?"

"Why, sure."

"I'll pay for that too."

"But, he said —"

"Let me pay for that too," said Digby. "That's the right thing."

"That's what I want to do — the right thing."

"That's half the battle," said Digby, "*wanting* to do it."

"Too bad about O'Connal," said Mr. Harris.

"Yes," said Digby.

"He was a fine man."

The grandmother sat by her open window. Maggie was all right — good stuff in Maggie. There had been the time she held the lantern in the barn while John worked over the hired man. If she could just cry; more than anything she needed the release of tears. He had been a fine man.

Mrs. Abercrombie looked down the table to her husband. "How much?" she said.

"Twenty thousand," said Mr. Abercrombie, "payable in monthly income."

"What would his estate —"

"Can't tell yet," said Abercrombie. "There's the business too. Don't sit sideways at the table, Mariel. He was a fine man."

Nothing seemed any different, thought Brian O'Connal, as he lay in his bed with Bobbie asleep beside him; things should be different when your father was dead. They were different for Sean, his great, roaring uncle with his deep and booming voice hardly a whisper now, and his fierce eyes like ringed knotholes, no longer fierce — just hurt.

It was the same look that lay in his mother's eyes, the dull apathy of a trapped thing that has given up the struggle. She had not cried.

The fall wind was gentle at his window screen; carelessly it stirred a tissue of sound through the dry leaves of the poplar outside. He wondered what his mother was thinking, alone in her room. He got up from his bed.

Her door was slightly open, and he could see pale moonlight

242

sifting through her window and across her bed. He went in quietly and stood by her bed.

Her long braids lay black down the white pillow. Her eyes were closed. He leaned over, kissed her cheek. It was quite dry.

Her eyes opened and stared at him. She was not seeing him.

He started back to his room. She had not seen him at all!

The funeral was held in the house with Mr. Powelly standing in front of the fireplace, his fine voice dipping and soaring in deliberate strophe. He said, among other things, that Gerald O'Connal had been a fine man.

Mrs. Abercrombie sang "There's a Beautiful Land on High". Brian did not cry.

His mother and grandmother did not go out to the cemetery, nor did Brian and Bobbie.

After everyone had left, he stood before the house, the inexplicable longing within him deepened by the clarity of the fall day, a longing made more intense as the breeze stirred and he felt the halfhearted warmth of the sun dying from his cheek. The smell of burning leaves came to him, and across the street he saw blue smoke threading slowly up. Leaves on the trees detached themselves to fall hesitantly. The branches showed. Wishbones, he thought, curving up like wishbone arms.

He looked down at a poplar leaf by his toe, slick and broad, with a fat bulb where the stem joined the leaf part. If a person were going to cry at all, he would cry at a funeral.

The walk was dark-and-light with shadow and sunshine its entire length; blocks down, where the yellowing trees met the hedges, it tunneled to the round disk of light at its far end, the prairie end. Brian began to walk toward it.

He'd never see him any more; he was his father, and he would never see him any more. A tickling came to the end of his nose and his forehead; he brushed at it; it persisted. The long threads of spider webbing that floated upon the air were invisible until they caught the sunlight that slid glimmering down their length. It didn't mean that he hadn't loved his father. He stared at a clump of dandelions by the walk, pin-pricked cushions, each with an untidy fringe below.

It was like getting a licking and trying to make yourself cry so you wouldn't get it so hard. A grasshopper clicketed briefly; he heard its dry thud on the walk behind him. That must hurt. He was sad. He was sad that his father had died. He was very sad.

He was at the end of the street.

He walked on with the tall prairie grass hissing against his legs, out into the prairie's stillness and loneliness that seemed to flow around him, to meet itself behind him, ringing him and separating him from the town.

Mrs. MacMurray ascended the stairs slowly and with difficulty, sliding her hand along the banister ahead of her; halfway up she rested on the landing, then started up again. She opened her door quietly, snicked it shut behind herself. She sat down on the brass bed; carefully she lifted her stiffened leg, then lay back with her eyes closed.

The curtains breathed out into the room and were sucked back again; sunlight gleamed from the brass bed with the soapstone plaques of Mary Queen of Scots and John Knox about it.

She opened her eyes, and from the commode by the bed she picked up a worn leather Bible. She got slowly from the bed and sat in the walnut rocker by the window.

This is Maggie Biggart's Book. It was given to her on her wedding day in Dunlop, Scotland. May, 1832. . . .

She turned another page, brittle and yellowed with staining age; she looked for a minute at the hair-fine writing that spidered there: *John Ross MacMurray married Maggie Gibb Biggart, Sept. 1874. . . .*

To The Most High And Mighty Prince,
JAMES, . . .

Even one thing, she thought. She began gently to rock, and as she rocked, her lips moved, the words now aloud, now whispered,

244

her old mind making no distinction between thought and overt speech.

" . . . when the sound of the grinding is low." The curtains flapped and were sucked from the room as though the window had drawn its breath. "Or ever the silver cord be loosed . . . " — the curved sides of the chamber pot caught and held the afternoon light in pearly gleams — "or the golden bowl be broken . . . " The gilt-framed picture of John MacMurray stared unseeing from the wall. " . . . Shall the dust return . . . " *Ticket-a-roo — ticket-a-roo*, said the pigeon under the window.

When Brian turned he could just pick out the water tower, the gumdrop dome of Lord Roberts School, the spire of the Catholic church. All around him the wind was in the grass with a million timeless whisperings.

A forever-and-forever sound it had, forever and for never. Forever and forever the prairie had been, before there was a town, before he had been, or his father, or *his* father, or *his* father before him. Forever for the prairie; never for his father — never again.

People were forever born; people forever died, and never were again. Fathers died and sons were born; the prairie was forever, with its wind whispering through the long, dead grasses, through the long and endless silence. Winter came and spring and fall, then summer and winter again; the sun rose and set again, and everything that was once — was again — forever and forever. But for man, the prairie whispered — never — never. For Brian's father — never.

And as the boy stood with the prairie stretching from him, he knew that things were different now — forever and forever — forever the dark well of his mother's loneliness, forever the silence that could never end.

His mother! The thought of her filled him with tenderness and yearning. She needed him now. He could find them sliding slowly down his cheek; he could taste the salt of them at the corners of his mouth. There were no catches of breath, simply tears as he stood alone in the silence that stretched from everlasting to everlasting.

A meadow lark splintered the stillness.

The startling notes stayed on in the boy's mind.

It sang again.

A sudden breathlessness possessed him; fierce excitement rose in him.

The meadow lark sang again.

He turned and started for home, where his mother was.

PART FOUR

TWENTY-SEVEN

Although Brian thought often of his father in the first months after his death, in time he found himself aware with sudden guilt that he had gone for more than a week without remembering him. He frequently dreamed of him, dreams in which he was sure that his father had just gone away and was not really dead. The boy woke after them with a faint yearning that sometimes stayed with him throughout an entire day.

There was a new and warmer relationship with his mother now that he turned to her for some of the comradeship he had formerly shared with his father. Maggie O'Connal talked with the boys about their father, carrying out her determination to keep his memory alive in his sons. She told Brian that he was the older of the boys, that he was the head of the family now, and that she depended upon him. And there was in Brian a growing consideration for the other members of the family; he taught Bobbie to skate and to swim; he insisted that his brother be allowed to play ball in the informal games the boys got together, even though it was only as fielder. It seemed too that as he got older his grandmother had come to meet him spiritually in her declining years; for all his gravity he was still a child. He was now eleven.

The grandmother had failed noticeably since Gerald O'Connal's death. She sat in her room from morning until night and had her meals brought to her. Cataracts threatened her sight. Brian went often to visit her as she sat in her rocker by her open window and told him stories of his grandfather and the old homesteading days on the prairie.

Each Sunday Brian's growing sense of responsibility received impetus from visits to the cemetery. In spring and summer, Sean O'Connal would drive his old Ford into the town and take Maggie and her sons to the slight rise in the prairie a mile from town. They would stand together among the carved stone lambs and scrolls — with the wind in the tall grass, now and then the song of a meadow lark, the squeak of a gopher. They would look down at the ground slightly raised, with everlasting flowers under a huge glass dome at the head of the grave, at the rough granite headstone "LOVED BY ALL WHO KNEW HIM. *Gerald Fitzgerald O'Connal —* 1892-1935". On such occasions Brian would think resolutely of his father, would caution Bobbie about walking over the tops of graves lost in prairie wool. He would wonder too, with regret, that he had never had a return of the old excitement since he had heard the meadow lark sing to him the day of his father's funeral.

In the two years since, he had seldom thought of the yearning that had harried him as long as he could remember. Fragments of remembrance would return to him from the past: the dimly recol-

250

lected picture of a dead pigeon, a tailless gopher lying on the prairie, something about a dewdrop. . . . Once he had recalled the two-headed calf to Fat and Art; they remembered it, but that was all. Then on one occasion early in the spring of 1937 he had gone out on the prairie for the express purpose of recapturing the feeling. He had gone to see Saint Sammy.

"I'm gonna stook the thoughts for Him!" Sammy had cried. "Gonna harrah the thoughts an' one-way the thoughts — gonna summer-fallah fer the Lord — gonna plow down all the Sodom an' Go-mores that's growin' like wild buckwheat — spreadin' their sprawly fingers an' chokin' God's yellah-thought wheat!"

Brian had returned sadly home.

Perhaps it was the lustier interests of another year of age that were defeating him; that too might have been responsible for his finding it difficult to keep alive the memory of his father. He was captain of the Lord Roberts ball team; the previous winter he had played right wing in the Rotarian Pee Wee Hockey League.

One thing had not changed — the Young Ben's attraction for him. It was almost as if his father's death had brought the two closer together, for after that event Brian began to visit the Young Ben and to walk with him over the prairie or along the town streets whenever the Young Ben delivered washing. It was a taciturn association, almost a communication by silences. That winter the two of them had run a trap line together, baiting it and setting it on the clear, cold days after school and on Saturdays.

With spring and baseball, Brian had drifted away from his association with the Young Ben, but seldom a week went by that he did not have momentary contact with him — at recess, noon, or after four. He was the only child in the school who spoke to the Young Ben or to whom the Young Ben spoke.

The Young Ben was in Digby's room; he sat near the window, his strange gray eyes as always staring out over the prairie that spread from the schoolyard. As Miss Thompson had done, Digby sought to relieve the tension in the boy. He was no longer able to ignore the Young Ben's truancy, for Mrs. Abercrombie was on the school board now. She was not sure that Digby was a strict enough disciplinarian; it had been a shame that Miss MacDonald had left the school several years ago. Something like Miss MacDonald was needed, she thought; only a man, of course.

It was possible that Mrs. Abercrombie's doubts about Digby were helped along by Mr. Powelly; the Principal was a stubborn man, he had told her often; there had been the case of the Young Ben and the stolen twenty-two rifle the year before. He would be glad to acquaint Mrs. Abercrombie with any infractions of discipline that came to his notice, especially in regard to the Young Ben. Mr. Powelly was keeping a close watch on the Bens. He suggested that the school board appoint Jake Harris as probation officer. He pointed out also that Digby never attended church, that he spent much time with Milt Palmer, and was seen often talking with the Ben. It was his duty, felt Mr. Powelly, to bring these things to the board's attention. Mrs. Abercrombie thanked him; Mariel was not doing so well in school as she ought to. She had never forgiven Digby for telling her that her daughter was lazy.

For Digby it had been an intolerable winter. He alternately cursed and blessed the fact that he and Miss Thompson worked together. When he was not with her, he could hardly wait for the candid and temperate friendship of her company; when he was with her on school business, he wished with all his heart that the woman were a thousand miles away. The smell of her hair, the casual touch of her arm, simply the nearness of her, were torture. He wished that the school term would hurry its end; he wished that the school term would never finish. With spring and blandishing chinooks, he became, for the first time in his teaching career, irritable and unreasonable. When he himself realized it, he went down to Milt Palmer's, talked philosophy, drank the Ben's brew, and got very drunk.

That was the spring the Ben was responsible for a special bit of ordinance-making on the part of the town council. There now existed a town bylaw to the effect that there must be no urinating under the strung lights of First Street, including Saturdays and Sundays. The Ben's still remained undetected under the floor of his cow barn; four feet of manure have little difficulty in absorbing the alcohol fumes of one still.

It was that spring Brian first saw the owl which the Ben kept in

252

a chicken-netting coop tucked in one corner of the fence tilting around his place. The Ben had made this addition to the population of his yard the year before, and had that spring moved the owl down from the barn loft where he had kept it in a cage.

The Ben had not caught the owl because he wanted a pet for the Young Ben: he had felt like catching an owl; he had. Now it was his owl to put into a chicken coop.

After his visit to Saint Sammy, Brian had returned home by Haggerty's Coulee, and as he climbed under a strand of the fence around the Ben's place, a sharp, snapping sound had come to him, like the clear punctuation of dead underbrush cracking and popping. He straightened up and heard a wild, harsh hissing, a fierce sibilance deep in the owl's gray throat. He looked up and into two eyes of amazing brilliance, eyes that blinked deliberately with the coming down of their untidy gray lids. They were the lids of an old, gray man, thought Brian. He saw that the pupils were dead-black with nothing in them to tell that they lived.

Transfixed by the cold and unholy glow, he stood for minutes with the insistent, persistent husking incessantly in his ears. And he was suddenly aware that the gray wing-shoulders were weaving tirelessly from side to side in a frantically uneasy glide born of restraint, a soul-burning compulsion that stirred within him an ineffable urge to tear the netting away.

With a feeling of relief he let his eyes drop to the owl's white, feather-panted legs, to the black twig-toes growing into talons gripping the Saskatoon sapling perch. He turned away with the hissing real in his ears, the lemon eyes like lingering after-images glowing on in his mind. He felt his body, against his will, sway with a hint of empathy. He knew that owl could never be tamed to the chicken coop and the Young Ben bringing it the limp bodies of gophers and field mice.

Brian heard a footstep beside him and looked up to see Mr. Digby. Silently the two stared at the owl. Digby turned, and as Brian looked up he saw an expression that told him the schoolmaster must be experiencing the same feeling he'd had himself upon first seeing the owl. There was more, a quality that Brian could not define.

"It shouldn't be in the coop," said Brian simply.

"No," said Digby.

"It's wild," said Brian. "They got to be out — they hate it."

"Like the Young Ben," said Digby.

Brian stared silently at the owl. He suddenly remembered the quality of compassion that was on Digby's face; it was the one he had seen often in school, one saved for the Young Ben. When he turned he saw that Digby was making his way toward the Ben shack. Brian started for home.

Within the shack, Digby found Mrs. Ben uninterested in the Young Ben's school attendance, the boy's father completely drunk over the kitchen table. As he picked his way back through the welter of mud and manure in the yard, Digby avoided the chicken coop.

The memory of the owl stayed with Digby for a long time after; its image came to him unbidden, in classes, while he sat and smoked with Mr. Briggs in his cellar retreat at recesses, while he sat alone in his boarding-house room. And then, at the end of the spring term, it ceased to bother him. With the sudden lift of a reprieve, he heard the news that Miss Thompson's wedding to Svarich had been put off till fall.

The course of love was again not running smoothly for Peter Svarich and Miss Thompson. There had not been the fiery complications of the old affair, but there had been a certain just-missing-harmony that marred. With the engagement, Svarich's old self-assertion had appeared again. There was the night late in spring when Peter had taken Miss Thompson for a drive and had stopped the car on the slight rise of ground by the town water tower. He had turned off the switch.

The night had the diffusing clarity of all prairie nights. It was of the sort that prompted prairie people to tell Easterners, "The days are hot, but the nights are always cool."

"What's on your mind?" Peter asked, his hand on hers as it lay in her lap.

She turned her head to him, for a moment unable to give the distinctness of expression to her thoughts. "Nothing, Peter. Just thinking."

254

"Thinking of what?"

"Different things."

Peter frowned with a slight movement of his dark eyebrows. He took his hand away and sat staring ahead. Miss Thompson felt a tightening around her heart. He had asked her what she was thinking; she had not told him; he resented it. She remembered suddenly that her mind had been casually on Peter's car, a long and shining Buick. She had been thinking that he took great pride in it as he did in the new medical building that he had built, with its broad windows and shining, metal-tubed office furniture. She had been struck with the thought that the key to Peter was his need for respect and attention, that and his distrust of it when it was given him. "Peter."

"Yes?"

"What's wrong?"

"Nothing — nothing's wrong." He said it with an edge of irritation on his voice.

"You know — I'm an individual too. I'm not you, Peter. I'm another person with feelings and wants and thoughts. You can't have all of me."

"What the hell are you talking about?" He was looking full at her.

And Miss Thompson, who was too honest to say he was too possessive—that was not exactly it—and who was too confused to put her finger exactly upon what was wrong, said, "Forget it, Peter."

"Now — what have I done?"

"It's just me. I'm tired." She turned to him and tried to smile. "Please, Peter, let's not. I couldn't give you much of a fight tonight."

Peter looked at her a moment. She began to roll herself a cigarette.

He drew a package of cigarettes from his pocket.

"Have one of these."

"No thanks, I prefer — all right, Peter," she said wearily.

As the spring term went on, her doubts and anxieties increased, and yet she could not bring herself to call the thing off;

she had hurt him once before, she had become engaged to him again, well aware of what it would involve. In her unsettled state, she found herself turning more and more to Digby's company, finding there more and more relief from tension that was wearing her down. At first there were only the usual school associations, then more frequent outside meetings — at the post office at mail time — in Nelson's Bakery, where they had tea together. It was there that Miss Thompson told Digby she and Peter were postponing the marriage till fall, since Peter was going away that summer for a refresher course. After Svarich had left, the meetings were more frequent.

It was that summer that the Reverend Powelly's bitterness bore its first fruit. Dolly, the Ben's mare, was the betrayer; led by the Young Ben she entered the barn while Jake Harris was paying one of his hopeful visits. Before Jake's protruding eyes, she stumbled just inside the door, caught herself only to have her hind leg disappear up to the hock. As Jake strained with the Bens to release her, a fruity gentleness, as of rising bread dough, teased at his nostrils. Dolly's hoof came suddenly free, and the usually solid smell of manure within the barn became unbelievably heady and exotic. A rotten board in the still's cave had given way.

The Ben came up for trial three days later. Mr. Powelly attended.

Judge Mortimer customarily held court in the town hall, a great, gray building partitioned horizontally through its middle like an upended box, the top half again sectioned into the council chambers and Jake Harris's apartment, the lower also sliced and containing the stables of the two roan fire- and garbage-wagon horses. Here, seated at a fumed oak desk, amid the pervading sweetness of alfalfa, hay, and green feed—soothed by the smell of horses' bodies, touched with just a tinct of ammonia — the Judge dispensed justice.

Later, while riding with Joe Pivott on his dray, Brian O'Connal heard of the Ben's trial. The Ben had stood before the Judge, his hands trembling with a two-day drouth, one clear, amber bead of tobacco juice dewing the silver stubble at the corner of his mouth, his raw-rimmed eyes steady upon the face of his best customer. He kissed the Gideon Bible borrowed from the Royal Hotel for the occasion, then pleaded hoarsely "Not guilty." Jake Harris brought out the still pot and coil, a kerosene burner, and a half-filled demijohn of whiskey. He told of finding the still. The Ben changed his plea to guilty.

The Judge picked up his metal-rimmed glasses, perched them on his nose, blew out the ragged fringes of his mustaches, and looked down into the well of the desk.

From below came the blurred thudding of hoofs; through the opened window, the quick, skipping lift of a meadow lark's song, from the dented spittoon by the desk, a juicy spattering of sound as the Judge spat. The Ben, the town secretary, Mr. Gillis, Milt Palmer, Joe Pivott, and others who had attended the trial, waited. The Judge was not ruminating over the case; he had left his "Criminal Code" book at home and was now pawing through his desk papers, looking for it. He uncovered a spring mail-order catalogue and realized then that he had brought it by mistake. He opened it, read:

Semi-step-in model of fine quality rayon satin — for snug fit — $2.98.

He blew out his mustache and with a careless flick flipped over a quarter-inch of catalogue.

Team harness—Black Steerhide. Popular and useful 5-ring-style breeching. De luxe. Sh. wt. 68 lbs. — $92.95.

He looked up to the Ben, leaned forward, and said: "Ninety dollars an' costs."

Mr. Powelly leaned forward to Mr. Gillis. "Er what?" prompted the town secretary.

"Huh? Oh — " He drew in his chin, looked down at the catalogue and up again. "Er—ninety days." He extended his chin. "Not includin' time in custody." He spat with a distinct plop into the spittoon.

As he finished his account of the trial, Joe Pivott, like the Judge, had spat. "Damn shame," he said and it was more than the knowledge that his favorite liquor supply had been cut off that made him say it.

With his mother and Bobbie, Brian sat in church the Sunday after the Ben's conviction and looked up to the benign and smiling Mr. Powelly. For his scripture reading the minister turned to the little book of Nahum; his reverently timbred voice rose and fell.

"'Behold, upon the mountains the feet of Him that bringeth good tidings, that publisheth peace! O Judah, keep thy solemn feasts, perform thy vows; for the wicked shall no more pass through thee; he is utterly cut off.'"

For a moment Brian felt a return of the fright he had experienced years before, a sudden and physical fear of the Lord, who had stricken down the Ben. But at the same time he felt there was a wrongness in the Lord's punishment and with this he experienced a feeling of guilt at being upon the Ben's side rather than that of Mr. Powelly and the Lord. It was a feeling that deepened as the weeks followed.

The Ben had taken the jail term; Mrs. Ben had no intention of selling any one of her fifteen cows. The Young Ben cared for his father and the owl; he brought the Ben tobacco and news or just himself, and to the owl, gophers and field mice. The owl had to be fed; the Ben had threatened to "thin his hide" if he didn't come and stand by the jail window half-imbedded in the ground at the side of the town hall.

The Ben found imprisonment hard to bear, and that was a strange thing, for he had never before been so comfortable in his life. The Young Ben brought his meals each morning before school and at noon, from the Chinaman who had taken over the Bluebird Café at Wong's death; the food transcended anything to which the Ben had been accustomed. He slept between sheets and on a flounced Winnipeg couch that stood in one corner of the twelve-foot-square room that served as his cell. These luxuries served only to sharpen the restraint the Ben endured with difficulty for three months.

Several times Brian accompanied the Young Ben on his visits to see his father, and he stood with the other boy, staring at the

Ben's face close to the barred window, his gray hair wild, his startling eyes deeper than ever in their sockets.

At first there had been outbursts of fury, during one of which the Ben had purpled the Young Ben's face with a flung wedge of Saskatoon pie. These ceased finally; or rather the pent energy of the man sought outlet in the continuous overflowing of movement that would not let him alone for one second of his waking hours.

Once Brian and Fat and Art had sneaked up to the jail window and watched the Ben in his cell. Compelled from within himself, he moved like all caged things — from the bed to the chair, from the chair to the table with its china pitcher and red-rimmed basin, from the table in a twitching turn to the bed again, to the chair, to the table, to the bed, again and again and again.

Watching him, Brian felt that he was seeing more than was actually before him, and the feeling he experienced then had an undertone of helplessness and of failure. The Ben's wild eyes made him think of Saint Sammy, and it was on a Saturday in early summer, after seeing the Ben through the cell window, that Brian decided to pay a visit to Saint Sammy out on the prairie.

TWENTY-EIGHT

Saint Sammy, Jehovah's Hired Man,
lifted the sacking from the front of his piano box and looked out
over the prairie sweeping to the horizon's bare finality.

Today was the fifth day.

The first day after Bent Candy's visit had not been the day; the
Lord had been busy; for one thing he had been lightening and
darkening His earth by slipping the melting edges of slow clouds
over the prairie.

260

The second day after Mr. Candy's visit had not been the day. Saint Sammy had known that as he walked to the corner of the poplar pole corral, one shoulder high, walking as though he had a spring under one heel. Far to the West, he decided, the Lord was occupied with a honing wind and a black dust storm that needed His attention.

The third day after Bent Candy's visit had not been the day. That day there had been no frightened feeling in the pit of Sammy's stomach. So the third day had not been the day.

Nor was the fourth day. That day had been the Lord's hail day. He had been mixing up a batch of hail. Hail to the Lord that was mixing hail! Hail to the bunging brown grasshopper that leaped! Hail to his bulging shanks! Hail to Saint Sammy too!

Today, the fifth day, was the day. As he watched Habakkuk and Hagar cropping the grass by the empty wagon box and the others, Hannah, Naomi, Ruth, Hosea, Joel, Malachi, and the two colts, Corinthians One and Two, in the far corner of the pasture, Saint Sammy knew that today was the Lord's day to punish Bent Candy. The Lord wasn't letting him get any Clydes!

Bent Candy, the caterpillar man, had added another five sections to his holdings that year; he had put all his land into flax, and with his usual luck had managed to have a moderate amount of rain fall on his crops. Some of it was burned, but most of it would still return him enough to show a profit, small though it was. He was called "the Flax King" now.

Time and again since Candy had first made an offer for the horses, Sammy had been visited by the voice of the Lord, reminding him always of the day ten years ago. That had been the bad hail year, when Sammy had stood on the edge of his ruined crop, looking at the countless broken wheat heads lying down their stalks.

As he stared, the wind, turning upon itself, had built up a black body from the topsoil, had come whirling toward him in a smoking funnel that snatched up tumbleweeds, lifting them and rolling them over in its heart. The voice of the Lord had spoken to him.

"Sammy, Sammy, ontuh your fifty-bushel crop have I sent

hailstones the sizea baseballs. The year before did I send the cutworm which creepeth an' before that the rust which rusteth.

"Be you not downcast, fer I have prepared a place for you. Take with you Miriam an' Immaculate Holstein an' also them Clydes. Go you to Magnus Petersen, who is even now pumping full his stock trought. He will give ontuh you his south eighty fer pasture, an' there you will live to the end of your days when I shall take you up in the twinkling of an eye.

"But I say ontuh you, Sammy, I say this—don't ever sell them Clydes, fer without them ye shall not enter. I will take them up with you when I shall fill the air with Cherubim an' Serubim from here to the correction line.

"Even as I did ontuh Elijah an' Elisha an' John will I speak ontuh you just like now. So git, Sammy—git to Magnus Petersen before he's finished of pumping full that stock trought an' shall commence to stook the oats which I have made ready for him.

"There will you find the box off Miss Henchbaw's pianah, which Magnus will give ontuh you together with his stone boat fer hawlin' it.

"Hail, Saint Sammy!" the Lord had said. "Hail, Jehovah's Hired Man!"

And today was the Lord's smiting day, decided Sammy as he walked over the prairie to the Lord's corner. It was a perfect smiting day.

Ahead of Saint Sammy the sun haloed the soft heads of fox-tails bending in the rising wind; it glistened from the amber wings of a red-bodied dragonfly hovering; it gleamed from the shrunken surface of the slough. High in the sky a goshawk hung, over the prairie flat as the palm of a suppliant hand, inscrutable and unsmiling, patched dark with summer fallow, strung long with the black crosses of telephone poles marching to the prairie's rim.

The vengeance of the Lord upon Bent Candy would be awful. Mr. Candy would wish he'd never tried to get Saint Sammy's horses; he'd wish he had never ordered them off the Petersen pasture. The vengeance of the Lord would be enough to give a gopher the heartburn.

262

Saint Sammy thought of the day that Bent Candy had called on him.

He had climbed under the barbed wire and had said, "I come to see was you gonna sell them there Clydes."

"Over the breadtha the earth there ain't no horses like mine!" Saint Sammy cried, "an' the voicea the Lord come ontuh me sayin', 'Sammy, Sammy, don't you sell them there Clydes.' An' moreover I say ontuh you, I ain't!"

"Like I thought. Figgered to give you one more chance. You ain't takin' it. Got a week to git off of here."

Saint Sammy's mouth made a little round hole in his gray beard, and as he looked into Bent Candy's expressionless red face under white hair, the wildness of panic came to his eyes. "All a this here land was give ontuh me an' the herb thereoff fer me an' my critters! Magnus Petersen he—"

"Sold her."

"But — the Lord, He wouldn't—"

"No blaspheemy. Sell er git off. My land now. Them horses ain't no good to anybody—way they are. You ain't broke 'em. You don't work 'em. Sell er git off!"

"But — Magnus — he wouldn't—"

"He did."

"From here to the ridge there ain't no pasture fer—the Lord hath mighty lightnin', Bent Candy."

"Mebbe He has."

"An' He moves in—"

"Sell er git off!"

"The Lord hit a man I knew an' it come to pass between the well an' the back stoop an' the Lord's lightning burnt every stitch of clothin' from off of him an' left him standin' bare-naked with a bucket of water in each hand — once."

"I got no time to listen—"

"An' his wife she arose an' she went fer tuh emp'y the slop pail an' she was sore afraid when she saw him there an' she yelled an' he come to with a great start an' spilt the water from them red-hot buckets over him an' got scalded nigh ontuh death."

263

"You got a week."

"The Lord will — "

"Sell er git off!"

After Mr. Candy had gone, Saint Sammy had been afraid. He had gone into his piano box and lain there. He plunged his hand deep into the raw sheep's wool and binder-twine bits to bring out the tin box with its broken glass and pebbles and twigs and empty matchboxes and labels. He had counted them as he always counted when troubled. Count your labels, count them one by one.

It did not help. He put the red and blue underwear labels back, and for a long time he watched the wedge face of a field mouse sitting just outside the piano box opening.

When the fence post shadows lay long over the prairie and the whole pasture was transfigured with the dying light of day, he went out to milk Miriam and turn the calf loose on Immaculate. Then he started across the prairie to Bent Candy's. He found him in the act of rolling gasoline barrels off his truck that stood by the barn. It was a new barn, hip-roofed and painted red, a thing of beauty and of pride. The metal runner and pulleys on the broad door were hardly rusted yet, since Candy had built the barn only that spring. It was the barn that was to become the home of Saint Sammy's Clydes, a barn built by a man who did his farming by tractor, and who, although he had no use for horses, had been obsessed for years by a desire to possess Sammy's.

He turned upon Saint Sammy. "Whatta you want?"

"I come to see would you — ain't there any way me an' my critters could dwell on — "

"Jist sell me them ten heada horses — stay as long as you please."

"But — the Lord He won't take me up in the twink — "

"You got a week."

"The Lord might knock yer flax flatter'n a plattera — "

"You heard me."

Saint Sammy's long arm came slowly up, and the finger pointing at Bent Candy trembled. "The glory of the Lord come outa the East an' His voice was the wind a-comin' over the prairie's far rim!"

On Mr. Candy's red face there was a look of discomfort; in the district, he enjoyed the reputation of a religious man; he was serving his fifteenth year as Baptist deacon. "Now—don't you go startin' nonea that—"

"An' the voicea the Lord come ontuh me, sayin', 'I kin do the drouthin' out an' the hailin' out an' the hopperin' out an' the blowin' out till Bent Candy gits good an' tired out! She shall come to pass—'"

Mr. Candy reached behind himself and knocked with his knuckles against the manure-fork handle leaning against his new barn. He *was* a religious man, and years of prairie farming had deepened in him faith in a fate as effective as that of Greek drama. There had been a mental struggle through the years since he had first seen and wanted the Clydes. Before he could go to Magnus Petersen and secretly buy the land, it had been necessary for him to want the horses badly.

"' . . . Sorra an' sighin' shall come to Bent Candy, for he hath played the sinner in the sighta the Lord, an' it shall come tuh pass the horned owl mourneth an' the kiyoot howleth.'" Saint Sammy's arm had come down.

For a long time after Sammy had left, Bent Candy stood by his shining barn. Then as he walked back to his house he looked up to the evening sky, where high clouds still caught the lingering light of day and held it, unexpected, there. His Baptist conscience told him that Clydes were only horses after all. A killdeer sadly called. The church, thought Bent Candy, could use new pews.

Coin clear, the sun had sunk to leave an orange stain behind on clouds above the prairie's western line.

And now, thought Saint Sammy, waiting in the Lord's corner of the pasture, the fifth day was the day. He said it aloud to the weasel a short distance away with its slant head bolt upright in Presbyterian propriety, toy ears round.

The rising wind tossed the prairie grasses now, stirring Saint Sammy's long and tangled beard, lifting the gray hair that hung to his shoulders. A butterfly came pelting by to pause on a goldenrod, its wings closed up like hands held palms together; it untouched itself to go winking and blinking, now here, now there, echoing itself over the empty, wind-stirred prairie.

265

And off toward the town a small boy's figure could be seen, leaning into the strengthening wind, as it walked toward Saint Sammy's. Brian wished that he had not decided to call on Sammy; he would have turned back now in the face of the threatening windstorm, but he was closer to the Petersen pasture than he was to the town. So, while Saint Sammy waited for the Lord to button up the top button of His work smock, give a hitch to His "Boss of the Road" pants, and call for a whirlwind, Brian walked on. The grasses all around him tossed like demented souls, their sibilance lost in the voice of the strengthening wind.

Brian reached the Lord's corner of the pasture just as Sammy shaded his eyes with his hand and looked out over the prairie. "An' the Heavens will be opened up!" Saint Sammy cried, "just southa the correction line! Sorra an' sighin' shall come to Bent Candy today!"

"It's going to storm, Sammy!" shouted Brian.

Sammy plucked the yellow head from a flower at his feet, crushed it, and stared down at the threads of gum stringing from the ball of his thumb. "The vengeance of the Lord shall be tenfold on Bent Candy — an' it shall be somethin' fearful!"

Calm and peace were in Sammy now; the terror had left him as he watched the far cloud hung low on the horizon, perceptibly spreading its darkness up the sky. "The Lord is on His way! He shall smite Bent hip an' thigh an' shin, an' there shall be none to comfort him!"

A tumbleweed went bounding past the boy and the old man, caught itself against the strands of the fence, then, released, went rolling on its way. An unnatural dusk that had grown over the whole prairie made Brian strain his eyes to see through the spread darkness of dust licked up by the wind in its course across the land. His ears were filled with the sound of the wind, singing fierce and lost and lonely, rising and rising again, shearing high and higher still, singing vibrance in a void, forever and forever wild.

As far as the two could see, the grasses lay flat to the prairie earth, like ears laid along a jack rabbit's back. They could feel the wind solid against their chests, solid as the push of a hand. It had plastered Sammy's beard around his cheek. Brian felt it sting his

266

face with dust and snatch at his very breath. He was filled again with that ringing awareness of himself.

He looked at Saint Sammy and saw that the old man had his head cocked on one side in a listening attitude. From the darkness all around, scarcely distinguishable from the throating wind, the voice of the Lord came to Saint Sammy:

"Sammy, Sammy, this is her, and I say ontuh you she is a dandy! Moreover I have tried her out! I have blew over Tourigny's henhouse; I have uprooted Dan Tate's windbreak, tooken the back door off of the schoolhouse, turned over the girls' toilet, three racks, six grain wagons; I have blew down the power line in four places; I have wrecked the sails on Magnus Petersen's windmill!

"In two hours did I cook her up; in two hours will I cook her down! An' when she hath died down, go you ontuh Bent Candy's where he languishes an' you shall hear the gnashing of teeth which are Bent Candy's an' he shall be confounded! Thus seth the Lord God of Hosts, enter intuh thy pianah box an' hide fer the fear a the Lord! Take the kid with you!

"Count yer labels, Sammy, count them one by one!"

"C'mon!" cried Sammy to Brian, and as the boy stared questioningly up to him, "He's invited you in! C'mon!" He took Brian by the shoulder and led him toward the piano box.

In the dark depths of Sammy's house, they crouched and Sammy did the Lord's bidding, going over his collected underwear labels by the light of the flickering lantern.

In town a bounding garbage can, flung by the wind, clanged against the bars of the town hall basement window plastered with papers and tumbleweed. For the first time in his jail term the Ben was still, standing in the center of his cell, his wild eyes up to the swirling darkness outside.

By her open window on the second floor of the O'Connal house, Brian's grandmother sat quite still in her rocker, her hands black with blown dust driven into the room between frantic curtains. Maggie O'Connal entered, struggled with the window, then turned anxiously to her mother.

Mrs. Abercrombie and Mr. Powelly, their planning of the Auxiliary garden party interrupted, stared at each other from uncomfortable throne chairs; they felt the large frame house around them shake like a spaniel after a swim. Over the sound of the wind came a rending crash; the house jumped.

"Let us pray!"

"What!"

"Let us pray!" Mr. Powelly called again.

"Oh."

The two got down on their knees with elbows on the rich velvet of Renaissance chairs.

The light of Sammy's lantern had become weak, and, outside, the light of day had become strong again. Saint Sammy lifted the sacking.

The wind was discreet in the grass; Brian saw that just the loose blow-dirt, piled slightly higher, sharply rippled as the sand of a creek bed engraved by the water's current, showed that the Lord's wind had passed. Silence lay over everything; Brian and Sammy stood just outside the piano box. A jack rabbit, startled, ears erect, went off past the fence in an exuberant bounce.

With his right shoulder high and his walk punctuated as though he had a spring under one heel, his arm swinging wide, Saint Sammy started off over the pasture. Brian, drawn, followed. The prairie grass clung at their pants legs; looping grasshoppers sprang sailing ahead of them and disappeared to lift again in brief, arcing flight. Here and there the yellow petals of black-eyed Susans hung about their chocolate domes.

They crossed the road before Bent Candy's farm.

Mr. Candy stood where his new red barn had been.

Sammy and Brian halted; they stared at the utter, kindling ruin of what had once been a barn. No stick stood. In the strewn wreckage not even the foundation outline was discernible. The barn might have been put through a threshing machine and exhaled through the blower. Certainly the Lord's vengeance had been enough to give a gopher the heartburn.

270

There was awe in the old and quavering voice of Saint Sammy as it lifted in the hush of Bent Candy's farmyard.

"The Lord hath blew! He hath blew down the new an' shinin' barn of the fundamental Baptist that hath sinned in His sight! Like He said, 'Sorra an' sighin' hath cometh to Bent Candy!' "

Candy turned to Saint Sammy; he looked into the old man's eyes, water-blue, mildly wild with a fey look which said that he was either childlike, senile, or gently insane. He looked at the squeezed intensity of Sammy's face, and he thought of the spreading fields of flax he had planted, even now thirsting for moisture; he thought of the years of drouth and rust and hail and the many wheat plagues which had touched him only lightly. He said:

"You kin stay."

Brian watched Saint Sammy lift his arms wide.

"I looked an' I beheld! The Heavens was opened up, an' there was a whirlwind a-comin' outa the East, liftin' like a trumpet a-spinnin' on her end, an' there was fire insidea her, an' light like a sunset was all around about her! Plumb outa the midsta her come the voicea the Lord, sayin', 'Sammy, Sammy, git up from offa thy knees fer I am gonna speak ontuh you! The prairie shall be glad, an' she shall blossom like the rose! Yay, she shall blossom abundantly! The eyesa the blind shall see, an' the earsa the deaf shall hear! The lame is gonna leap like the jack rabbit, an' the water shall spout ontuh the prairie, an' the sloughs shall be full — plumb full!' "

Saint Sammy's arms came down.

"Amen," said Mr. Candy.

TWENTY-NINE

Mr. Abercrombie and others estimated the damage to the town at approximately fifty thousand dollars. The porch of the Abercrombie house had been wrecked by an uprooted poplar. Several shacks on the wrong side of the river had been destroyed; the frame of the new implement shed on the back of the MacDougall Implement building, in the process of erection, had been twisted into a tangle of studding and rafters.

The town streets were littered with branches; one of them in falling had caught Gaffer Thomas over the head and sent him to the hospital with a slight concussion. With its shattered plate glass and its tattered awnings, the downtown section had a forlorn look in spite of the flat dignity of its false-fronted buildings.

For several days after the storm, Maggie O'Connal worried about her mother, who had sat by her open window for several minutes before she had been able to get to her. The grandmother, however, seemed to have drawn new life from the storm, and in the week that followed even came downstairs for several meals. Sean on a visit to town showed a strange jubilance over the storm; no damage had come to any of the buildings on his farm.

Sean was a calmer man now; perhaps it was the loss of his brother; perhaps it was that the anger and bitterness in him had gone too deep for expression. Ab had given up hope of converting him, and devoted all his attention to his wife and family. In July of 1937 Annie had given birth to twin daughters. "Never thought he had it in him," Sean had said at the time, then added almost sadly, "'Twill be the only seed to yield a crop around this goddam place this year." He was forgetting the garden, which had flourished under the small irrigation system he had laid out five years earlier.

It had taken Brian O'Connal several days to get over the excitement of the storm. The Young Ben was more restless than usual in school, and treated himself to a week of truancy.

The Ben's jail term ran over into fall and partly into the first month of school. It was just three days before his incarceration ended that the pencil-sharpening incident occurred. Digby had a standing rule that no pencils were to be sharpened during school hours, a rule that, while it did not take into consideration the fallibility of pencils and the break in monotony their sharpening afforded, did quench the pencil-sharpening hysterias that frequently swept that part of the room the schoolmaster was not teaching.

The sharpener lifted its grind of sound three days before the Ben's release. It was the Young Ben standing there by the window, his eyes lost in the expanse of prairie stretching from the schoolyard edge to the distant line of the sky with the town's seven grain elevators lifting their sloping shoulders.

Digby dropped the intricacies of percentage; the low hum of the classroom faltered and was stilled. A crow flying low over the schoolyard took that moment to repeat its deliberate call, each echoing caw diluting itself with more and more prairie stillness, withdrawing, fading to silence.

"Ben!"

The boy turned, startled.

"You're sharpening your pencil!"

The Young Ben looked down at the chewed end of the pencil guiltily protruding from the sharpener.

"Take it out, Ben."

He did, then looked at Digby, uneasily shifting his weight from one bare foot to the other.

"Take your seat."

When the four o'clock bell rang, Digby called the Young Ben to his desk. He saw that Brian O'Connal lingered behind, then sat down in a back seat to wait.

"How old are you, Ben?"

"Fourteen."

"Not fifteen?"

"No."

Digby reached for his register. He opened it. He picked up a red correction pencil from his desk and drew a line through the Young Ben's name. He said:

"Ben — I think I better let you go."

The Young Ben looked at the schoolmaster; he looked at the pencil sharpener, then left the room. Brian rose and went with him. They walked in the direction of the town hall.

By the basement window they stopped and waited beside a tremble-leaved rosebush. The Ben's head, with its gray hair in tufts at either temple, appeared; then his hands with their chickenfoot knuckles and their spade nails clutched the bars. His eyes stared up to the Young Ben and Brian from red rims. Brian could hear the Ben's breathing, harsh with a shrill edge to its rhythm. The huskiness was familiar.

The Young Ben told his father that he had dropped school. He

274

stood there in the slanting rays of the fall sun, rubbed the back of one leg with the bare instep of the other. The Ben's head, with its two eyes, moved slightly from side to side as with impatience, as though to move the bars from his line of vision.

Finally the Young Ben said he'd better be getting home for the chores. The cows had to be milked. The owl had to be fed.

Low along the prairie sky the dying sunshine lingered, faintly blushing the length of a lone, gray cloud there.

The Ben looked at it a moment.

"Let that there goddam owl go."

THIRTY

In her room on the second floor, Brian's grandmother sat by her window; it was open and she could see the yellowing leaves of the poplar outside, shot through with the blue of the fall sky. Her window stood usually open now, teasing her old nostrils with the softness of spring, the richness of summer, or the wild wine of fall.

The eighty-two years of her life had imperceptibly fallen,

moment by moment piling upon her their careless weight; and now it seemed that her years were but as yesterday; the little time that was left to her seemed as much as she had lived. Her world now was that of her window.

She had tried to explain to Maggie, had tried to tell her not to pull the window down. It wasn't fair. The rippled pane had no right to distort the clouds, the leaves of the trembling poplar. When the world was completely through with her would be time enough to lose the sounds of the street below: the tack-hammer strokes of women's heels on the walk, hoofs dropping quick cups of sound, children calling. Maggie could wait — draught or no draught.

The electric clock on the commode said five. Brian would be in to see her. He never failed to call when school was over. He would bring the wool — black and yellow. He had set his heart on long hockey stockings — wasp-striped. She would knit him his stockings.

As she rocked, she thought of other days, prairie days. In her mind she lived them over, picking crocuses if she willed it; freckle-throated tiger lilies, Saskatoons, wild strawberries, pin cherries — she picked them all as she once had. There was silver wolf willow from the bank of the river running by the homestead hut; the faint, honey smell of it remained long with her as she reminisced.

Brian stood before her with his dark eyes steady upon her face. He held two balls of wool in his hand. When he had got her needles from the drawer of the dresser, she began to cast on stitches, her arthritic, swollen knuckles making the work difficult.

She told her grandson again the story of his Grandfather John and the bobcat with tassels on its ears.

"For about three weeks he hung around the sod hut," she went on. "He kept pretty well out of sight, and we used to hear him only at night. It was winter—nineteen six and seven—the year of the blue snow. Every morning we'd find his tracks in the snow all around the back, and the second week after we first saw his tracks, we saw him. John had gone out to split up some birch chunks, and he looked up, and there was the bobcat spang in the middle of a branch of the poplar by the woodpile. John looked at him and he looked at John and ye should have seen his eyes. They were green and they were slitty-like; they didn't blink the while he stared at John. He kept right on setting there, staring like John oughtn't to be there. And John told me later he thought to himself, 'There isn't any bobcat going to stare me down. No siree bob.' John kept looking right back up at him. It was the only time he ever stared a bobcat down. The only time."

The poplar moved. A wavering wedge of geese crossed the window.

"The bobcat finally gave up," said the grandmother. "He turned his head like he hadn't been trying to stare John down at all. When John came in the hut to bring me out, the bobcat was gone."

The old lady talked and knitted on. She told of how the bobcat had sneaked into their shack and stolen a tin of John's chewing tobacco. He had trailed it, she said, by following the tobacco juice trail the cat had spit brown upon the snow. He had killed it.

"It was a fine hide, as nice a bobcat hide as ever I saw. I made a cushion out of it. Just left the tassels on the corners for decoration."

The bedroom door opened and Maggie O'Connal stood there.
"Mother."

The grandmother looked up from her knitting.

"Don't you think it's a little chilly to have your window up? It isn't good for — "

"I'm warm, Maggie."

"But—even I feel it cold now that I'm in here. Please let me put your window down. Oh — you're knitting."

The grandmother did not answer her. She continued to knit on the sock, her hands trembling noticeably. It worried Maggie O'Connal that her mother used her eyes for knitting; she wasn't sure that it was good for them now that cataracts were forming.

"Mother, I don't think it's good for you to be straining your eyes doing that — "

"I'm all right — leave me be, Maggie!"

"If you would only do a little at a time, Mother. But you go right on and—I'm going to have to put down that window. You'll catch your death of cold." She went to the window.

"Leave my window alone!"

278

"I'm sorry, Mother."

Although she had not intended it to, the window gave suddenly and came down with a bang. Maggie turned away. She picked up the wool and needles from her mother's lap. "Leave this for a while now, Mother." She went out, hoping that the old lady, given time, would forget about the knitting.

Mrs. MacMurray sat in her rocker, waiting for the blood to stop hammering in her ears and the calm to come back in her. Long after Brian had left the room, she got up laboriously and with difficulty opened her window. She sat down again, her hands half-closed over the arms of the rocking chair. Motionless she sat, watching the sun-chinked pattern the poplar leaves made along the side of the window.

When Maggie brought in her supper, the old woman still sat by the open window. Her daughter set the tray down on the commode top and stood hesitantly looking at the window. She finally went to the bed and returned with an afghan which she threw over her mother's shoulders.

The grandmother continued to sit, leaving the tray untouched. For a long while, as the leaf pattern in the window dimmed, and the autumn sunlight thinned to the pale violet of dusk, she stared. When there was nothing in the window for her, other than the clear moon high over the dark trees across the street, and a careless wind now and again stirring among the dead leaves, she began to wonder.

She wondered why she had been. A girl, a woman, and now an old woman. She did not find it frightening; just senseless. She sneezed twice. She got up from her rocker. She went to bed.

She'd make the boy his hockey stockings.

When Brian came to see her the next day, she sat in her rocker. He said nothing about the stockings nor did his grandmother. She told him about the tame coyote named Tom. Gray, its eyes had been, and it had belonged to a Cree, Little Johnny Whiskeyjack, who had a squaw named Sally Eagleribs. Little Johnny, she told Brian, trained Tom to howl tenor. It was very pretty to hear Tom carry the harmony when coyotes out on the prairie howled at night.

She looked at Brian. It was no use. He wanted hockey stockings.

Through the open window came the sound of a carpet being beaten. *Whap!* The sound bounced off the sides of the house outside and slapped at the still afternoon. They could hear the penny thunder of coal for winter, chuting into the cellar of Sherry's house.

"Do ye know where your mother's put the knitting?"

Brian looked at her eagerly. "It's on the mantel," he said. "There's an armchair right beside."

"Make sure your feet are clean."

When he had come back, she began to knit again. She talked as she worked.

Telesphore Toutant was a man who shot a brown bear cub in the East; he raised the cub on a bottle. He brought the cub with him when he came West, and one day he played with the bear when it didn't want to play. The rest of his life Telesphore used a purple Saskatoon berry for a glass eye. There was a tickling in the back of the grandmother's throat near the end of the story.

She had just stopped coughing when they heard Maggie's footsteps upon the stairs. Brian shoved the needles, wool, and knitting into the top drawer of the dresser; he was just closing it when his mother entered the room.

"You're coughing, Mother," said Maggie O'Connal anxiously and accusingly.

"Was I now?" said the grandmother.

"And no wonder!" Down went the window. *Her* window.

The grandmother did not get another opportunity to work on the stockings. Maggie made her go to bed just because she had been coughing a bit. She put a burning mustard plaster upon her mother's chest. Then she went downstairs and phoned Dr. Svarich, who promised that he would come over later.

Svarich drove Miss Thompson to the school board meeting that evening. After his return from his refresher course, the wedding had been postponed again, to the Christmas holidays, at Peter's request. He gave her no reason; simply said that it would be more convenient then. Tonight, after he had picked her up at her house on the other side of the river, and while he drove her to the town hall where the board meetings were held, he was silent. They sat for a moment in the car before she got out.

He said casually, "Ruth, I don't think you would have liked a Ukrainian wedding."

"Peter, whatever are you talking about?"

He looked at her with his old, quizzical expression, the lines deep at his mouth. "Both times — a mistake. More mine than yours. I knew. You—you're blinded by an overdeveloped maternal instinct. I advise children—lots of them—your own." He looked down at her. "And Digby's."

"But I don't — "

"Come on. Get in to your meeting. I've got a call."

"Oh, Peter — I'm sorry!"

"It wasn't your fault." He put the car in gear. "It's all right."

She watched the car move off down the street, then turned into the town hall.

Mr. Thorborn, chairman of the school board, looked down the long table in the council chambers with reddened eyes and a heavy feeling in his chest. It was a bad time of the year for colds. Mr. Harris blew his nose frequently.

In spite of her cold, Mrs. Abercrombie seemed in high spirits, and tonight threw herself into discussions with abandon, handling the trivia of school business with a sureness and confidence and liberality of quotation and platitude. The minutes of the last meeting were accepted; the matter of extra coathooks for the primary boys' cloakroom (the reason for which Miss Thompson had been summoned) was disposed of. They came to the question of whether or not Mr. Arley should get the painting of the school walls again this year (Mr. Thorpe would do it two cents an hour cheaper). Mrs. Abercrombie reminded the board that Mr. Arley had done a good job in former years; he had a family of five; his wife was in the hospital. "The quality of mercy," Mrs. Abercrombie explained, "is not strange."

Miss Thompson in her chair beside Digby, slightly removed

from the school board group around the council table, paid little attention to what went on, her mind busy with what Peter had just told her. From time to time she stole a glance at Digby's rough face under the untidy lock of sandy hair. A slight breathlessness possessed her; she wondered if her face was flushed; surely the emotional storm within her must be evident.

"And now," Mr. Thorborn cleared his throat, "we come to another matter — the uh — " He looked over to Mr. Digby, "the one we asked you to — Why, we have our Principal here with us tonight."

Digby saw that Mrs. Abercrombie's little eyes were steady upon him, her mouth slightly parted. He glanced at Mr. Harris with his faintly bewildered expression and at Mr. Gillis with his staring eyes.

"It — We find it rather painful," went on Thorborn, "to have to call certain things to your attention, Mr. Digby." He looked down at the papers on the desk before himself, shuffled them uncomfortably a moment. With horses things were simpler; a horse was either a gentle horse, or a snuffy horse; pretty nearly always the latter could be brought around to one's way of thinking. If not — it could be sold. He looked at the note on the paper before him. "Discipline — not strict." The handwriting was full and round.

"We — the board's of the opinion, Mr. Digby, that you don't keep strict — you ought to keep a little tighter rein on the kids — pupils."

Digby's eyebrows rose slightly.

"Another thing's been worrying us some is we feel that you could — uh — set a little better example in the community — when you're not in school."

"I don't think," said Mrs. Abercrombie, "that a teacher can be careless of his associates. Mr. Palmer — the Ben — "

"Mind you," said Mr. Thorborn, "the board is only trying to be helpful. We try to do our best."

"Is there anything else?" asked Digby quietly.

"Yes. The — kids aren't educated just inside the schoolroom. We feel that their spiritual life — you should be taking more interest in the church, and we figure it wouldn't hurt if you was to take a Sunday school class each Sunday."

Mr. Harris and Mr. Johnson nodded their heads in agreement; neither attended church, but their wives and children did—regularly.

"The main point though," said Mrs. Abercrombie, "is the Young Ben."

Miss Thompson saw Digby's face tighten. "What about him?"

"He's not attending school," said Mrs. Abercrombie.

Digby jerked around to her. "I released him. I've crossed his name from the register."

"How old is he?" asked Mr. Gillis, who knew very well, since each month he took the school register to his office to make out attendance returns.

"Fourteen," said Digby.

"School Act says he can't leave till he's fifteen," said Mr. Thorborn.

"Yes," said Digby.

"We think it rather high-handed of you," said Mrs. Abercrombie, "deliberately disregarding the regulations of the School Act."

"Just what am I expected to do?"

Mrs. Abercrombie took over. "We aren't interested in having that boy in our school, but we must have some regard for the Act. I have suggested that he—be sent away to a school—an institution of correction."

"But—to correct just what?" asked Digby.

Mrs. Abercrombie chose to ignore the question. She turned to Mr. Harris. "That theft from your store last fall could be reopened."

"Could it?" said Mr. Digby.

"Yes. Then—when he was—was sent away, he would no longer be a bad influence on the other—"

"Why not just say that he is a bad influence and expel him?" suggested Digby. "The board can do that. There's no need to send him away—"

"No," said Mrs. Abercrombie flatly. "We feel that what we have in mind is best."

"I don't think so," said Digby. "I don't think you can expect me to throw in with you on — "

"In that case," said Mrs. Abercrombie with a gleam in her eye, "we should have to ask for your resignation."

So that was it. Digby felt sick. He ought to have known there was more behind it than what appeared. She wanted him out. She had carefully laid her trap; he had stepped into it. He looked at Mr. Thorborn, who in turn looked at the papers before him.

"I see." She had him either way.

"So we feel that you'll see it our way, Mr. Digby," Mrs. Abercrombie was saying, "that you'll be reasonable in this and the other things Mr. Thorborn has pointed out."

No, thought Digby, she doesn't want to get rid of me. It's the Young Ben; she actually wants to see the boy in reform school. That was what Powelly had meant by his parting shot the night he had visited a year ago.

"But Mr. Digby is a young man."

The members of the board and Digby looked at Miss Thompson with surprise. She stood by her chair with her dark head slightly back and her candid eyes on Mrs. Abercrombie.

"I don't see what his age has to do — "

"Oh yes," Miss Thompson interrupted; "he has several more years in which he'll have to live with himself." She looked around the room at the other members of the board. "It seems to me there's something that ought to be cleared up here. And it seems to me that this whole thing goes back several years to an incident that occurred in the Presbyterian church. Isn't that right, Mr. Thorborn?"

The chairman looked at her in astonishment.

"May I refresh your memories? A still blew up. It was the Ben's still. I don't think Mr. Powelly has ever forgiven the Ben or his family for that and I don't think he ever will. And I think I can see the fine hand of Mr. Powelly in the board's direction to Mr. Digby tonight. The Young Ben's father has served a jail term; evidently Mr. Powelly and Mrs. Abercrombie will not be satisfied until the Young Ben does too. I suppose there is some justification

284

for visiting the sin of the father upon the son, though not—" she turned to Mr. Thorborn—"not nearly so much as upon our school board chairman. I understand that the Ben evaded justice by the skin of his teeth at the time that his still blew up. Strange that there was no evidence for Jake Harris—Mr. Thorborn."

In an agony of embarrassment, Mr. Thorborn looked down at his papers. How in hell had she found out?

"And Mr. Mortimer," she addressed the Judge, "was it not with regret that you sentenced the Ben to three months in jail—or had you been foresighted enough to lay in a good supply of—"

"I'm afraid we haven't time to listen to—"

"Oh, yes, Mrs. Abercrombie. Mrs. Abercrombie, very soon after I came to teach in this town, I saw evidence of your influence—the insensitive and vindictive persecution of the China Kids by your daughter, Mariel—"

Mrs. Abercrombie's face flamed. "You—that's the most—"

"The deliberate spoiling of their birthday party is still to me even more—more—wicked than the callousness that led to Old Wong's suicide! You have asked Mr. Digby either to resign or help you. I find it hard to believe you people—all of you. Tonight you've shown me the heart of darkness—you, Mrs. Abercrombie. It is in you—all of it—in your dark, dark soul!" She turned to the rest of the board. "Isn't it about time for a little sweetness and light around here? A little backbone?"

She turned and walked toward the door. She stopped. "I resign." She left the room.

For a moment there was shocked silence. Mr. Harris blew his nose loudly. Judge Mortimer cleared his throat, looked almost helplessly around for a spittoon. Strangely it was Mr. Harris, a slight, sad little man with thinning hair and a rather narrow face, who spoke first.

"Seems like an awful lot of fuss—losin' two teachers in one crack 'counta one kid. I don't know so much about that there School Act—has it got anythin' to do with sendin' the Young Ben to jail?"

Digby got up and went quietly out of the board room.

"Not jail," protested Mrs. Abercrombie. "Just to—"

"Isn't so much difference," said Mr. Johnson. "I didn't know the Young Ben was giving trouble — "

"Gentlemen!" Mrs. Abercrombie was standing; her voice for the first time in the meeting was shrill.

"I have been insulted by that—that woman!" Her full cheeks shook slightly; her small mouth quivered with indignation. "I have only tried to do my duty as a member of this board. I thought the board would be interested in doing — what — was right. But I see that — "

"I figger, Mr. Chairman, that — "

"I'm still talking, Mr. Mortimer!"

Wrath sparkled in the magistrate's eye. He had never forgiven Mrs. Abercrombie for having the spittoons removed from the town rooms; she had crossed him continually since she had come on the board. "Hurry up an' git her said!" He exploded, and defiantly took a plug of tobacco from his pocket.

"Mebbe we ought to leave this matter over for a while till we git sort of cooled down a bit," suggested Mr. Thorborn. "Isn't any use in — "

"We will not!" Mrs. Abercrombie had completely lost the complacent restraint that made her a formidable antagonist. "If this is shelved tonight, you can carry on without—I will not be here when you come to take it up again!"

Mr. Thorborn leaned eagerly forward. "You mean *you're* thinking of resignin'?"

Mrs. Abercrombie had never resigned from anything in her life; she was a tenacious fighter, and her words had been intended only as a threat. "Why — I — if something isn't done I — "

"I move we accept the resignation," rumbled Judge Mortimer and spit on the floor.

"I second her!" said Mr. Harris in a rather strident voice; then drunk with the wine of rebellion, "I'm gittin' tireda bein' pushed around."

"Wouldn't be a bad idea to move a vote of confidence in Mr. Digby an' Miss Thompson," suggested Mr. Johnson.

"There's already a motion before the board," said Mr. Thorborn. "But we will — we will."

Mrs. Abercrombie had recovered her poise. She looked around at the other board members. She rose majestically, turned; all eyes were upon her broad back as it went through the door.

There was upon the faces of the board members the same look: that of a boy who has waited for the explosion of a giant cannon firecracker, and has been given instead the long and disappointing *whoosh* of a dud.

THIRTY-ONE

Her chest had been aching that morning, and the flat, hard cough came oftener and with greater intensity. The evening before, Dr. Svarich had come with his stethoscope, thermometer, tapping fingers, and the bitter smell that doctors always have. After the examination, the grandmother had heard Maggie and the doctor talking out in the hall. The voices subsided, then she heard Svarich's footsteps going down the stairs.

Maggie had come into the room and told her that she was to stay in bed. With the window down.

So she lay now, looking at the flat faces of four walls and a ceiling, at the log-cabin quilt that covered her, at the commode by the head of the bed, at the spoon there and the beaded water glass and the bottle of dark medicine. The clock bothered her; it was an electric clock with a thin, gold thread of a hand to push time around its square face. Crazy, quivering, enamel box trying to tell all the time in all the world. It had measured out little of her past life, and now it thought it was going to dole out what was left.

Brian killed it for her; he pulled its plug and turned it around on the dresser. Then, at her request, he got the knitting from the dresser drawer. She told no story as she knitted the stocking; it required all her concentration to keep the needles going.

The next morning unpleasant things were happening to the pane of her window; the center of it had crinkled. Harsh waves spreading out, like wrinkles from a pebble tossed into the center of a pond, filled the window. She could taste them. Over the wallpaper they snarled and, rolling jagged up the quilt, broke over her face. All day they did. And the next, while the old woman's breath sounded impatiently short and roupy through the still room.

And then for a brief while the window glass was smooth; the wallpaper was calm; she lay in her bed, filled with inexplicable sadness.

Brian came in to see her. He seemed ill at ease as he stood by her bed.

"Have ye got the knitting?"

He said that it was in the dresser drawer.

"Do ye expect it to knit itself there?"

She was almost half through the first sock. She had done hardly one row when the windowpane began to wrinkle. Over there part of the wallpaper's pattern had begun to sag.

"Open—" Her voice thinned. She tried again. "Open—my—window."

Brian went to the window. He lifted; it refused to move at first, then, as he struggled, it gave, only to stick again a few inches above the sill. He bent his knees and placed the heels of his hands on the bottom of the window. It slid the full length of his arms, and the warm room was suddenly filled with the mint freshness of the outside. Stray flakes of the winter's first snow floated out of the afternoon and into the room, to melt in mid-air.

As he turned around he saw that the knitting had fallen upon the quilt and that his grandmother's head lay back on the pillow. Her eyes were closed.

He tiptoed from the room.

Flakes of snow floated softly down as he walked along Sixth Street, carrying his skates by their leather laces. He hated the sloppy feel of dull skates, the slipping sideways when he pushed on them. It would be another couple of weeks yet till skating season, he thought, but he might as well take them in to Mr. Palmer's for sharpening; the hockey stockings would be ready then too.

The bell above the door tinkled as Brian entered the shoemaker's shop; he was welcomed by the richness of leather. The shearing ring of an emery wheel came from the back of the shop, and for a moment he watched a million sparks star the darkness as they fell. As he laid his skates on the counter, the bell tinkled again.

In the back of the shop, Mr. Palmer turned off the motor, laid down the skates he had been sharpening, and walked toward the counter. He picked up Brian's skates and looked past the boy.

"Hullo, Jim."

Why did his insides slip a notch whenever he saw Mr. Digby? thought Brian. He didn't act like a principal.

"Afternoon," said Digby. "Hello, Brian."

Brian mumbled hello.

As Mr. Palmer placed his hands flat on the counter, Brian saw that they were netted indelibly with black lines of dirt, the nails pale against the dark skin. "I read that fella, Barkly."

"Did you, Milt? Like him?"

"Just the way I figgered—same thing—a little cleaner, that's all—nothin' outside—all sensations."

"That's right," said Digby.

"All insidea me," went on Palmer in his metallic voice, his

290

inverted V eyebrows high on his forehead, his nose bright in the dimness of the shop; "shop's insidea me — town's insidea me — whole damn shootin' match insidea me."

Digby nodded.

Milt Palmer drew in his breath. "Who the hell's me?"

"Town shoemaker," said Digby.

"That don't answer. Shoes, folks, churches, stores, grain elevators, farms, horses, dogs — all insidea me. You — the kids — this shop, insidea me — me insidea my shop; so that means I got me insidea me. Who the hell's me?"

Fascinated, Brian stared at the shoemaker; he thought of Saint Sammy; he thought of the feeling. "You got a feeling?"

"Huh?"

"You — do you get a funny feeling — like — well — you wanted to know something, only you don't know what you — Have you got a feeling?"

Mr. Palmer looked down at the skate he held in his hand; he pursed his lips, then bent down. He came up with a jug. The sound of the cork, drawn, was reluctant on the silence; the jug gurgled. Milt Palmer wiped his mouth with the back of his hand.

"It's like you are going to spill over," said Brian. "And you're all — "

"No," said Mr. Palmer, "can't say I got that in there, kid. I got a hell of a lot, but — I guess that ain't there no — more." He said it, thought Brian, sadly. The shoemaker turned to Digby. "I still don't know who 'me' is."

"An idea."

"Whose?"

"God's."

"Oh."

"You're inside Him, Milt. When I get outside that door, I'm out of you, but I'm still inside Him."

Mr. Palmer stared at Digby. "That what he says — Barkly?"

Digby nodded his head.

"Hell," said Mr. Palmer. "Oh, hell! 'Nother good one gone on the rocks — he — did he live on prairie?"

"No," said Digby.

"I could feel her stickin' out—I could feel her edges stickin' out—I—oh, hell!"

"When'll my skates be done, Mr. Palmer?"

"Thursday." He bent down at the counter again, straightened up. To Digby he said, "Yours'll be ready Friday—the shoes. That soon enough?"

"I think so," said Digby.

"Best of luck," said Palmer.

"Thank you," said Digby.

Outside, the flakes fell lazily, silently.

"About Mr. Palmer," Brian said.

"What about him?"

"I was just wondering—is he all right?"

"Yes."

"I'm not inside of anybody."

"Aren't you?"

"No—what's he mean?"

Upon Digby's angular face was a faint look of frustration. "I don't—I don't think you're old enough."

"I wouldn't understand?"

"Name something."

Brian thought: skates—ice—snow—road apple—"Ice?"

"All right—what is it?"

"Something you skate on."

"Then you can feel it—you can see it—taste it. That's all it is—a sensation of sight, taste, and touch. Anything you can think of is just such a bundle of hearing, smelling, feeling, seeing. That's all. The post office."

Brian looked at it—solid, square, brick-red with its tower pointing out the dull sky.

"That's just a set of sensations—nothing else. They're yours. They're inside you."

Brian tried to work his way through the seething sees and feels. "I guess you were right," he said.

"I was afraid so," said Digby. "Don't let it bother you."

"But it does!" Brian looked up to the Principal's face. "I've

292

been trying to — to figure out for a long time, and it won't! Everything has to figure out, doesn't it?"

"No — not everything."

"But — if it doesn't figure out —"

"Just some things."

"I never told anybody — if I have to know about sense — sense—"

"You just keep on trying," Digby said.

"I'll know some day?"

Digby looked down at him without saying anything.

"I get the closest—I used to—when there's a feeling. Is there a feeling?"

"Yes."

"Then, I'm on the right track?"

"I think you are."

"A person can do it by feeling?"

"That's the way," said Digby.

"Then, I'm on the right track." Brian said it with conviction.

The black branches of the trees along Sixth Street were edged with white, the staring white that belongs to a child's paintbox. Feathering lazily, crazily down, loosed from the hazed softness of the sky, the snow came to rest in startling white bulbs on the dead leaves of the poplars, webbing in between the branches. Just outside the grandmother's room, where she lay quite still in her bed, the snow fell soundlessly, flake by flake piling up its careless weight. Now and again a twig would break off suddenly, relieve itself of a white burden of snow, and drop to earth.

THIRTY-TWO

Mrs. MacMurray's death did not come with the shocking impact of her son-in-law's; it was followed by a gentler sadness more akin to nostalgia than to deep grief. She managed a departure typically Scotch and Presbyterian in its restraint, a predestined event of logical finality. In her own words, her time had come.

Mr. Stickle filled two front-page columns of the *Times* with

294

the story of her life, pointing out that she had come West to a homestead in the *métis* rebellion year of 1885. As she had requested, she was buried beside Gerald in the prairie cemetery just outside the town.

It was Sean who handled the funeral details and arrangements for Maggie. He came into town in a cutter, and stayed at the house for a week. One evening, as he sat with Maggie before the fireplace after the boys had gone to bed, he asked her what plans she had for them. She told him she hoped to send them to the university.

Sean was silent for a moment, his eyes upon the flames of the fireplace. "Do you think Brian will be takin' over the store?"

"It's a long time yet," said Maggie. "You seem to have put an idea in his head."

"Me? What?"

"He says he'd like to be a — dirt doctor."

"Dirt doctor!"

"He's heard you say that the prairie's sick. Evidently you've told him what has been already done about rust—that there could never be another rust year like 1935. He has mentioned a new wheat too — being developed in Russia — a perennial." Maggie gazed a moment at Sean. "I'm told that you think it would be the— clear rig for this country—for feed—to prevent soil drifting. Brian tells me it wouldn't winter-kill. His last composition for Mr. Digby was, 'Why People Should Raise Cows in Southern Saskatchewan'."

"The hell it was!"

Maggie nodded her head. "Irrigation."

Sean got up. He stood with his elbow on the mantel, his red mustaches moving jerkily. "You figger you can swing it? University?"

"I think so."

"Next summer," said Sean, "wouldn't be a bad idea if he was to come out with me for part of the holidays."

"Why — Sean, that would be very — "

"Be doin' me a favor—have somebody 'round listens to what I say—an' I'll learn him. I'll learn him to be a dirt doctor." Sean went back to his chair. "You got that there composition around?"

"It's in my sewing basket," said Maggie.

"Let me have a look at the goddam thing," said Sean.

Two days after Sean had left for the farm, Brian walked home with Mr. Digby. The schoolmaster noted the intentness on the boy's face; he spoke of a coming hockey game; then just as they were about to part at MacTaggart's Corner, Brian said:

"I've thought a lot about it since my grandmother died — about what I was telling you in Mr. Palmer's that day. I've thought about it ever since."

"Have you?" said Digby.

"You're the only one I ever talked to." He looked up to the schoolmaster. "I don't get the feeling any more. I — don't think I will — get it any more."

Digby was struck by something more than familiar in the serious eyes under the broad band of the toque with its red pom. His mind went swiftly back to the first day of school some six years ago when Brian had faced him in the office. He thought of the Young Ben, who no longer attended his school. That was it — the look upon Brian's face — the same expression that had puzzled him on the Young Ben's: maturity in spite of the formlessness of childish features, wisdom without years. "Intimations of Immortality," he thought.

"Perhaps," said Digby to Brian, "you've grown up."

Brian walked the rest of the way home alone. No one answered his call at the doorway of the house. He hung up his scarf and coat and toque, then went through the living room and up the stairs. He opened the door of his grandmother's room. Before he entered, his eye caught the glinting of winter sunshine on the dimpled knobs of her brass bed.

He looked up at John Knox with his beard cascading to the opened Bible in his knotted hands, a staring John Knox unaware of Mary, Queen of Scots beside him. Her index finger pointed to the scroll in her left hand; the ruff around her neck made Brian think of Christmas candy, the stiff and convoluted kind. They were like brother and sister, he thought; both of them possessed the same

296

long and bridgeless nose, cameo lips, pinpricked pupils. Their unseeing stare filled him with a feeling of guilt. He should not be in his grandmother's room. She had been dead two weeks now.

The sight of his grandfather, gaunt and dark in his oval frame, reassured him. He thought of Telesphore Toutant, a bobcat with tassels on its ears, a buckboard creaking over wide and rustling prairie. He stepped into the room.

He missed the staring white of teeth and orange, wax gums hanging tilted in the half-filled water glass on the commode. He missed the chamber pot on the shelf below.

As he turned he saw his grandmother's leg brace lying down the bed. Left behind. It was as though she had just taken her leg out of the hooping straps, as though she would return to put it on at any minute. The feeling of guilt deepened again as he looked at the rocker with its arms invitingly wide. In the pieces of the log-cabin quilt his eyes found out the velvet that had been her Sunday dress, pin-striped cloth once a vest of his grandfather's, pepper-and-salt tweed from a pair of his father's trousers. He suddenly felt that he was being watched, and he was sure he could smell a faint and winy trace of tonic on the air. She would be back. She had just taken the teeth from the glass and snicked them into place. She would return to find him uninvited in her room.

As he turned toward the door, he was suddenly aware of an emotion long familiar to him; it was as though he were recognizing again an experience that his memory had stored for him, but not too well. Perhaps it had been there only since his father's death; he was not sure. Death had come to many things that he had known.

And still the feeling that his grandmother was not dead persisted in him. He looked up again at the soapstone plaques. *They* had died. For hundreds of years they had been dead. His own father had died and *his* father, and his father, and his father before him.

Outside the door of his grandmother's room, he remembered the meadow lark that had sung the day he had been unable to cry. He remembered it with an aching nostalgia that he strained to keep within himself as he went down the stairs and as he took his coat and scarf and toque from a peg in the hallway.

The freshly fallen snow protested under his feet. Why did people die? Why did they finish up? What was the good in being a human? It was awful to be a human. It wasn't any good.

Goose-gray above him, the prairie sky had a depthless softness undetermined by its usual pencil edge, melting invisibly into the spread and staring white of the land. He walked over the prairie, his ankles turning to the frozen crust of hummocking summer fallow and stubble fields. No living thing moved; and he saw only the domino tracks of jack rabbits, the sidling wells of a trotting coyote's trail, the exquisitely stamped tracks of prairie chicken. These things filled his mind against his will. Sun glinting from a wild rosebush branch caught his eye; looking more closely he saw that it was crowded with crystals, each one pointed and veined, all of them growing away from him. He kicked at the branch and watched the frost drop in a white shower. He looked out over the prairie again.

All kinds of people had died. They were dead and they were gone. The swarming hum of telephone wires came to him, barely perceptible in the stillness, hardly a sound heard so much as a pulsing of power felt. He looked up at rime-white wires, following them from pole to pole to the prairie's rim. From each person stretched back a long line — hundreds and hundreds of years — each person stuck up.

It had something to do with dying; it had something to do with being born. Loving something and being hungry were with it too. He knew that much now. There was the prairie; there was a meadow lark, a baby pigeon, and a calf with two heads. In some haunting way the Ben was part of it. So was Mr. Digby.

As he turned back toward the town he saw the moon pale in the afternoon sky, a gray ghost half-dissolved. And the town was dim — gray and low upon the horizon, it lay, not real, swathed in bodiless mist — quite sunless in the rest of the dazzling prairie.

Some day, he thought, perhaps when he was older than he was now, he would know; he would find out completely and for good. He would be satisfied. From the weeds tall along the barrow pit, twinkling light appeared and disappeared as the sun glinted from bowed stalks and frost-blackened leaves.

298

Some day. The thing could not hide from him forever.

A startled jack rabbit leaped suddenly into the air ahead of him. Ears ridiculously erect, in seeking spurts now to one side, now to the other, it went bounding idiotically out over the prairie.

The day grays, its light withdrawing from the winter sky till just the prairie's edge is luminous. At one side of the night a farm dog barks; another answers him. A coyote lifts his howl, his throat-line long to the dog-nose pointing out the moon. A train whoops to the night, the sound dissolving slowly.

High above the prairie, platter-flat, the wind wings on, bereft and wild its lonely song. It ridges drifts and licks their ripples off; it smoothens crests, piles snow against the fences. The tinting green of Northern Lights slowly shades and fades against the prairie nights, dying here, imperceptibly reborn over there. Light glows each evening where the town lies; a hiving sound is there, with now and then some sound distinct and separate in the night: a shout, a woman's laugh. Clear — truant sounds.

As clouds' slow shadows melt across the prairie's face, more nights slip darkness over. Light then dark, then light again. Day then night, then day again. A meadow lark sings and it is spring. And summer comes.

A year is done.

Another comes and it is done.

Where spindling poplars lift their dusty leaves and wild sun-flowers stare, the gravestones stand among the prairie grasses. Over them a rapt and endless silence lies. This soil is rich.

Here to the west a small dog's skeleton lies, its rib bones clutching emptiness. Crawling in and out of the teeth an ant casts about; it disappears into an eyesocket, reappears to begin a long pilgrimage down the backbone spools.

The wind turns in silent frenzy upon itself, whirling into a smoking funnel, breathing up topsoil and tumbleweed skeletons to carry them on its spinning way over the prairie, out and out to the far line of the sky.

W. O. Mitchell was born in Weyburn, Saskatchewan, in 1914. Although he has lived most of his life in Alberta and Saskatchewan, he has travelled widely and has been a lifeguard, deckhand, salesman, and high school teacher. For many years the most renowned resident of High River, Alberta, he now lives in Calgary.

In 1951, after working for several years as fiction editor for *Maclean's* magazine, Mr. Mitchell returned to the West to work as a free-lance writer. These years witnessed the creation and rise to popularity of his radio series *Jake and the Kid*, which was subsequently (1961) published in book form. In addition to *Jake and the Kid* and *Who Has Seen the Wind*, W. O. Mitchell has written *The Alien* (1953), *The Black Bonspiel of Wullie MacCrimmon* (1962), *The Kite* (1962), and *The Vanishing Point* (1974). He is also a widely respected dramatist whose most recent play, *Back to Beulah*, originated with Theatre Calgary and appeared in Toronto in 1976. His talents are undeniable. As Pierre Berton has said: "W. O. Mitchell is what I call an original...there is only one of him and there aren't going to be any more...."

Mr. Mitchell was made an Officer of the Order of Canada in 1973.

William Kurelek was born in Alberta in 1927. He graduated from the University of Manitoba in 1949 and briefly attended art schools in Toronto and Mexico before going to England in 1952. In recent years he has lived in Toronto.

As a painter Mr. Kurelek is largely self-taught and his distinctive style is immediately recognizable. His work has received significant acclaim both in Canada and abroad and has been exhibited in one-man shows and major group exhibitions throughout Canada, the United States, and Great Britain. His paintings hang in the major Canadian and American museums and galleries as well as in many noted private collections. He has travelled extensively in India, South Africa, Hong Kong, and northern Canada.

As an artist Mr. Kurelek's reputation is already secure. He has become equally regarded for his work in book illustration. Of his several highly successful books, two for children, *A Prairie Boy's Winter* and *Lumberjack*, have received the New York Times Award for "Best Illustrated Children's Book". His outstanding talent and prairie background combine to produce the ideal illustrator for the Canadian classic *Who Has Seen the Wind*.